MP NO

RED LIGHTNING

HUGH HOLTON

A TOM DOHERTY ASSOCIATES BOOK
NEW YORK

NOTE: If you purchased this book without a cover you should be aware that this book is stolen property. It was reported as "unsold and destroyed" to the publisher, and neither the author nor the publisher has received any payment for this "stripped book."

This is a work of fiction. All the characters and events portrayed in this book are either products of the author's imagination or are used fictitiously.

RED LIGHTNING

Copyright © 1998 by Hugh Holton

All rights reserved, including the right to reproduce this book, or portions thereof, in any form.

A Forge Book
Published by Tom Doherty Associates, Inc.
175 Fifth Avenue
New York, NY 10010

Forge® is a registered trademark of Tom Doherty Associates, Inc.

ISBN: 0-812-58912-2
Library of Congress Catalog Card Number: 98-3038

First edition: July 1998
First mass market edition: April 1999

Printed in the United States of America

0 9 8 7 6 5 4 3 2 1

This book is dedicated to Ms. Adele Walker, who was the first love of my life, whom I found again after we had spent many years apart. I look forward to us having many happy years together. And to my son-in-law Kevin Cook, who captured my daughter's heart and gave me the son I always wanted. To Warren Hatch II, who is too young (five years old) to read my books (he told me so himself). I am certain he will grow up to be a fine young man and make us all proud of him.

Hugh Holton
July 1998

In Memoriam

In memory of the Reverend Eugene Lionel Gibson of the Mission of Faith Baptist Church in Chicago, who passed away recently. The world has lost a brilliant man, who was dedicated to God, Family, and Church. You will be missed; and

In memory of General Franklin M. Kreml, founder of the Northwestern Traffic Institute, the West Point of the Law Enforcement profession. You led the way to true professionalism in police work. You will also be sorely missed.

Hugh Holton
July 1998

Acknowledgments

With each book I find that there are more people who have had an impact on my life and career. I'm always afraid that I'm going to miss someone and, if I have, I apologize in advance. However, if you are excluded, take heart, because I definitely plan to write more books.

Again, I would like to begin by thanking my agent Susan Gleason, my editor Robert Gleason, and the fellow participants in my authors' reading group—Barbara D'Amato and Mark Richard Zubro; Tom Doherty and Linda Quinton at Forge, who make me feel like a member of the family; Natalia Aponte and Stephen de las Heras, who get it done behind the scenes at Forge; and a special thanks to Karen Lovell, the best publicist in the publishing industry.

As I spend the majority of my time as the third watch commander in the Second District of the Chicago Police Department, I would like to acknowledge some of my colleagues, who in many ways are more interesting than my fictional characters: Commanders Donald L. Hilbring, John W. Richardson, and Joseph L. Logue, who are the best bosses on the CPD; Lieutenant Michael Zefeldt, who has proven himself to be a diabolical scientific genius of truly epic proportions; my fellow watch commanders Lieutenant Virginia Drozd, Captain Frederick Friedlieb, and Lieutenant Nolon Hawkins; Jack and Patrice Stewart, who give a new meaning to the term *partners;* and to Police Officer Nora Smelser, who is the best administrator in American law enforcement; and finally all the men and women assigned to the "Deuce"—Second District—which is the best police operation in the world.

An additional thanks to Randy Royals of the Target Stores, Jeff Wardford of UniMag, and Chip Crowell of Ingram Distributors.

Cast of Characters

The Chicago Police Department

Larry Cole — Chief of the Detective Division
Cosimo "Blackie" Silvestri — A lieutenant assigned to Cole's staff
Manfred Wolfgang "Manny" Sherlock — A sergeant assigned to Cole's staff
Judy Daniels, aka the Mistress of Disguise/High Priestess of Mayhem — A detective assigned to Cole's staff
Jack Govich — Superintendent of Police
Ray Bishop — First Deputy Superintendent of Police

The National Security Agency

Reginald E. Stanton — Special Agent
Ernest Steiger — Special Agent

The Chicago Department of Public Safety

Tommy Kingsley — Director

The Field Museum of Natural History

Nora Livingston — Curator
Silvernail Smith — Historian

The Press

Kate Ford — Freelance Journalist

Red Lightning Operators

Jonathan Gault — The Scientist
Christian Dodd — The Assistant

PROLOGUE

Astrolab Industries, Gary, Indiana

JUNE 17, 1998

10:10 A.M.

Colonel Robert Lee Watkins was at his desk in the administrative wing of the Astrolab research facility complex outside of Gary, Indiana, where he had been the commanding officer in charge for fifteen years, when the building shuddered violently.

Watkins clamped his back teeth together until his jaw muscles ached. Dr. Gault was conducting one of his strange experiments again. Experiments that had the citizens of the city of Gary and the Indiana countryside for fifty miles around up in arms.

All that, however, would soon come to an abrupt end. The Defense Department had decided to close Astrolab permanently. And the reason for this closure was the strange and diabolical Dr. Jonathan Gault.

Watkins got up from behind his desk and went to the coatrack across the room where his uniform blouse was hanging. Slipping on the olive drab garment with the insignia of a bird colonel on the shoulder epaulets, he stepped in front of a full-length mirror with an ornate antique frame that dated back to the Civil War. The mirror surface was of metal covered with a light-reflecting paint, which gave his image a slight distortion. Originally, there had been glass in the frame, but one of Gault's bizarre experiments had shattered it from over an eighth of a mile away.

The mirror was slightly off center. Before leaving the office he straightened the frame, noticing that there were cracks at the base of the cinder-block wall. Sighing, he realized that there was nothing that he could do about that now or for that matter in the forseeable future.

As Colonel Watkins left the office, the complex again shuddered. It was as if a violent thunderstorm were passing directly over Astrolab. Traversing the corridor leading from the administrative wing of the complex to the research wing, Watkins noticed that the entire place was coming apart. All of the windows had been destroyed and replaced by wooden boards, some of which had also been knocked loose by Gault's experiments. There was also a great deal of structural damage to Astrolab. The government building could not withstand the pounding much longer. In another year the white brick structure would be reduced to a pile of rubble. Colonel Watkins realized that Astrolab didn't have a year. And neither did he.

As he made his way along, he noticed frightened soldiers standing guard at various locations throughout the complex. A master sergeant, wearing a starched fatigue uniform, approached.

"Begging the Colonel's pardon," the sergeant said, after snapping off a salute, "but the jolts from the lab are getting more violent every day. The building foundation is cracked and the basement is in imminent danger of collapse. If that madman isn't stopped he's going to kill us all, sir."

Watkins returned the salute. "We won't have to worry about Dr. Gault much longer, Sergeant. In fact, I want you to start evacuating the troops from this death trap right now."

"Yes, sir," the sergeant said, hurrying to do his commanding officer's bidding.

The colonel continued on his way.

Robert Lee Watkins of Lafayette, Louisiana, was a West Point graduate. After receiving his commission as a second lieutenant, he had been assigned to the Army Corps of Engineers. When the Astrolab commanding officer's post became available, he had jumped at it. Within two years he had gone from a second lieutenant to the rank of captain and with the advances in military science they were making at Astrolab, he was easily able to envision himself earning a brigadier general's star in ten years. He could see himself eventually becoming the Chairman of the Joint Chiefs of Staff. Watkins was ambitious and perhaps had far-fetched dreams, but at that point in his career he definitely had a brilliant future.

The colonel entered the research wing of the Astrolab complex. The destructive deterioration caused by Jonathan Gault's experiments was more pronounced here. Walking along, Watkins kept an eye on the ceiling, which looked in danger of imminent collapse.

It was during Watkins's second year as the commanding officer at Astrolab that valuable experimental equipment and sophisticated military hardware started coming up missing. Then, when Sergeant First Class Bryce A. Carduci ended up dead in Chicago at the hands of an assassin and this same assassin started using the stolen ordnance, a certain cop named Larry Cole had gotten involved. When he discovered that Astrolab was the source of the weaponry, Watkins's career went into a tailspin.

A tailspin that was finally about to end with the inevitable crash.

Gault was seeing to that.

The double doors to the lab were located in a darkened corridor that ran the length of the research complex. At one time, this corridor had been illuminated by glass block windows filtering in light during the day and fluorescent ceiling light fixtures at night. Gault's experiments had destroyed the windows, which had been bricked over for security reasons, and damaged the ceiling lights beyond repair.

Because of the many years he had spent in this place, Colonel Watkins could have easily found his way along in the dark. However now, despite his military bearing and the parade-ground stride he had maintained so far in his journey across the complex, he hesitated and peered warily into the shadowy area in front of him. This caution was due to another of Dr. Jonathan Gault's peculiarities. That was an affinity for keeping large poisonous snakes as pets. Pets he experimented with.

The colonel possessed exceptional hearing and could detect the almost undetectable slithering movements of Gault's poisonous reptiles. Now Watkins proceeded carefully.

At one point, before Jonathan Gault had shown up at Astrolab, Watkins thought that the army had forgotten the security problem caused by Bryce Carduci. He had been promoted through the ranks of major, lieutenant colonel, and finally to full colonel on schedule. However, he was never reassigned from Astrolab. This caused him to be viewed from two very contradictory positions by his contemporaries in the military officer corps. One faction saw Watkins's promotions, while remaining at the same duty station, as evidence that he was being groomed for bigger and better things in the United States Army. The other faction saw the Astrolab assignment as a dead end. Needless to say this latter group was right.

The colonel arrived at the lab door and found it securely locked, forcing him to knock in order to be admitted to a section of the facility he commanded. The one consolation was that he would never again have to knock on this door in order to gain entry. He banged his fist against the metal surface and waited. A full minute passed before the sound of numerous locks being undone became audible in the dark exterior corridor. Then one of the double doors opened a crack and a shaft of light pierced the darkness.

The cherubic face of a young man with large hazel eyes and

a head covered by curly brown hair appeared. Watkins frowned. The boy's name was Christian and he was not authorized to be on the grounds. The colonel had argued with Gault about this before and even ordered the scientist to keep Christian away from Astrolab. But the crazy scientist ignored this and every other directive that Watkins had attempted to make him follow.

"Doctor, the general is here," Christian called back into the lab without opening the door all the way to permit the commanding officer inside.

"Let Bobby Lee in, Christian."

These were more thorns in the Astrolab C.O.'s side. Christian could never get Watkins's rank straight and Jonathan Gault refused to use the colonel's military title at all when referring to him. Finally, the door swung open.

As Watkins stepped into the laboratory, Christian rolled away from the entrance in a wheelchair. The young man with the face of an angel had lost both of his legs in a train accident. This infirmity and his devotion to the strange scientist gave another bizarre twist to this place.

Referring to the inside of Dr. Gault's lab as "macabre" would have been an understatement. Electrical equipment of every size and description was mixed in with beakers, Bunsen burners, computer workstations, printed research volumes, and notebooks containing pages and pages of Jonathan Gault's hastily scrawled handwriting. The lair of a nutty professor or more appropriately, the fabled mad scientist. But Gault had added another element to this incredible scene. The place was alive with uncaged, slithering snakes.

Steeling himself, Colonel Watkins counted the snakes. There were six that he could see: four rattlesnakes, an enormous cobra, and a black-gray thing that he couldn't identify. Another upsetting element was that the serpents were not caged or controlled in any way. They were allowed to wander around the lab, at will. To a man like Watkins who detested snakes, this was less than acceptable. Another part of the Jonathan Gault equation that would soon come to an end.

"I need to speak with you, Doctor," Watkins said, keeping a watchful eye on two of the rattlesnakes, which were coiled in a corner of the lab and appeared to be eyeing him.

Jonathan Gault was on the opposite side of the lab tinkering with one of his inventions. Now, when the colonel spoke to him, he turned around.

To say the least, Gault was startling in appearance. It was evident from his sharp features and dark complexion that he was of Native American extraction. He was in his middle years, but it was impossible to estimate his age. The brown, unwrinkled skin could have belonged to a man under fifty. He wore his long black hair, which was liberally streaked with gray, combed back off his forehead into a ponytail held in place by a silver clasp shaped in the form of a coiled serpent. Then there were the eyes.

Dr. Jonathan Gault possessed what in some cultures was known as the evil eye. One orb was flat and black as a diamondback's, the other an opaque sky blue. He was of medium height and weight, but he moved with feline quickness. When he smiled he displayed very even white teeth. There was also an aura of keen intelligence, insatiable curiosity, and a difficult-to-define, mysterious quality about him. A mysterious quality possessing definite undertones of evil.

"Come ahead, Bobby Lee," Gault said with a deep voice holding a definite note of authority. "You're among friends."

Watkins stiffened at the familiarity and started across the large room. He was aware that the two rattlesnakes had now uncoiled and were following him. He glanced at Christian, who had rolled his wheelchair off to one side and was watching the army officer and the reptiles with obvious anticipation. Watkins didn't like this at all.

The colonel reached the area where Gault was working and

turned around to find that the rattlers were coming straight at him. Watkins gasped and looked frantically at Gault. The scientist's evil eyes glistened and he appeared to be enjoying the military man's distress immensely.

The snakes coiled at Watkins's feet and their rattles began transmitting their intention to strike. The colonel stood stock-still expecting to feel the sharp sting of deadly bites at any second. Then Gault spoke.

"Christian, I think it's time to feed Jean-Claude and Marshal Ney before they decide to make a meal of Bobby Lee here."

The handicapped youth appeared visibly disappointed at the order. Then Christian clapped his hands together and the snakes stopped, uncoiled, and began to slither back the way they had come.

Colonel Watkins was badly shaken and it took him several moments to compose himself. This had never happened before during his infrequent prior visits and he was glad that he would never have to come here again.

As Watkins fought to bring himself under control, Gault said, "I must say that the process of domesticating dangerous reptiles is not one of my more laudatory accomplishments, but, as you can see, I have succeeded. Did you enjoy our little demonstration?"

Watkins was still attempting to recover and had his mouth shut tight as he struggled to keep down the contents of his stomach.

"No," Gault answered his own question. "Well, in a combat zone having my little crawling warriors, as I like to call them, on your side could have quite a devastating effect on the enemy. It actually took me years to come up with the method of control."

Watkins watched the snakes crawl across the lab. Christian opened the gate of a large wooden crate and they entered docilely. Gault was still talking.

"No doubt you're here because of the noise, Bobby Lee. I'm sorry, but that couldn't be helped. I've managed to develop a new explosive," he said, pointing to a vial on the table, which contained a murky, blue liquid. "A couple of ounces of this substance is equivalent to ten kilos of dynamite."

Colonel Robert Lee Watkins had now completely recovered from the scare the snakes had given him. He straightened up, squared his shoulders, and said, "I have just received orders from the Department of the Army that this facility is to be closed at once, Doctor. All of this equipment and your research notes are to be turned over immediately for transfer to National Security Agency headquarters in Washington, D.C."

Gault listened patiently and then said, "And what about me and Christian, Bobby Lee?"

Watkins could not hide the satisfaction he felt as he replied, "Your employment with the United States government will be terminated in two weeks." The colonel paused to allow a slight smile to play at the corners of his mouth. "Of course, you may appeal this decision in writing to the director of the NSA."

"Won't such an appeal take time?"

Turning to leave, the colonel said over his shoulder, "Usually, six months to a year." At the door to the lab he turned and looked back at Dr. Jonathan Gault and Christian. "And, Doctor, I want those snakes out of here by seventeen hundred hours or I'll send a platoon of soldiers with automatic weapons to kill them."

With that he stepped out into the hall and was gone.

Colonel Robert Lee Watkins didn't have much in the way of personal items to pack. Everything he had accumulated during his fifteen years as the commanding officer of Astrolab fit neatly into a single cardboard box. The only item of furniture in his office that he wanted to take with him was the antique mirror. Two enlisted men had just left with the mirror, which would be shipped to the colonel's next duty station, when the master sergeant entered the office.

"You sent for me, sir?"

"Yes, Sergeant. I want you to make sure that Dr. Gault vacates the premises and takes those damned snakes with him."

"The doctor's already gone, sir, and I'm pretty sure he removed those little beasties when he left. He had these crates loaded on a handcart. Him and that poor handicapped lad pushed it out to that old motor home of his. A couple of my troopers offered to give him a hand, but he told them, and this is a quote, sir, 'Save the help for Colonel Bobby Lee. He's the one who's going to need it.' That Gault is one odd bird, if you ask me."

"Okay, Sergeant," Watkins said, feeling as if a weight had been lifted from his shoulders now that he was rid of Gault, "let's get out of here."

With the sergeant carrying the colonel's cardboard box, they walked to the front door of the complex. Before stepping out into the parking lot, Watkins turned and looked around at the shabby interior. He recalled that long ago day when he'd arrived here. Then the place had been brand new and as modern as any facility in the U.S. military. Now, thanks to Jonathan Gault, it was fit for the wrecking ball. There was a tear in the colonel's eye, as he turned to leave Astrolab for the last time. He had a hollow feeling inside of him. Robert Lee Watkins realized at this moment that nothing of any lasting importance to the army had ever been invented here. It saddened him that both Astrolab and his career had amounted to nothing.

A vial of Gault's concentrated explosive was left behind on the scarred table in what until only a short time before had been the scientist's bizarre lab. Before he and Christian carted their deadly pets and few belongings out of the building, the scientist had added a catalytic agent to the volatile mixture. Now it was beginning to darken from a murky blue to blood red. The substance started bubbling and the vial was emitting smoke.

Gault drove his aging Winnebago a quarter of a mile from the Astrolab complex. He pulled onto the shoulder of the road and got out. After helping Christian into his wheelchair, he handed the young man a pair of specially treated sunglasses. He donned a pair himself and turned in the direction that Astrolab was located. He consulted his watch.

"It's time to say good-bye to our former employees, Christian."

The amputee nodded in anticipation.

At that instant a bright flash of light lit up the sky followed by a horrendous roar. The wind picked up and Gault and Christian were forced to brace themselves against the side of the Winnebago. A mushroom cloud rose into the sky.

"I would say that Colonel Bobby Lee and his band of toy soldiers are no more. Now we need to find ourselves a new sponsor."

"Where will we do that, Doctor?"

The scientist's mismatched eyes glistened. "In Chicago, Christian. In Chicago."

PART 1

"I'm certain she was murdered by Jonathan Gault," said an anonymous voice on the telephone.

1

Chicago, Illinois
JULY 7, 1999
2:55 A.M.

The black Lexus LS 400 was parked on Chestnut Street a quarter of a block east of Rush. Its finish reflected light with a mirror clarity and the sleek lines of the body had graced the covers of every major automotive magazine in the world. It was a popular vehicle, although there were few of them found on city streets. This was due to their high cost.

However, the Lexus LS 400 was in great demand. In fact, it would fetch twice the retail sticker price when resold on the overseas black market. This markup made the luxury car one of the favorite targets of auto thieves.

The auto thief considered himself a professional. He was thirty-six, which made him a bit old for his chosen line of work, but he wasn't what could be considered your average car booster either. He was a specialist. He went after only top-of-the-line luxury cars like the Lexus LS 400.

The thief worked alone, but he did employ a driver. On this hot, humid night the driver was a woman. Actually, she was a girl who had yet to reach her seventeenth birthday. But she was good. In the thief's estimation, very good.

They had been cruising the Near North Side streets for an hour searching for a suitable high-performance, high-sticker-price car to steal. The thief was a rapier-thin African American with ebony skin and short, curly hair. He'd dropped out of high school before the end of his sophomore year, but he could read an automobile technical manual with the comprehension of a Harvard Engineering School graduate.

The girl was a petite redhead, who'd been a member of a notorious West Side street gang since she was thirteen. Her initiation into the gang had entailed her drinking a fifth of scotch and then having sex with ten gang members consecutively. By the time she was fifteen she had a record of twelve arrests, all of which were for felonies. Then she met the thief and learned to drive.

They saw the Lexus LS 400 at the same time. Without a word spoken between them they went into action.

The thief retrieved a black attaché case from the backseat of the souped-up Chevy. Opening the case revealed two racks of hand-sized remote-control devices with numbered keypads on their faces. Removing one, he began punching in various numerical combinations. Between each formula he depressed a red button on the side of the device. Then he waited, his eyes fixed on the target car's taillights. On the third try the lights flashed indicating that the thief had defeated the legendary LS 400's keyless locking device.

Without a word the thief closed the case, returned it to the backseat, and got out of the car. The driver double-parked the Chevy at an angle, which would block anyone from seeing the Lexus from the opposite side of the street. Using her mirrors, she maintained a constant vigil in case a police car showed up. When the thief got the car started, she would follow him. If a cop did get on to them, she'd use the Chevy to block the pursuit long enough for the thief to escape. A reckless driving charge was a lot easier to take than a felony criminal trespass to vehicle.

The thief opened the driver's side door of the Lexus LS 400 and got in. Despite the heat, he was wearing a long-sleeved black jumpsuit with breast and sleeve pockets to accommodate the collection of precision car burglar's tools he carried. Using a couple of slender picks from a sleeve pocket, it took him ten seconds to get the Lexus started. The thief smiled. His price for this car would be a cool ten K. He'd been boosting cars for fifteen years and at the rate he was going, in another year, he could retire an independently wealthy man.

The engine purred softly and the car thief reached for the gearshift lever. He was contemplating buying a Lexus LS 400 after his car-stealing days were over. Of course he planned to install a much more sophisticated security system than the one he'd just defeated. He had no way of knowing that this vehicle's owner had already done that.

The gearshift lever in this car felt different from the ones in other Lexus LS 400s he'd stolen. This one was longer, thicker, and had . . . The electrical charge that coursed through him spasmed his body rigid. The air was trapped in his lungs and he could neither inhale or exhale. With all of his might he attempted to pull his hands away from the steering wheel, but the limbs would no longer do the brain's bidding. Then he started to burn.

The girl in the tail car realized that something was wrong. The thief had told her not to stick around if a problem developed before he got rolling. She was about to do just that, but the code of the ex-street-gang member made her hesitate. Then with a "to hell with it" snarl, she jumped out of the Chevy and ran over to the Lexus.

She looked through the driver's-side window at the thief. He was sitting, eyes open, as rigid as a soldier at attention. She could see the wisps of smoke drifting from every orifice in his body. His short, curly hair was standing on end and a blackened tongue protruded from his mouth. Despite her street-gang background, she'd never seen a dead body before; however, she knew that the thief was dead. Slowly, she backed away before turning to run back to the Chevy. Getting in she peeled rubber and rocketed away. She had retired permanently from the auto-theft business at the age of sixteen.

2

JULY 7, 1999
4:30 A.M.

Chicago Police Chief of Detectives Larry Cole was on a stakeout; however, it was not official. He was alone in his black police car in Jackson Park just west of Lake Shore Drive. He was approximately fifty yards from the exterior southeast wing of the National Science and Space Museum and seventy-five yards from the old wooden bridge leading onto Seagull Island. An island that, until two years ago, had also been known as Haunted Island.

Cole, a tall, well-built black man, was waiting for a woman. A woman whom he was at once in love with and whom he believed to be an imposter.

He stared at the bridge, which he had crossed on a late summer night in 1997. Little did he know at the time that he was charging headlong into one of the most bizarre cases he'd ever encountered. But he'd also met someone who had become very important to him and he was here to find out who she really was.

Cole's car was parked in a small grotto with trees casting dark shadows obliterating the moonlight and reflections from the few streetlights in the area. The park had officially closed at 11:00 P.M. and Cole had taken up his surveillance at 10:30. Waiting had never been his strong suit; however, what he was doing now was very important. He had come prepared to wait all night.

On the front seat was a cooler containing a couple of sandwiches, a candy bar, some fruit, and a bottle of water. Only once had the mind-numbing boredom of the surveillance made him drowsy. He had quickly snapped out of it and forced himself to go over the reasons why he was sitting in Jackson Park in the middle of the night.

In the fall of 1997 Larry Cole, who was then a commander in the Organized Crime Division, discovered that since 1902 over 188 people had disappeared either inside the National Science and Space Museum or from Seagull Island. After he was injured by a century-old booby trap, which was still in operation out on the island, he had begun an investigation into these disappearances. An investigation that had nearly gotten him killed, but had brought him and Detective Edna Gray very close together. He had also discovered that Edna's sister, who had vanished inside the museum at the age of four and had been missing for twenty-five years, was under the influence of an ancient crone known as the Mistress. During a terrifying encounter with Edna's sister, who as the then-curator of the museum was known as Eurydice Vaughn, Edna and Cole had nearly drowned in a subterrenean chamber beneath the museum. Even when it was over there were still a few secrets that the National Science and Space Museum had managed to keep. Now Cole was back to uncover these secrets.

There was movement out on the island. Cole tensed and kept himself completely motionless. It was initially too dark for him to make out anything but a black silhouette. Then, as it came closer, he could discern a black-hooded, full-length cape covering the body from head to toe. He studied the motion of the body beneath the cloth. He could tell that it was a woman, but not just any woman. She crossed the wooden planks of the bridge with long, graceful strides. He recognized Edna Gray's walk. Eurydice Vaughn, aka Josie Gray, who was in a mental hospital, also had a similar walk.

Without looking back, she moved rapidly toward the museum. The area she was heading for had no entrance. At least not a visible one. If Cole's suspicions were correct, the woman in the black cape would find her way inside. Before she could disappear into the shadows, Cole got out of the car and followed her.

She stopped at a wall beneath a statue of the Greek goddess Aphrodite. Cole, who was dressed in a black short-sleeved shirt, black slacks, and black soft-soled shoes, had maintained a discreet distance, but never took his eyes off her. He also stopped. Then she vanished.

He was less than twenty-five yards away, but when he reached the wall there was no sign of her. The wall was made of solid stone with no seam. There were no indentations or protrusions. Nothing that could house a triggering mechanism to open a secret passage leading into the museum. But he knew she had come this way so it had to be here somewhere. Cole ran his fingers across the wall's flat surface.

He missed it the first time. He found it on the second try. There was an irregularity in the stone, which would have gone unnoticed by a less experienced investigator. But this was exactly what Cole was looking for. The irregularity was rectangular in shape with four-inch-by-two-inch dimensions. It extended an eighth of an inch from the smooth stone surface. He pressed it with his hand, but nothing happened. The stone was totally unyielding. He pressed again. Again nothing happened. He tried combinations of twos and threes in rapid succession. Still nothing. He stepped back and looked up at the wall. He had seen the woman in the black cape vanish right here. He was certain of it.

Eurydice Vaughn knew every secret passageway in the museum. She had learned of them from the Mistress, who was discovered to be Katherine Rotheimer. One of the most intricate of these passageways was concealed behind a two-ton display in the previous "Glassware from Around the World" hall. The case itself was virtually immovable by an application of brute force, as was the wall Cole was standing in front of. Later examination revealed that a system of pulleys and levers had been installed behind the case enabling it to move with an astonishing ease. Behind it was a secret passageway leading down into an ancient railroad station lying beneath the museum.

Now, as he stood behind the museum in the predawn hours of this summer morning, Cole recalled that the case in the "Glassware from Around the World" hall had two triggers installed to activate the opening mechanism. Cole began searching for the second trigger.

It took him longer to find the second one than it had the first. It was at the base of the wall on his right, whereas the irregularity was on the left at waist level. Stepping forward, he simultaneously pressed the irregularity in the wall while pressing his foot against the indentation. The wall swung sideways so quickly and silently that it startled the policeman.

A dark passage led down beneath the museum. Having come too far to turn around now, Cole stepped through the opening into the National Science and Space Museum.

The area beyond the entrance was immersed in pitch blackness. Pulling a small but powerful flashlight from his pocket, Cole illuminated the darkness in front of him. He was on a stone-floored ramp, which slanted down at a twenty-five-degree angle. The walls were of raw brick and the ceiling, which was so low Cole's head nearly touched it, was of the same rough stone as the exterior of the museum. Cole had to use one hand to steady himself against the brick surface as the incline continued for a hundred feet before leveling off.

He realized that he was now far below the National Science and Space Museum. He attempted to get his bearings and estimated that the underground cavern, which had been the train station and now housed the museum's "Transportation of Yesteryear" exhibit, was somewhere off to his right. He swung his light in front of him only to have the beam vanish in the vast darkness up ahead. He shivered, as memories of him being trapped beneath the museum all those months ago came back to him. He considered returning to the surface and waiting for the woman to emerge. Then he would confront her and find out the truth. But what if she lied or refused to tell him who she really was? How could he disprove that lie or uncover the truth? The only thing he could do was continue his search down here until he found her.

Cole started forward again. The National Science and Space Museum took up over 100,000 square feet and it appeared to Cole that the subterranean chamber where he was now was just as large as the museum above. He continued to walk in a straight line, because if his search proved fruitless it would be a simple matter to turn around and retrace his steps. He refused to think what would happen if the light malfunctioned or the batteries failed.

He had been walking for perhaps five minutes, but the surrounding darkness and his being alone made it seem twice as long. He noticed that there was no dust or signs of vermin infestation. This was undoubtedly due to the museum's cleanliness and air-filtration system. For this Cole was grateful. It was bad enough being down here in the dark alone without having bugs, spiders, and rats running across his feet or watching him from the shadows. He was just about to make the decision to turn around and go back when he heard voices. He stopped and listened. They were coming from somewhere directly ahead of him. He switched off the flashlight.

The darkness enveloped him with the suddenness of an unexpected physical attack. He steeled himself and waited for the initial wave of panic to recede. Slowly his eyes became adjusted, enabling him to make out the light source up ahead. He turned his flashlight back on, adjusted the beam to emit a less intense light, and started forward again.

He could detect the familiar voice of Edna Gray. Then there was a male voice. A male voice Cole recognized, which was spoken with the slow deliberation of someone who not only had a speech impediment, but whose mind had never developed beyond the age of twelve.

The door from which the light came led into a tunnel. Cole remained in the darkness and peered inside. The tunnel was large enough to accommodate a locomotive and about twenty yards of track remained. However, it was obvious to Cole that the tracks were very old, as the iron had rusted and the wooden ties were rotted.

The train tunnel had never been completed and ended less than fifty yards from the door. Electric lights were strung at ten-foot intervals along the walls and the area was air-conditioned by way of a ceiling vent making the tunnel's interior twenty degrees cooler than the dark passageway Cole had just come through. The abandoned tunnel was also occupied.

There were a few old pieces of furniture, a Formica-topped table with the legs of tube-shaped metal, a couple of scarred wooden chairs, a television set that was wired into the electric lighting system, a refrigerator that received power in the same fashion as the TV, and an old army cot.

The woman was standing over the cot. Her back was to Cole, but he was able to see past her to the figure lying on the bed. When the police officer recognized who it was, he reached for the semiautomatic pistol he carried in a belt holster beneath his shirt.

The man on the bed was Homer, a seven-foot-tall giant who was badly deformed, had the mind of a child, and the strength of ten men. He was also very dangerous, especially when he dressed in a Halloween death costume and kidnapped people inside the museum. After the incident two years ago, he was the only member of the Mistress's band who had escaped.

Cole stepped into the room keeping the gun down at his side. He was aware that Homer was not only extremely strong, but also agile and fast. Then Cole saw that the giant had changed dramatically since they'd last met.

From the barrel-chested, mammoth figure he had once been, Homer was now a skeleton. The flesh of his face and arms hung slack and his skin possessed a yellowish color. His eyes were closed and his body covered with sweat. Cole noticed a familiar odor in this century-old train tunnel. The cop had been exposed to it many times before during his career. It was the smell of death. Cole put his gun away and stepped up beside the woman.

She continued to stare at Homer. In a very soft voice she said, "He was so lonely down here. It was almost like a child being abandoned in a graveyard."

The giant's eyes opened, revealing his startling cobalt blue irises. He looked at the woman, totally ignoring Cole's presence.

"Tell Eurydice that I said good-bye, Edna."

Edna Gray reached down and grasped his hand. "I will, Homer."

Then the giant was gone.

3

July 7, 1999
7:15 A.M.

The burglar was in a van parked a quarter of a block away from the targeted house. The sign on the side of the van proclaimed it as one of a fleet of vehicles utilized by the Evans Exterminating Company to eliminate RODENTS, ROACHES, AND OTHER VERMIN. Such vans were seldom seen in this upscale South Side of Chicago neighborhood. After all "rodents, roaches, and other vermin" were not tolerated here.

The burglar was in the back of the van hidden behind a curtain in which he had cut holes to accommodate the lenses of his binoculars. He had been parked on the quiet street for less than ten minutes. He could only hope that none of the residents or their servants, occupying the expensive mansions on either side of the street, had observed the van's arrival and that no one was getting out of it. This wasn't a critical error as, up to this point, he could pass himself off as a legitimate exterminator. However, if someone did call the cops he would have to abandon his target for anywhere from three to six months. This would also mean that the four weeks of research and legwork that had gone into the job would have been wasted.

Up the block a tan Mercedes backed carefully out of the driveway of a white brick house, which rested on an acre of land and possessed a front lawn large enough for a professional football team to scrimmage on. The Mercedes was driven slowly, almost tentatively. With a jerky stop-and-go motion, the gears were shifted and the luxury car began moving forward. The burglar watched it go.

The driver of the Mercedes was the doctor's wife. She had her hair done every Wednesday morning at eight-thirty. Her beautician was located in a suburb just south of the city. Ordinarily, the drive would take no more than thirty minutes, but the doctor's wife was a particularly bad driver so she allotted twice the usual time.

The burglar expected to be through before she even arrived at the beauty shop. He checked the street. Nothing was visible moving inside any of the houses. There was no traffic, either pedestrian or vehicular, in evidence. As an added precaution he checked his sixth sense. It wasn't always reliable, which was one of the reasons why he'd spent seven of the last twenty years of his life in jail. But he had gotten away with more crimes than he'd been caught, tried, and convicted for.

Now it was time for him to make a decision. He took a deep breath, exhaled it slowly, and whispered an urgent "Go!" into the emptiness of the van.

A moment later he was cruising down the street toward the doctor's house. His speed was almost as slow as the doctor's wife's had been. Anyone seeing the van with the exterminating company logo on the side would have surmised that the slow speed was due to the driver searching for an address.

As he came up to the doctor's house he thought about the physician who lived in such conspicuous opulence. The burglar's thoughts made him sneer. He remembered when his mother began hemorrhaging and he rushed her to a local hospital with an overcrowded emergency room. She had bled to death during the six-hour wait for a doctor to see her. Her death had left him bitter. The reason his mother had died was not because of the failed abortion, but because she had no money.

The doctor who owned this huge house on this enormous

grassy lot had a great deal of money. He was a plastic surgeon who charged his clients dearly for his services. Burglarizing his house would be a deeply personal act and the burglar planned to give it a particularly personal touch.

He cruised slowly past the house and stopped at the corner. A couple of cars heading east went by on the cross street, but the drivers didn't even look in his direction. Still he had yet to see a single individual on foot in this little slice of urban suburbia known as the Highlands. He made a right turn and pulled into the alley behind the doctor's mansion. A six-foot-tall wooden fence surrounded the backyard. On this fence prominently posted signs proclaimed BEWARE OF DOG! The burglar had done his homework well and knew that the doctor not only didn't own a dog, but actually hated animals. This thought made the burglar smile. He didn't trust people who didn't like animals.

Now it was crunch time and the burglar began moving very fast. Carrying a canvas carryall bag, he was out of the van and at the dead-bolt-locked fence gate in less than ten seconds. He unlocked the gate and was on the property in a shade more than an additional five seconds. It took him twenty seconds to defeat the sophisticated electronic alarm system and gain entry through a patio door. Exactly one minute after he'd left the van he stood in the doctor's dining room staring at the contents of the glass-doored china cabinet. The stuff in there looked expensive, but there was no way he could carry it out of here. Even if he could he didn't know of any stolen-good fences who dealt in second-hand dishes. He planned to trash them on the way out.

The burglar was crossing the entrance foyer when he heard a noise. He froze. The empty, silent house loomed above him. He held his breath to enhance his exceptionally acute sense of sound. Then he heard it again. Slowly, he moved toward its point of origin.

He reached the sunken living room, which was as big as his

entire apartment. In a far corner, beside a set of glass doors leading out into a flower garden, was a grandfather clock, its mechanism swinging a pendulum with a steady, loud tick-tock-tick. But the burglar was certain he'd heard something else in addition to the ticking noise. He crossed the living room.

The clock was handmade and so expensive it didn't have a manufacturer's name on its face. The hands and trim were solid gold and the housing consisted of black sandalwood. The burglar wasn't an expert on clocks, but he had an eye, developed by long years in the thief's trade, for expensive things. And he could tell that this timepiece was expensive. However, there was something not quite right about it.

Deciding that he didn't have time to fool around with this antique, he was turning away when the clock emitted a soft click. Startled, he spun back and searched for the source of the noise. A small door in the clock housing had snapped open and a beam was shining from it. A beam that made a small red dot on his chest. Before he recognized the danger, it was too late.

A two-inch dart was fired from inside the clock and penetrated the burglar's chest. The pain was minimal, but the effect on the thief was devastating. The projectile was hollow and equipped with an internal mechanism that forced its contents out of the tip into the burglar's chest cavity. Six ounces of deadly reptile venom entered his system and he began to die.

Terrified he ran to his illegal entry point at the rear of the house. Bolting through it without any regard for the alarm system, he ran to his van, tossed the canvas bag on the front seat and jumped behind the wheel. The engine turned over efficiently and he was reaching for the gearshift lever when the first seizure hit him.

He managed to get the van rolling and even drive two blocks before he collided with a tree. The police unit responding to the accident found him wedged between the front seat and the steering wheel, which had been shoved into his chest on impact. His rib cage was crushed. It wasn't until the autopsy that they discovered the poisonous dart. However, the presence of this foreign object would go unreported.

4

July 7, 1999
8:20 A.M.

Kate Ford was a freelance investigative reporter, who had won a Pulitzer Prize two years ago for her investigation of how the city of Chicago treated, or more appropriately mistreated, the homeless and disenfranchised. She was a graduate of the Columbia College Writing Program and could have been equally adept at writing fiction as she was with nonfiction. But she preferred the stark reality of facts and would do whatever was necessary, within the tenuous realm of the bounds of reason, to get a story. Now she was, as she liked to term it, "on the case."

Born Kathryn Anne Ford on the South Side of the city, she had been educated in the public school system and worked her way through Columbia College at such odd jobs as waitress in a Loop restaurant and fare taker on the Chicago Rapid Transit subway lines. She was a petite, nicely put together, five-foot-three-inch blonde with the features of an imp and light brown eyes under long lashes. Her looks made her the target of amorous pursuits by a number of men, but she generally discouraged their advances. She simply didn't have time to go through the mental and emotional tussles it took to maintain a heterosexual relationship in the twenty-first century. So she made her work her life. And she was quite serious in this regard, which could be evidenced by her attempt to sneak into a restricted area of the Cook County Morgue on this summer morning.

Kate was sitting in the public waiting room. She was dressed in a white cotton blouse, a knee-length denim wraparound skirt and open-toed sandals. A pair of oversized sunglasses and a wide-brimmed straw hat obscured her features. It wasn't much of a disguise and she really didn't think she needed one at all. She doubted if very many of the people frequenting the morgue today would recognize a freelance writer.

She had just picked up a copy of *Pathology Today* magazine when a tall black man, who'd been sitting in one of the plastic chairs in front of her, turned around and said, "Excuse me, aren't you Kate Ford?"

For just a moment she was too startled to speak. What was that thought she'd had a couple of seconds ago about nobody recognizing her? She considered responding with a lie, but then there was something familiar about the inquirer.

"Yes, I'm Kate Ford."

He extended his hand. "Larry Cole, Ms. Ford. We met at a Mystery Writers of America dinner a couple of months back."

She recalled the dinner meeting. She'd been the guest speaker. But she didn't remember this guy. Studying his arms and the muscles of his upper body she was certain that if she had met him she'd remember. Then she realized that he probably hadn't been dressed in a T-shirt that night.

"Oh, are you a writer?" she asked.

He smiled, but she noticed he looked tired or rather sad. "No. I'm a friend of Barbara Zorin and Jamal Garth."

Impressive company, Kate thought. *But if he's not a writer . . . ?*

A white-coated man with hairy forearms and an expression as animated as that of a cheerful cadaver called from the glass-partitioned cubicle across the room, "Chief Cole, the M.E. will see you now."

Even the attendant's voice sounded like it came out of a corpse.

"Thanks," Cole said, getting to his feet. "You have a nice day, Ms. Ford."

Then he strode over to the door separating the public area from the restricted one and was buzzed through by the white-coated man. Then she remembered who the black man was.

He was Larry Cole, the Chicago Police Chief of Detectives. That's why she hadn't recognized him. She didn't make the connection with him being a cop, and he had been sitting less than five feet away. Some criminal she'd make. She was going to attempt to sneak into the morgue right in front of the chief of detectives.

Wait a minute! her brain screamed. *Enough of this self-incrimination crap.* Cole being here might be just the break she needed.

Kate Ford had been studying the comings and goings from the public area into the restricted one for the past forty-five minutes. She was looking for a rhythm she could exploit to gain access to the area behind the locked door the cadaverous-looking attendant stood such careful guard over. She was waiting for a propitious moment to slip inside unnoticed. But she had seen nothing that would help her. No break in the security routine. No lapses in the vigilance of the man behind the glass partition. Then Cole had spoken to her, which might just be the opportunity she was looking for.

Casually she got up and crossed the waiting room to a water fountain next to a row of public telephones and a couple of battered vending machines. This took her out of sight of the attendant. She looked around. The waiting area was about half full and she'd been concealed behind an obese woman, who was in the front row facing the attendant. It was possible that the attendant hadn't seen her. But suppose he had? She explored the possibility. It was a chance she'd just have to take. She headed for the glass partition.

"Good morning," she said cheerily to the attendant, who looked up at her with cold black eyes that gave her a chill despite the humidity of the poorly air-conditioned room. When he didn't respond to her greeting, she forged on, "I'm with Chief Larry Cole."

The man's unrelenting gaze never left her. She was thinking about making a run for it when his face split into a very uncharacteristic grin. With his teeth on display he wasn't half bad. *What's with you today, Kate Ford?* she questioned herself. *Have you gone man crazy? First Cole, now Doctor Frankenstein's helper here.*

Her thoughts were interrupted as he said, "You must be Detective Daniels. Chief Cole and Mr. McGuire are expecting you. You do know where the office is?"

She hadn't the slightest idea, but she answered, "Sure thing." Then the buzzer unlocking the door sounded and she walked into the "Authorized Personnel Only" section of the Cook County Morgue.

5

July 7, 1999
8:32 a.m.

Larry Cole sat across from Bill "Soupy" McGuire, the Cook County Medical Examiner. McGuire was a dead ringer for screen star Christopher Reeve, who had played Superman in the movies. One of the pathologists working in the morgue had noticed the resemblance and stuck McGuire with the nickname Soupy, which was short for Superman.

Cole had known McGuire since the pathologist had first come to work in the M.E.'s office. The cop and the doctor didn't always get along, but Cole had found Soupy McGuire to be a valuable ally when it became necessary to take shortcuts in cases in which dead bodies had to be autopsied. Now Cole had come to ask for a favor.

McGuire had offered Cole a cup of coffee, which the cop had declined. Soupy also noticed that Cole appeared to be under a great deal of stress and hadn't had much sleep lately. It was Soupy's understanding through the M.E. staff's rumor mill that the chief of detectives had accompanied a body that was delivered by a Third District wagon. Soupy's understanding was that the corpse was discovered in a hidden subterrenean chamber beneath the National Science and Space Museum. Soupy had also heard that the body was that of a monster.

So Soupy McGuire had poured a cup of coffee for himself and sat down behind his desk to see what had brought the CPD chief of detectives to see him on such a hot morning.

Cole started it off exactly the way Soupy figured he would with, "I need a favor."

Soupy listened and what Cole was asking really wasn't very complicated. All he wanted to do was keep a press lid on this monster thing. It wouldn't be difficult since, during the years he'd spent in the M.E.'s office, Soupy had seen many sights that could qualify for the label monster. Each of them, no matter how badly burned, bludgeoned, or mutilated, had turned out to be of human origin. Soupy didn't know what particularly horrible qualities the new arrival possessed, nor could he figure out what personal connection the corpse had with Cole, but it would be easy to keep it out of the press. In fact, Soupy doubted very seriously if there would be any members of the media interested in an ugly stiff, unless there was a really juicy background story involved. He expressed this opinion to Cole.

The chief of detectives looked away from McGuire before answering, "There is a story, Soupy, but it's probably too fantastic to be believed."

"You want to share it with me?" the M.E. asked.

Cole studied McGuire for a moment. He was debating what, if anything, he could divulge. Then he decided to tell it all.

When Cole was finished, Soupy McGuire stared back at him with unconcealed awe. "Jeez, Larry," he finally said when he found his voice, "I heard rumors about the National Science and Space Museum, but I never gave them any real credence. I remember when you got hurt a couple of years ago and I recall a couple of mummified bodies being brought in."

"The bodies were those of Katherine Rotheimer and Jim Cross," Cole said. "Homer was the only one left."

"What about the young woman who was kidnapped inside the museum when she was a child?"

McGuire noticed the fatigue lines in Cole's face deepen. "She doesn't need to be dragged into this. She's in a place where she can't cause any problems. However, if the press gets a hold of this they might not only begin hounding her, but also her sister."

Now Soupy understood. At least most of it. "I don't think you're going to have a problem with the press at this end, Larry. We don't get too many of them sniffing around here after a story unless it's something really big. No pun intended."

Cole understood what he meant. Despite air-conditioning and the utilization of a strong disinfectant, the smell of death hung over the place like a shroud. He didn't know whether Soupy was attempting to make a joke, but Cole was beyond seeing the humor in death at this point.

"Well, you've got one reporter outside in the waiting room," Cole said. "Actually she's more of an investigative journalist, who goes in for writing something called nonfiction novels. Her name is Kate Ford."

Soupy's eyebrows arched in surprise. "Do you think she's here about this guy . . . uh . . . ?"

"Homer," Cole said. "I don't think so, but she was sitting out there when I arrived. I met her a couple of months ago and it is my understanding that she's not only got an uncanny ability to uncover the truth, but she's also been known to do whatever is necessary to get a story."

Now Soupy frowned. "But didn't you say she was here when you arrived?"

"She could have a snitch out in the Third District who tipped her off. I tried to keep everything fairly quiet when I called for the wagon to bring the body over here. But if she's not here about Homer, then why is she here?"

Soupy shrugged before suddenly stiffening with alarm.

"What's wrong?" Cole said.

The M.E. was reaching for the telephone. "I think I know what's she's looking for." When the switchboard operator responded, Soupy barked, "Get me the front desk!"

6

July 7, 1999
8:45 a.m.

Kate Ford was lost. Once inside the restricted area of the morgue she'd had no idea where she was going. The one thing she knew was that she didn't want to run into Larry Cole. The corridors were dimly lighted and cool; however, there was an odor present. Nothing overpowering, just something in the air that was unclean or decaying. She steeled herself and forged on.

An intersecting corridor to her left bore the sign on one wall that read MEDICAL EXAMINER—ADMINISTRATION. She glanced down the corridor, noticed it was empty, and kept going. The next intersecting corridor she came to bore the sign LABS AND RECORDS. This was what she was looking for. At least the place where they kept the records.

There were people in this area and a couple of them eyed her suspiciously. She adopted her Mask of Confidence, as she liked to call it, which entailed walking with a purposeful stride and saying a cheery, "Good morning." This got her past the curious stares to the office with the door marked RECORDS.

"Bingo!" she said out loud before she could catch herself.

The door, as was the case with all the other doors in the corridor, had a large glass window set in its upper half. This allowed her to see that the inside of the office was empty. However, it possessed the equal disadvantage of allowing anyone passing to see what she was doing once she got inside. That was just the chance she'd have to take.

Hoping the door was unlocked, she reached for the handle and turned. Her luck held and she slipped inside.

She had memorized the names of the persons, or rather the deceased, whose records she'd come here to look up. There were four of them, all of whom had died since April. There was a desk facing the door at the center of the room. This was probably where the person who manned this office sat. If Kate knew bureaucrats, the record keeper wouldn't get here before nine. That didn't give her much time.

There was a computer workstation beside the desk, but she didn't have time to fiddle with it. Computers always came with passwords and she would have to hope that whatever password was being used was concealed somewhere within reach of the person seated at the desk. Then it could also be memorized, which would put one very tenacious investigative reporter out of business. The walls were lined with sturdy, old-fashioned filing cabinets. They would be her salvation. That is if they weren't locked. They weren't. Then she was confronted with another problem. The contents of the file cabinets were arranged by a letter prefix followed by a six-digit, numbered code. She didn't understand this filing system so how could she locate the information she was looking for? *Think, woman, think!*

She selected a file from the first drawer she'd opened and scanned its contents. The date listed was February 12, 1995. That was four years ago. She scanned the three sheets of paper clipped inside the cardboard folder. They related the homicide and autopsy of one Louis Gillette, an African American male aged twenty, who had died of gunshot wounds inflicted at 5428 South State Street. She selected another file from the back of the drawer. This one covered the death and autopsy of Betsy Stevenson, a Caucasian female aged seven, who had died in an auto accident at 3902 North Southport on April 17, 1995. She checked the case numbers of both folders. The one for April 17, 1995 was higher than the one for February 12, 1995. The files were arranged not only by the number-letter code, but also by date.

It took her less than a minute to find the file drawer covering the autopsies she was looking for. Now she began moving very quickly. First she would locate the file, then carry it over to the desk and photograph the pages using a spy camera she always carried in her purse. One, two, three then she was back at the drawer replacing the last one and retrieving the next. She carried the final file back to the drawer and replaced it. She had what she'd come after. She hadn't been able to read the files, because she didn't have time. She could do that after she got her film developed. Now she had to get out of here.

She was heading for the door leading to the corridor when she heard voices. She froze and listened. Whoever was out there was coming closer. Kate looked around frantically for a hiding place.

There was nothing she could see that would conceal her except ducking beneath the desk. She rejected that option and was just about to come up with a halfway plausible lie when she saw the other door. It was at the far end of the office. She hadn't noticed it before because she'd been concentrating on the file cabinets.

As fast as her legs would carry her, she dashed across the office and through the door. She made it to the other side just as someone entered the records room. She closed the door as quietly as possible.

"I don't understand what you're so worked up about, Soupy," Kate heard Larry Cole say. "What do you think she's going to steal? A body?"

"That's not funny!" another man snapped angrily.

She could hear file drawers being opened and closed. If they discovered she'd been there they'd start searching. She looked around for an escape route.

The room she was in was dark, because the shades were drawn and the overhead lights off. There was enough light from the corridor for her to see by, although most of the room was in shadow. She began moving forward and then the smell hit her.

It was the same stench of decay she'd detected earlier, but now it was much stronger. In fact, it was stifling. She felt her stomach lurch and her hand flew up to her mouth. She fought to hold her breakfast down, as she staggered toward the corridor door.

She bumped into something. It was a table. Her eyes became adjusted to the dimness and she could make out something on the table. It was a body. The large, terribly ugly body of a nude man. And as she looked on, with her stomach in an uproar and her lungs screaming for the air she refused to breathe in this stinking place, Kate Ford would have sworn she saw the body move.

7

July 7, 1999
8:53 A.M.

Cole watched Soupy McGuire stomp around the records room of the morgue. He'd never seen the M.E. so agitated and he didn't think it was simply because he had mentioned that Kate Ford was sitting out in the waiting room. After Soupy called the front desk and found out that the reporter, whom Cole had described, had gained entry to the morgue posing as Detective Judy Daniels, the M.E. had thrown a mild fit. Then he'd dashed from his office straight to the records room. With mild curiosity, Cole followed him.

Now Cole watched the M.E. checking file cabinet drawers for any signs of tampering. But Cole noticed, despite the fact that Soupy checked four drawers, he was only interested in the contents of one. This was the one he gave the closest scrutiny to, even checking the contents of two of the case files it contained. The others drawers were checked, Cole surmised, because Soupy was either being thorough or attempting to make Cole believe there was important material in them too.

Cole perched on the desk in front of the room, folded his arms across his chest and waited. When the M.E. slammed the final drawer, Cole asked, "Is everything there?"

"Yeah," Soupy said, attempting and failing badly to regain his composure. "But I'm going to have to do something about security around here. That door and these cabinets should have been locked."

Cole was about to ask him why when a dull thud came from the next room. At the sound, Soupy McGuire almost jumped out of his skin.

"Nobody's supposed to be in there now," the M.E. said in a hoarse voice, as he stood rigidly in place staring at the connecting door.

Cole unwound himself from his perch on the desk and crossed the office. He was about to open the door when Soupy said, "What are you doing?"

"Checking out this room for you, Soupy," Cole said, "and when I'm through we'd better talk about you taking some time off. You're jumpy as hell."

When Cole opened the door the stench hit him. It was similar to the smell of death he'd experienced back in the old tunnel beneath the National Science and Space Museum. Removing a handkerchief from his back pocket, he held it over his mouth and entered the room. Slowly, Soupy followed him.

It was dark inside and Cole looked around for a light switch. He checked the walls on either side of the door, but found nothing. The corridor door was on the other side of the room some thirty feet away. Cole started toward it, figuring there had to be a light switch over there somewhere.

The smell was nearly overpowering, but his freshly laundered handkerchief helped screen out some of the odor. He was forced to walk carefully, because visibility in here was bad and he didn't know what obstacles he might run into. On cue, he ran into something, which almost made him lose his balance and fall to the floor. He reached down to brace himself and touched cold flesh. He recoiled and took a step backward just as two banks of overhead fluorescent lights flashed on. Soupy had located a light switch on the wall opposite the door leading in from the records room.

The sudden illumination had the effect of a flashbulb going off in Cole's face. But before he could blink he saw what he'd run into and what he had touched. The metal table bearing the body of the giant Homer was less than two feet away.

When his vision cleared, Cole was shocked to see how close he'd come to the dead man, not because of any aversion to the corpse, but because Homer's eyes had not completely closed when he died. In the initial shock of the bright lights coming on, the dead man appeared to be staring at Cole.

The policeman quickly checked the autopsy room. Except for him, Soupy McGuire and the corpse of the dead giant, it was empty.

Cole kept the handkerchief pressed to his face. "You should do something about the smell in here, Soupy."

Still agitated, the M.E. crossed to the corridor door, opened it and looked out. Over his shoulder he said to Cole, "This is an autopsy room. Last night we did a body in here that had been decomposing in an abandoned building for three weeks. You should have smelled it before it was disinfected."

Cole could only imagine, but he didn't plan to stick around here any longer. He joined the M.E. out in the corridor and shut the door to the autopsy room behind him. The smell still lingered.

"You will take care of that matter we talked about, won't you, Soupy?"

The M.E. was looking up and down the corridor with eyes that Cole could only characterize as frantic.

"Sure, Larry," he managed. "Now, if you don't mind showing yourself out, I've got a lot to do."

With that he walked rapidly away down the corridor heading in the direction of his office. With a shrug and still holding the handkerchief over his mouth, Cole followed.

There was a commotion going on at the security station when Kate Ford exited the restricted area of the morgue. A young woman, dressed in a very similar fashion to the reporter, was arguing with the attendant. Kate only caught snatches of the argument.

"But I'm Detective Judy Daniels."

"Don't give me that, lady," the attendant shot back. "Detective Daniels is already in there."

The woman was opening her straw bag to extract a black identification case just as Kate reached the exit and escaped into the fresh air and sunshine.

When Soupy McGuire got back to his office he locked the door behind him and snatched up the phone. A moment later he said, "I need to talk to the director right away. Yes, it's urgent!"

8

JULY 7, 1999
9:05 A.M.

Thomas Edward "Tommy" Kingsley was the city of Chicago Director of Public Safety. A thin, dark-skinned black man of medium height, his authority extended over the police, fire, streets and sanitation departments. He had replaced Edward Graham Luckett, who had been on paid medical leave for two years. Luckett had suffered from a number of ailments that included emphysema, obesity, and a bad back, but he had staunchly refused to retire. It had taken some fancy political maneuvering, but Tommy had succeeded in getting Luckett dumped by the mayor. Then, with the right political backing, Tommy'd gotten himself appointed to the post.

Kingsley had been born fifty-six years before in Weaver, Alabama. He was the third of seven children and his father had been a sharecropper. Tommy recalled that when he was coming up, he and his brothers and sisters could only go to school half a day because they had to help their father in the cotton fields. The work was backbreaking to the point that, as he got older, Tommy developed a deep hatred for any form of manual labor.

Growing up he developed a number of deep-seated hatreds. His aversion to being poor made him develop a hatred not only for the rich, because they were financially better off than him, but also the poor, whom he felt were weak and allowed themselves to be victimized by the wealthy. He hated the better educated than he was, because he felt they'd had more opportunities than he had, but he also hated the less educated because he saw them as inferior. He hated anyone in a higher social position, because he felt they were snobs. He hated anyone in a lower social position, because he felt they were trash.

The event that had the most telling impact on Tommy Kingsley's life occurred when he was seventeen years old. It was the 1960s and the civil rights movement was gaining momentum in America; however, to the sharecroppers of Weaver, Alabama, the events occurring in Memphis, Tennessee, and Little Rock, Arkansas, were as far removed from their existence as they would be, had they occurred on another planet.

Tommy's father, Henry Kingsley, was appointed the overseer of the Weaver plantation, a thousand acres of farmland owned by Mr. Theophilus Weaver, the great grandson of the town's founder, Colonel Clyde Weaver of the Confederate States of America. At the time Theophilus was seventy-two. The only time Tommy ever met the plantation owner was at the 1965 Juneteen Day picnic. Prior to the introduction, Henry Kingsley instructed his son to, "Keep your tone of voice respectful, boy, and don't go eyeballing the man."

Mr. Theophilus, as the plantation owner was called, was an emaciated, liver-spotted heavy drinker. That day, despite the humid ninety degree Alabama heat, he'd worn a black wool suit with a bright red vest adorned with a gold watch chain, and a planter's wide-brimmed straw hat. The plantation owner was accompanied by a stunning black woman he referred to as Miss Bessie. Tommy would later discover that Mr. Theophilus called all "nigra" women Miss Bessie. He also referred to all black people as nigras. That is when he wasn't displeased.

Tommy was presented to Mr. Theophilus, who was seated at a picnic table beneath a red-and-white striped tent. After his father made the introduction, Mr. Theophilus put down a water tumbler filled to the brim with Jack Daniel's and studied the young black man. Tommy only glanced at the plantation owner following his father's admonition not to eyeball Mr. Theophilus. After a full minute of this scrutiny, which was making Tommy so nervous he was sweating profusely, the old man said, "You got a lazy, shiftless nigra here, Henry. I can tell by just looking at him."

"Yes, sir, Mr. Theophilus," Henry gushed. "Tommy sure is a lazy one. I've had to keep my foot in his behind every day or he'd be off somewhere screwing around."

Tommy felt himself swell with outrage. He worked damned hard and his father knew it. Why was he letting this old white man say these things about him? But Tommy held his tongue and waited until he and his father were alone before raising the issue.

Henry Kingsley responded angrily to his son's questioning of Mr. Theophilus Weaver. "Let me give you the facts of life, boy. Number one is, Mr. Theophilus Weaver is 'the man.' He owns the land we work. He kick us off that land, we don't work. We don't work, we don't eat, and last time I looked, you seemed mighty fond of eating. Now if he wants to call you a lazy, shiftless nigra then that's his right, because he's the boss. When you become the boss, then you can say what you want to say. You understand me?!"

Tommy responded with a respectful, "Yes, sir."

It wasn't wise to argue with Henry Kingsley, because he had an explosive temper that could erupt into violence in the blink of an eye. Five years later he would die of a heart attack while in the act of physically chastising Tommy's stepmother. But despite his acquiescence, Tommy was still deeply stung by the false allegation that he was a "lazy, shiftless nigra." For the rest of his life he would strive to ensure that no one would ever believe that about him. He learned one more thing from his humiliation at the hands of Mr. Theophilus. What his father had said about the boss being able to do whatever he wanted to do was true. So Tommy Kingsley set out to become the boss.

* * *

The office of the Director of Public Safety was located north of Randolph on LaSalle Street approximately one block from City Hall. Since taking over the post, Tommy Kingsley had the suite of offices remodeled at a cost of over a million dollars. He'd made sure that every remaining vestige of his predecessor's presence, including the staff, was removed. In place of Luckett's pre–World War II antiques and wood paneling, everything Tommy had installed was ultramodern. Many had commented that the decor resembled something out of a Star Trek movie. Even the paintings possessed a surrealist, futuristic motif. However, the office did not reflect Tommy Kingsley's tastes, but those of his wife, Anna. She'd been dead since April.

In place of E. G. Luckett's staff, which was exclusively composed of the former director's family members, Kingsley had selected a patronage staff of his own. None of them were related to the new director in any way. In fact, he would not have employed any of his own relatives, because he didn't trust them. Plus everyone he knew from down in Weaver would find it difficult referring to him as anything other than Tommy. He wouldn't tolerate this from any subordinate, although he cultivated such usage of his first name among his superiors and equals. He felt that such familiarity made him seem less threatening.

He had replaced E. G. Luckett's staff with personnel that had certain things in common in their backgrounds. One was that none of them were native Chicagoans. Although he served the city of Chicago in one of the highest appointed posts in municipal government, he didn't trust anyone who had been born and raised here to work for him. Instead he preferred people with a similar history to his own, African Americans who had been raised in the rural South. He also looked for certain traits in those he hired, such as diligence, a capacity for unlimited hard work, and, most of all, subservience to him. This last trait he valued higher than any of the others. After all, he didn't want to be eyeballed by any of his workers. He'd learned this from his encounter with Mr. Theophilus Weaver over thirty years ago.

Tommy had been at his desk since eight-fifteen. He always arrived early and stayed late. He was also thorough to the point of being tedious. He had been known to study reports and statistical printouts until the ink faded. Though this caused numerous bottlenecks to develop in his office, he didn't see this as a bad trait. He was also fond of kicking back reports with scathing memos attached asking for elaborate explanations for minor irregularities or discrepancies. A few of the administrators in the offices of the department heads had begun calling him Terrible Tommy and he'd had a run-in with Police Superintendent Jack Govich that had nearly led to blows. Because of this he was particularly interested in the Chicago Police Department. However, his problem with Govich was not the only reason for this interest.

Tommy's secretary, a fairly attractive young woman in her late thirties who'd been born and raised on a small farm near Money, Mississippi, buzzed the director of public safety on the intercom.

"Yes, Mary?"

"The Cook County Medical Examiner, a Mr. McGuire, is on line four for you, sir."

The secretary spoke with a lisp caused by a missing front tooth. Tommy had once recommended that she have the tooth replaced. She had responded with tearful embarrassment that she was afraid of dentists.

Tommy punched the button over line four.

"Kingsley."

"Tommy, this is Soupy McGuire." The tension in the M.E.'s voice was evident.

"How's it goin', Soupy?" Tommy said, allowing his black Southern accent to deepen. "How's your family?"

"Everyone's fine, Tommy, but I think we've developed a problem here at the morgue."

Tommy Kingsley sat up a little straighter. He had no authority over morgue personnel, as they were employees of a county office, and his position was with the city. However, in order to have obtained the post of director of public safety he possessed a great deal of political influence. Influence he had brought to bear on Soupy McGuire some months ago.

"What kind of problem are you talking about and do you think it's something we should discuss over the telephone?"

Soupy paused for a moment. Then he rushed ahead with, "Let me just say this: earlier today an investigative reporter named Kate Ford snuck into the restricted area here. I believe she went to the records room, and took a look at some files."

"Which files?"

"Those of certain autopsies done in April, May, and June of this year."

"Why didn't you have her arrested?"

"I didn't actually see her do it, but Cole told me she was here and she impersonated one of his detectives to get past the security station."

Tommy's face became set in grim lines. "Are you talking about Larry Cole?"

"Yes."

"What was he doing there?"

"I'll fill you in on that later, but I don't think it has anything to do with the reporter."

"Are you sure of that? Cole could be the one interested in the files and only used the reporter as a smoke screen."

There was another silence from Soupy's end. "I don't think so, Tommy. I've known Cole for a long time and that's not the way he operates. If he'd wanted something like that, he would have come out and asked me. Or he'd have come in here with a court order and seized the files."

"If you trust Cole so much why are you calling me?"

"I'm not calling you about him. I called because of the reporter."

Tommy thought for a moment. "Okay, I'll look into it and get back to you. By the way, Soupy, you've got two more bodies coming over this morning. A car thief and a burglar. Two less criminals this city will have to worry about."

"Could you tell me how much longer this will go on?" There was a panicky edge in the M.E.'s voice.

The director of public safety's tone was harsh. "As long as I say it goes on."

A silence ensued, which was finally broken by the M.E. "You will get back to me before the end of the day?"

"I said I would, so just stay cool and keep your mouth shut." With that he hung up.

For a long time Tommy Kingsley stared at his telephone console. Then he snatched up the receiver and punched the button over his private line. He dialed a number from memory, which was answered after only one ring. However, no one spoke.

"I need to see you."

"When?" asked a deep, well-modulated male voice.

"Now."

"As you wish."

Then the call was terminated.

9

July 7, 1999
10:17 A.M.

Larry Cole stood under a hot shower letting the water cascade over his head and face. He had lathered himself twice with a bar of deodorant soap and washed his hair, but somehow the stench of the morgue was still with him. After getting out of the shower and toweling himself dry, he brushed his teeth, gargled with a strong mouthwash and splashed Woodland aftershave on his cheeks. Now he could no longer smell the stench, but he could still feel it.

Donning a black terry-cloth robe he walked into his bedroom. The sun shone brightly through the windows of his twenty-seventh floor condominium overlooking Grant Park. He had moved into the two-bedroom condo after he'd sold his South Side home six months ago. Since he was divorced and lived alone, Cole no longer needed the ranch-style home with the two-car garage. His apartment had plenty of room and required much less upkeep than the house. It also had the advantage of being less than a ten-minute drive from headquarters.

Cole sat down on the side of the bed he hadn't slept in in over twenty-four hours. As usual he ignored the gritty, burning sensation in his eyes and the general discomfort signals coming from various parts of his body, which were signs of fatigue. Picking up the phone he dialed Edna's number. After the third ring her answering machine clicked on.

He waited for the beep before saying, "It's me. I need to talk to you about last night. I'll be in the office in about an hour. Call me."

When he hung up the phone he sat staring at it.

After Homer died that morning, he and Edna had said little to each other. Cole made arrangements for the Third District wagon to pick up the body and supervised the removal from the bowels of the museum. Then, as he was about to get into his car, he turned to her.

"Do you want to ride with me?"

She looked at him with a blank stare and said, "No."

"Do you want me to drive you home?"

She shook her head no.

He was about to leave when she said, "Were you following me this morning?"

He was too tired to offer any explanations at this point, so he responded simply, "Yes."

Then he watched her turn slowly and walk away.

Throughout the morning this had troubled him. Could what he had done been construed as stalking Edna Gray? Playing his own devil's advocate Cole was able to respond confidently, "No." What he'd been doing was closing the books on a two-year-old case. He cross-examined himself in his own mind.

"Chief Cole, did you follow Detective Gray to the National Science and Space Museum on the morning of July seventh, 1999?"

"No. I was already there when she arrived."

"But how did you know she would be there at that time?"

"I didn't. I was acting on a complaint I received personally from Dr. Winston Fleisher, the museum chairman. He told me that a woman in a long black cape had been seen in the early morning hours mysteriously approaching the exterior of the museum from the bridge connecting the museum grounds with

Haunted Island. These citings had been made by three citizens over a period of ten days."

And on his first night out he'd found her.

The ringing phone snapped Cole out of his reverie. He snatched up the receiver, "Hello."

"It's me, boss," Lieutenant Blackie Silvestri's gruff voice came over the phone. "Sounds like you were expecting someone else."

"Not really, Blackie," Cole lied. "I was just close to the phone. What's up?"

"We got a funny case a little while ago I think you should know about."

Cole's fatigue evaporated. He knew that Blackie wouldn't call him at home unless something really serious was going on.

The lieutenant continued, "We've got a corpse in the front seat of a Lexus LS 400 sedan, which was parked on Chestnut just off Rush. The dead guy's a well-known car thief, who managed to bypass the alarm system and use lock picks to start the car. But he didn't go anywhere. The owner, an accountant from Highland Park, was shacked up with one of the local high-priced ladies of the evening. When he got back to his car he found the engine running and our dead thief. Then he dialed nine one one."

"What did the thief die of, Blackie?"

There was a snort from the lieutenant's end. "A beat car from Eighteen and a fire ambulance responded. The crime lab wasn't available, but the Eighteenth District's evidence technician was. When they discovered the guy was dead, the E. T. checked the body. It looks like this guy was electrocuted."

"Electrocuted," Cole repeated with a frown.

"Yeah, boss. His hands, which were still wrapped around the steering wheel when he was found, were burned to a crisp, his hair was standing on end, and there was smoke coming out of his nose and mouth when the beat cop got there."

10

July 7, 1999
11:02 A.M.

Detective Judy Daniels, who was known throughout the Chicago Police Department as the Mistress of Disguise/High Priestess of Mayhem, was having a bad morning. She'd been assigned by Lieutenant Blackie Silvestri to meet Chief Cole at the morgue at 0830 hours. She had left her North Side apartment at eight o'clock only to discover that she'd left her headlights on all night and the battery in her five-year-old Toyota was dead. Without having the time to contact the motor club, she flagged down a taxi, which cost her twenty-two dollars to take her to the morgue. The driver, who had a West Indian accent, kept telling her how sorry he was about her loss even though she'd told him she was going to the morgue to meet her boss, who was very much alive.

However, her troubles did not end when she reached the morgue. Despite her identification, the Lurch the butler look-alike at the reception desk had accused her of being an impostor. Well, he didn't actually use the word *impostor,* but he had implied it by claiming that the real Judy Daniels was already in the morgue with Cole. By the time she'd gotten things straight, Cole was coming out. He thanked her for meeting him and then told her he really hadn't needed her here at all.

The one bright ray in a so-far dismal morning, was that Cole had given her a lift back to her place and charged her battery with jumper cables he carried in the trunk of his squad car.

But things hadn't improved that much when she got to Detective Division Headquarters. Before she could get her first cup of coffee, Blackie was at her desk with a stack of reports.

"These are accounts of the accidental deaths of a bunch of felons who got suddenly dead while in the act of doing a job or escaping from one. I want you to take a look at them and see if you can come up with anything. Probably your best bet would be to check with Soupy McGuire at the morgue."

Oh joy! Judy thought. Another visit to the morgue was all she needed to make this day a crowning success. But after she got her coffee and settled in to read the first report, while munching a cheese danish, she quickly forgot the problems of the day. Blackie had handed her a fascinating mystery.

Six career criminals had died either while in the commission of or shortly after committing a crime. There were three burglars and three auto thieves, with the last burglar and auto thief discovered that very morning. One of the burglars was found dead inside a Hyde Park mansion he was looting. Each of the auto thieves was found sitting quite dead behind the wheel of the car they were in the act of stealing. The remaining burglars, one in May and the one who was found that morning, managed to get a short distance from the scene of the crime before they died.

Judy checked the Medical Examiner's Autopsy Summary sheet, which accompanied each case file. The autopsy reports of the burglar and auto thief found that morning were not included, but the others were. Three of the other four were classified as fatal heart attack victims. The last cause of death, which was for a burglar who'd broken into a South Shore Drive penthouse, was classified as death due to "undetermined" causes.

Judy scanned the case reports of the criminals found that morning. The burglar had rammed his van into a tree and the steering wheel had been shoved into his chest on impact. That could be a definite cause of death. But what caused him to lose control of the van? She read the report on the car thief. Everything was exactly the same as the others who were found in cars they were attempting to steal. Except that the one this morning had been electrocuted.

She pulled a legal pad from her desk drawer and made two lists. In one she placed the occupations of the dead men: three professional burglars and three auto thieves. In the second she listed their targets. When she finished, she compared the two.

Burglar	Found dead outside the elevator serving a south Lake Shore Drive penthouse.
Burglar	Found in the private antique collection room of a millionaire's Hyde Park mansion.
Burglar	Rammed his van into a tree after gaining illegal entry to a doctor's Jackson Park Highlands residence.
Auto thief	Found dead in the front seat of a 1998 Mercedes Benz.
Auto thief	Found dead in the front seat of a 1999 Porsche.
Auto thief	Found dead in the front seat of a Lexus LS 400.

A comparison of the lists confirmed what Judy had suspected. The residents of expensive houses and the owners of luxury automobiles had taken the security of their property up a notch or two. They were killing thieves. Judy had no love for criminals. That's why she'd become a cop. But there were various levels of crime and murder was a great deal more serious than either burglary or auto theft.

She was about to take her conclusions to Blackie when something else occurred to her. In fact, a pair of something elses. The murders had been committed at various locations across the city and at first glance the individuals who were the targets of the dead thieves didn't appear to have anything in common other than the fact that they had a great deal of money. They ranged from a plastic surgeon to a suspected drug dealer. So, Judy surmised, there had to be a third party. Someone who each of the six property owners went to and requested the deadly security service. But how do you give a bunch of crooks heart attacks?

She returned to the report of the auto thief who had died that morning. She wanted to take a look at that car.

11

July 7, 1999
11:31 A.M.

The lunch crowd was picking up on Cermak Road as Tommy Kingsley turned his official Lincoln Town Car into Chicago's Chinatown. He cruised slowly past the Kow Loon Restaurant on the south side of the street before parking in a bus stop. Flipping his passenger-side sun visor down exposed the CITY OF CHICAGO—DIRECTOR OF PUBLIC SAFETY—OFFICIAL BUSINESS tag, which would keep a nosey cop with nothing better to do from writing him a ticket. Tommy's car had received a number of citations in the past. That was one of the reasons for his recent flap with Police Superintendent John T. Govich.

Tommy dodged through vehicular traffic to the south side of

the street. He stopped and looked at the exterior of the Kow Loon Restaurant and Bar. It didn't look like much at all and he would have never set foot inside the place unless he absolutely had to.

The building in which the restaurant was housed took up a quarter of a city block and was home to a number of Oriental restaurants, which served a similar fare to the Kow Loon. Some years before, in an attempt to brighten the dull, weather-beaten red brick of the building's facade, a coat of yellow paint had been applied. Now, Chicago's harsh winters and tropical temperature summers had taken their toll, and the paint was coming off in large flakes, which were strewn across the sidewalk.

The windows of the restaurant itself were clean, but unimaginatively decorated with a pattern of red dragons intertwined with blue-fanged snakes. Each time Tommy saw the snakes he shivered, because they held a connotation for him which had a far greater significance than a simple window ornamentation.

Steeling himself Tommy entered the restaurant.

One of the seemingly unending line of young Oriental waitresses shuffled toward him. The meal attendants here were usually plain girls who dressed in the pajama-like attire of coolies. They seldom wore makeup or jewelry, could speak little English, but did their jobs quickly and efficiently with a minimum of fuss. However, Tommy Kingsley had no appreciation for the service. He was here on business that had nothing to do with dining.

"I just want to use your men's room," he said, attempting to walk past her.

She was too quick and managed to slip in front of him and recite in broken English, "Right this way, sir. One for lunch."

He rolled his eyes, as his jaw muscles rippled with the anger he was barely able to control. But he followed her to the rear of the restaurant where she stopped at a small table with place settings for two. She held a rickety wooden chair out for him and flashed a stupid smile. He kept walking past her to a door marked RESTROOMS AND TELEPHONES.

Beyond this door there were two pay telephones mounted on one wall and doors marked GENTLEMEN, LADIES, and PRIVATE leading off the corridor on the opposite wall. Tommy proceeded to one of the telephones, dropped a quarter into the slot, and dialled the same 312 area code exchange that he had called from his office earlier. The phone rang once before it was picked up. As had been the case with his previous call, after the receiver was picked up, he was met with silence.

"I'm here," he said, attempting to keep the tremble out of his voice.

Still no sound came from the other end. An audible click sounded behind Tommy. He hung up the phone and turned around. The door marked PRIVATE now stood partially open. After glancing up and down the corridor, he crossed to this door, went through it, and closed it securely behind him.

A steep staircase led down into the basement beneath the restaurant. Grasping the wooden handrail for support, Tommy descended slowly. At the bottom he found himself in a large room with walls painted in a red-and-gold scheme with the same pattern of serpent and dragon ornamentation that was displayed on the front window of the Kow Loon Restaurant. Down here the paint was also faded and flaking badly in spots.

There was a low ceiling, which was less than a foot from the top of Tommy's five-foot-ten-inch standing height. The basement consisted of one large, damp, musty room with a frayed, burgundy carpet on the floor. This place had once been one of the most notorious gambling dens in Chinatown, gambling dens that had been closed down in the late eighties in the midst of a municipal scandal that reached high inside the ranks of the Chicago Police Department. Now it had a much different function.

The room was lighted by four naked bulbs screwed into fixtures arranged at twenty-foot intervals across the ceiling. The walls were lined with wooden crates into which ventilation holes had been punched. There was detectable movement inside the crates, but Tommy Kingsley ignored this. He instead concentrated on the man sitting on a folding chair at a collapsible card table in the center of the room. This man was Dr. Jonathan Gault and each time Tommy set eyes on his host, he was reminded of the first time he'd ever had reason to come to this dreary place.

Tommy Kingsley arrived in Chicago in 1972. At the time he possessed a degree in botany from a Southern agricultural college and a fanatical desire to succeed. He'd debated long and hard as to where he would sink his roots once he left Weaver, Alabama. Along with Chicago, he'd considered Washington, D.C., New York, and Atlanta. The Windy City won out because Tommy's study of its politics revealed that Chicago was particularly well suited to a man of his temperament, ambition, and ability.

As Tommy saw it, the Windy City operated on a strictly ethnic patronage system. Although Chicago experienced a brief period of reform during the five years Harold Washington was mayor, the city was again mired in the same "it's not what you know, it's who you know" philosophy it had operated under since William Hale "Big Bill" Thompson was the city's chief executive and reported to gangster Al Capone. Tommy knew he could make his mark in such a town and he knew exactly how.

He started at the bottom. In the aldermanic ward, where he lived in a roach-infested kitchenette apartment, Tommy volunteered to work in the ward office. Initially, the only tasks given to the transplanted Southerner were sweeping floors and washing windows. Tommy accepted these jobs gratefully. Indeed he was grateful, because, although the politicians he came in contact with didn't realize it, he was on his way.

Slowly, Tommy moved up from sweeping floors to knocking on doors and passing out literature during election campaigns. It took awhile, but he finally managed to ingratiate himself with the four-term alderman and even become the alderman's administrative assistant. When the FBI began investigating the alderman, after an anonymous tip was received about his misuse of campaign finances, the Democratic Party decided to slate another candidate for the post. It came as no surprise to most political insiders when Tommy Kingsley was selected. And because of his notorious loyalty to the former alderman, who spent eighteen months in a federal prison following his conviction, it would have surprised a number of people if they found out that Tommy had not only been the anonymous tipster, but had also turned over incriminating photostatic copies of the crooked alderman's records to the FBI.

For the next twenty years Tommy made steady progress as a Windy City politician. He played the game of Chicago plantation politics so well that many of his peers considered him a master at the game. They also thought of him as a ruthless, unprincipled, lying asshole, but this was actually a compliment for a politician of Tommy's ilk.

During this period he had little in the way of a personal life. In fact, he didn't have time for one. Then, as he set his sights on the directorship of the Department of Public Safety, he met Anna.

"You're thinking of her," Jonathan Gault's voice rumbled through the stillness of the large room, snatching Tommy Kingsley from his memories.

The director of public safety found himself standing in front of Gault like a recalcitrant student forced on the carpet in front of the school principal. He stared at the seated man. Gault's eyes bore into Tommy. They seemed to have a hypnotic effect. And they were strange, ugly eyes with one of them being black and the other a light, opaque blue. The face was weatherworn, but unwrinkled and there was no way Tommy could guess his age. His hair was gray, worn long, and tied back in a ponytail. He was dressed in a black, long-sleeve, cotton shirt that was buttoned up to the neck despite the heat. His hands rested on top the surface of the table.

Tommy finally found the voice to answer Gault's question about his dead wife. "I always think of her when I come here."

Gault's gaze continued to hold Tommy Kingsley riveted to the spot. "Then remember," he said. And Tommy did.

Older men of means marrying younger women was not unusual, Tommy told himself on the day he asked Anna Lucas to marry him. At the time, she was half his chronological age at twenty-five. She was also very pretty, well built, and knew how to stay in her place. When he met her she worked in the building maintenance department at City Hall. In actuality, the woman Tommy Kingsley, soon to be the crown prince of Chicago politics, planned to marry was a janitor. However, this didn't bother Tommy in the slightest. In fact, he saw it as an asset. She wouldn't get uppity. She would stay in her place and know that he was the boss. She would understand that he was responsible for dragging her out of the ghetto and giving her a place of prominence in society. And things had gone exactly as Tommy Kingsley thought they would. For a time.

He was a generous and loving, but strict husband. Anna could go anywhere she wanted as long as Tommy gave his prior approval. Seldom was she allowed to go anywhere without him. Anna had been born and raised in Chicago and never advanced beyond her sophomore year in high school. When she got married, she wanted to go back to school and finish her education. Tommy forbade it. Since she was married to him, and he was an excellent provider, she didn't need any further education. She asked him to get her a better job in city government so she could have something to do with her time. He explained in a patient, but stern, voice that she already had a job being his wife. Anna's mother and two sisters lived on the South Side in the Altgeld Gardens public-housing development. Tommy didn't approve of them so he barred Anna from visiting them. After all he should be enough family for her now. And slowly he watched his young wife withdraw into a shell.

Tommy noticed this and was pleased, but what he thought was her acquiescence to his authority was actually his wife entering a deep depression. He began giving her more freedom and even brought her a new Toyota Camry in which he had a voice-activated car phone installed. Shortly after he bought this car, Anna perked up and even became giddy to the point that more than once Tommy was forced to tell her to calm down in public. Yet in bed she'd become remote and standoffish so that they seldom made love more than once a month. Although Tommy was twice his wife's age, he possessed a greater sex drive than that.

Then a month and a half after he took over the much-coveted post of director of public safety, Tommy Kingsley came down with a severe case of the flu. He left work early on that winter day and was so sick that he was driven home by a member of his staff. When he reached his Beverly house, the garage door was open and Anna's car gone. For a brief instant Tommy was simply too ill to worry about his wife's absence and rationalized that she'd gone out to the grocery store.

After he entered the house and was overcome by a wave of dizziness when he attempted to make himself a cup of tea, he wanted to know where Anna was so she could come home and take care of him. Staggering into his study Tommy punched in the number of her car phone on his communications console. There was no dial tone, but instantly sound came over the line. There were the sounds of music and two people; a man, whose voice Tommy had never heard, and his wife Anna's. A chill ripped through Tommy Kingsley's fever-racked body. The couple he was listening to was engaged in a passionate, near-violent sex act.

Denial was Tommy's initial reaction. This had to be one of those dial-for-sex numbers, which had accidentally gotten mixed up with his wife's car phone number. But as he listened, it became painfully clear that it was Anna, and Anna in the throes of passion with another man.

Shaking uncontrollably from a combination of his fever and the trauma of his wife's betrayal, Tommy Kingsley turned on the speaker phone and slumped in his desk chair to listen.

They went on for an hour, making love twice and talking intimately between sex bouts. He wondered where they were? How could they be anywhere in the city and remain unobserved while making love in a car? He wondered who Anna's lover was? How old was he? Was he one of those tall, curly haired, muscular types Anna had shown an affinity to before Tommy married her?

But Tommy didn't possess much imagination and that, combined with his depleted condition, made it impossible for him to conjure up any images in his mind. Then, with a horrid fascination, he heard them plotting to kill him.

"It's going to look like natural causes, baby," the man said. "This guy I know can put me in touch with someone down in Chinatown who is a wizard at assassinations."

"I don't know, Kevin." This was the first time Tommy heard his wife's lover's name. He filed it away for future reference. "Tommy's been very good to me. I could just leave him."

"And have what?!" Anna's lover's voice came across the phone line with a harsh coldness. His next words caused a chill to run through Tommy. "We've got to kill Tommy Kingsley, Anna. Then everything he has, including his insurance money, will be ours. Then we can live wherever we want and in style."

There was a long pause and then she said, "You're right. We've got to kill him."

A sharp pain lanced through Tommy Kingsley's chest and he passed out.

When he came to, he was in a hospital room. There was an oxygen mask over his face and an IV in his arm. Anna was standing over him, a look of concern on her face.

For just a brief instant he thought he'd dreamed the entire thing. He tried to speak, to tell her what he'd experienced, but he was too weak and the oxygen mask was over his face.

When she saw his attempt to speak, she leaned down and said, "Don't try to talk, honey. You've got pneumonia. We had to rush you to the hospital. I found you unconscious on the floor of your study. You were burning up with fever. You must have passed out right after you got home from work."

He closed his eyes. So it had all been a dream or rather a nightmare induced by his fever. Anna would never plot to kill him.

When he opened his eyes again Anna was gone and the room was dark. The oxygen mask had been removed, but the IV was still in his arm. He felt an overpowering thirst. He felt around on the bed for a button to summon a nurse to get him some water. Then a deep voice spoke from a dark corner across the room, "You didn't dream it, Tommy. Your wife and her lover are planning to kill you."

"Who's there?" Tommy managed with a terrified rasp.

"A friend," came the voice from the shadows. "Are you thirsty?"

Tommy squinted in an attempt to see into the darkness surrounding him, but the effort only succeeded in giving him a headache. Shutting his eyes, he waited for the pain to recede.

Then he felt a presence beside him and a cup was placed to his lips. He drank too quickly and choked, which triggered a violent coughing fit. The cup was removed. Tommy got himself under control and opened his eyes. He gasped when he looked into the one black eye and the other opaque blue eye of Jonathan Gault for the first time.

Now he was looking into those eyes once more. Eyes that he was certain were capable of peering into his soul.

Gault smiled revealing his startingly white teeth. "You didn't come here in the middle of a workday to talk about your dead wife and her equally dead lover."

"No," Tommy said, taking the seat across from Gault. "It's possible we're developing a problem at the morgue."

"What kind of problem?"

Tommy proceeded to tell Gault the gist of the conversation he'd had with Soupy McGuire. Throughout the narrative Gault sat motionless, while continuing to stare at Kingsley. When he was finished, Gault said, "Do you think this Larry Cole was using Kate Ford?"

Tommy frowned. "There have been a lot of stories going around about Cole over the years. He's tricky, smart, and doesn't always play by the rules. On top of that he's Jack Govich's boy."

"Do you think he'll jeopardize our operation?"

Tommy thought for a moment. "He could. He's not the type who can be easily controlled like Soupy McGuire. Before Cole became the chief of detectives, he had a run in with my predecessor." The director of public safety paused. "Perhaps it would be wise to dispose of him."

For the first time since Tommy Kingsley had arrived, a flicker of amusement crossed Gault's face. But his words held the sharp undertone of a rebuke. "You wouldn't have an ulterior motive for wanting Mr. Cole dead, would you?"

Tommy became flustered. "I don't understand what you mean, Jonathan. I just think it's a good idea to get rid of him because it will protect us and our business."

"Your concern for me and our unique commercial enterprise is touching, but I still sense that there is something else about Cole you don't like." Before Tommy could respond Gault snapped, "Tell me about him."

"What can I tell you about Cole other than what I've already said?" Tommy said, nervously. "He's a career cop and he's the chief of detectives."

"Describe him," Gault demanded.

Tommy looked away from his host's probing eyes. "He's tall, husky, has curly black hair, and a thin mustache. I don't know what else to tell you."

"Would you consider him handsome?"

"What kind of question is that to ask me?!"

The outburst didn't faze Gault. "Tall and husky with curly black hair," he repeated. "It was almost as if you were describing Kevin Quinn, your dear departed wife's dead lover."

"I'd rather not talk about that, if you don't mind."

The amusement vanished from Jonathan Gault's face. "I didn't mean to make you uncomfortable with unpleasant memories, but I need to know more about this Larry Cole. If he proves to be a threat to us, I will dispose of him. However, for the time being I would prefer to concentrate our attention on the journalist Kate Ford."

Tommy started to protest, thought better of it, and said, "As you wish, Jonathan." He got to his feet. "I'll find out what I can about Cole and get back to you later."

He was starting for the door when Gault said, "Perhaps you will consider doing something about Cole yourself. After all you are his boss."

Tommy stopped, looked back at Gault, and then let himself out without comment.

12

July 7, 1999
Noon

As Tommy Kingsley exited the Kow Loon Restaurant he almost collided with a young man in a wheelchair. The director of public safety stopped and looked down at what was left of the body seated in the portable chair. The face of an angel, beneath a size-too-big snap brim cap, looked up at him. Tommy's quick scan also revealed that the reason the young man was in the wheelchair was because he had no legs.

Tommy quickly averted his eyes and hurried to his car as quickly as he could. He did not look back at the double amputee. Tommy only hoped that the boy wouldn't call out to him asking for a handout. To the director of public safety, the amputee's sudden appearance had been an embarrassment.

Through hazel eyes set in the face of a Botticelli cherub, Christian watched Tommy Kingsley cross Cermak Road and get into the official-looking car parked in the bus stop. Many times during each day that he lived the young man experienced similar reactions to that of the well-dressed man who'd just left. In many cases the physically challenged, such as himself, were ignored and treated as if they were invisible. This was a contradiction of sorts, because many pitying stares were cast their way, as long as the ones staring couldn't be observed themselves.

Christian backed up and looked through the front windows at the interior of the Kow Loon. The lunch hour crowd was increasing and the waitresses were moving rapidly back and forth carrying trays of food between the kitchen and the diners seated in the restaurant. The young man carefully studied anyone he didn't know. Satisfied that there were no cops lying in wait, he rolled forward and yanked open the door.

He was able to roll through the restaurant without incident. The waitresses deftly avoided him and the patrons ignored him. He reached the kitchen and, using his hands to spin the wheels of his chair, propelled himself across the steamy room, where two Oriental cooks, a man and a woman, were so busy preparing food they didn't notice him.

On this hot day the kitchen, which did not have an air conditioner, had reached a temperature of a hundred and fifteen degrees. Against this oppressive heat there was a small fan going full blast on a counter by the backdoor, which stood open. However, the fan and open door did little to alleviate the stifling conditions. The two cooks seemed totally oblivious to the discomfort. They were working quickly and productively. There were no visible signs of sweat on their bodies. By the time Christian reached the backdoor he was sweating profusely and his cheeks were coloring from the heat.

Outside in the alley he gulped the ninety degree fresh air, which was tainted by the rotting smell of garbage piled up behind the numerous restaurants in the area. Stopping his wheelchair he checked the alley in both directions before rolling down a ramp descending into the basement below the Kow Loon Restaurant. At the bottom of the ramp was a metal door with no knob. Again he looked around cautiously to make sure there was no one in evidence to observe him. This was one of the doctor's secret places and he took precautions to make sure he was not followed. Then Christian pressed a button concealed beneath the right handle of his wheelchair. A remote-control device was activated and the door swung open. He rolled the wheelchair inside and the door shut behind him.

* * *

Jonathan Gault was still seated at the card table where he'd met with Tommy Kingsley. When the alley door opened he turned to watch the young man in the wheelchair enter. Gault's mismatched eyes softened slightly. "Good afternoon, Christian."

Christian rolled quickly over to Gault's table. Snatching off his cap revealed a head of curly brown hair, beginning to show streaks of blond bleached by the summer sun. "Hello, Doctor." He glanced at one of the wooden crates lining the basement walls.

"I think Twister and Jean Claude are kind of hungry." There was excitement in his voice.

"Do you want to feed them?" Gault asked.

"Oh yes, Doctor. Could I please?"

"Go ahead, but don't take too long. I have something I want you to take care of this afternoon."

Christian's spirits deflated a bit, his shoulders sagging and his large hazel eyes developing a near tearful expression. But he recovered quickly. Some fun was better than none at all.

The arena was a twenty-foot-square sandpit surrounded on all four sides by four-and-a-half-foot tall wooden walls. Square cages, the size of milk crates, were arranged on each side. These cages were occupied.

Christian maneuvered his wheelchair to one of the cages and lifted the lid. He was able to see over the edge of the arena, as two large Norwegian rats darted out onto the sandy surface. The rats had been caged, but well fed, for a long time. The space of the twenty-foot arena initially seemed like freedom and they scurried around looking for a way back to the garbage-strewn alley behind the Kow Loon Restaurant from which they had come. But there was to be no freedom for the rodents. They were on a killing ground and they were the prey.

While the rats explored the arena, Christian wheeled his

chair over to the other cage. He was about to open it and let the occupants into the arena when he felt a presence behind him. Turning, he looked up into the face of Jonathan Gault. A man who had befriended him after the world had turned its back on him.

Snatching off his cap, Christian said, "They are ready, Doctor."

"Good," Gault said quietly. "Now do it slowly, Christian. Let Twister and Jean Claude savor their prey before they dine. It will make the meal twice as tasty."

"Yes, Doctor," Christian said turning back to the arena, where the rats were exploring the sturdy wooden walls looking for a way out. Then he reached for the door of the other cage.

Despite the excitement, which was causing him to squirm around on his seat as if at any second he would lose control of his bladder, Christian lifted the gate of the second cage very slowly. Initially, nothing happened, but the rats suddenly stopped their scurrying and froze. The eyes of the rodents became fixed on the dark opening on the other side of the arena.

Then the two pit vipers, nicknamed Twister and Jean Claude, came out and began to slither toward their prey.

Together, Christian and Jonathan Gault watched the serpents first kill and then devour the rats.

13

July 7, 1999
12:50 p.m.

Kate Ford exited the Fotomat shop where she'd developed the pictures she'd taken at the morgue that morning. She slipped on sunglasses against the glare of the midday sun and emitted a soft sigh as she felt the heat shimmering off the concrete in waves. She'd left her car back in the parking space behind her Hyde Park town house and walked the half mile to the Fotomat, where she'd dropped off the film that morning. Now the trek home in the heat didn't seem too inviting. At least not immediately.

An alternative quickly came to mind. She was only a block from Sandy's, which was a combination restaurant, bar, and jazz club with a heavy emphasis on the latter. She hadn't eaten since breakfast, so her visit to Sandy's would serve a dual purpose. She could get in out of the heat, have something to eat, and enjoy her second love, which was jazz.

Less than five minutes later she was walking through the jazz club's front door.

Sandy's had an old-fashioned look. It was set in a brick building, which had been constructed during the Depression and over the years had been faithfully preserved by the building's owner, Sandra Devereaux. Madam Devereaux, whom everyone called Sandy, was also the sole owner and operator of Sandy's and despite being well over seventy, could still get up on the stage and belt out a song with the best of them.

Sandy Devereaux was originally from New Orleans and there were stories going around about some trouble she'd gotten into down there sometime after World War II. Trouble that had supposedly involved Black Magic. Kate had always promised herself that she'd do some research into Madam Devereaux's past, but she'd never gotten around to it. She was glad of this, as she didn't like investigating friends and Sandy Devereaux was perhaps the best friend the investigative reporter had ever had.

The windows of Sandy's were tinted a bottle green color, which added to the coolness augmented by central air-conditioning. The only sign in the window was one of white neon advertising the name "SANDY'S" in blinking script. The announcement that live jazz was available nightly wasn't necessary. If you had to be guided by an advertisement you didn't belong in Sandy's.

Every time Kate walked into the bar she felt as if she'd been transported to a jazz joint in New Orleans. And the place qualified as a New Orleans jazz club circa 1950, as opposed to 1999. There were green plants placed around the large two-tiered room in such proliferation that patrons got the impression that the main room was in a forest in Louisiana as opposed to a gin mill in Chicago. There was lots of old, varnished wood and ornamented wrought iron adding further character. There was a long wooden bar to the left of the entrance and the wood gleamed as brightly as it had when Sandy had opened the club in 1963 a week after the assassination of President John F. Kennedy. At night the tables were always covered with spotless white cloths and adorned with a candle in a golden holder. During the day the tables were bare revealing a slab of marble making up the top, which was supported by black iron legs. There was a balcony running completely around the upper level of the club and tables were set up there for couples only. But despite the bar, the plants and the ornate tables, the main focus of everything in Sandy's was the stage.

It was raised four feet above the floor and had a crescent shape. There was room up there for a thirty-piece orchestra in a pinch, but generally there was no more than a sextet present. The room's acoustics had been modified to allow the most effective transmission of sound with a minimum degree of amplification and it was a rule of the house that noise was to be kept to a minimum whenever there was a vocalist on stage.

There was a smattering of people eating lunch in the club when Kate walked in. Sandy's wasn't as popular for lunch as it was for dinner, because the menu, in this age of calorie and cholesterol watching, was a smaller version of the high-fat, meat-and-potatoes fare served at night.

Kate took a seat at the bar and glanced at the single sheet of Sandy's stationery on which the luncheon menu had been carelessly typed. Pork chops and fried chicken with french fries and cole slaw were featured along with gumbo and chili. In this heat Kate decided on a bowl of chili and maybe a cold beer or two to wash them down. She had just looked up from her perusal of the menu when Benny, the day-shift bartender, came over to wait on her.

Benny was a man who could only be termed ancient. He was probably as old as Sandy Devereaux and it was rumored that in New Orleans years ago they'd been man and wife. However, Benny's last name was Little, not Devereaux. He was a black man with snow white hair and a face devastated by fiercely intemperate dissipation. Kate had been told he was a heavy drinker, but she'd never seen him take a drink or appear under the influence of alcohol. From her observations from the patrons' side of the bar, Benny Little seemed to be a hard enough worker, but he had the disposition of a scalded snake. He was efficient at waiting on customers and filling drink orders, but he was gruff to the point of rudeness and never smiled or joked with customers. Over the years she'd been coming to Sandy's, Kate had gotten used to him and it was obvious that Madam Devereaux had no plans to replace him.

He stood across from her wearing a white bib apron over a natty blue pin-striped shirt and a bright red designer tie. He was polishing a wine goblet with a spotless white cloth. His bloated face, with its patchwork of burst veins, was expressionless. He didn't acknowledge her presence by either word or gesture.

Kate assumed an attitude of equal indifference; but, she'd been too well brought up not to give him at least a modicum of courtesy. "Good afternoon, Benny. I'll have a bowl of chili and a glass of Miller Draft."

Without a word he stalked off to fill her order.

Live entertainment didn't begin until after six o'clock. Now the jukebox was playing and Ahmad Jamal's "Poinciana" instrumental drifted through the bar. For a moment Kate listened to the chords of the master pianist. Then she opened her Fotomat envelope.

The pictures she'd taken with her spy camera had been enlarged to eight-and-a-half-by-eleven-inch size. On one of the photos there was a shadow that obscured some of the data on the autopsy report, but she could still read it. The rest of the pictures were as clear as the original reports they were copies of.

Basically, the autopsies related the causes of death of six people, who had all died since that past April. The first was the death of Anna Kingsley, who had been found dead in the bathroom of her South Side home. She had been discovered in the tub by her husband Tommy Kingsley. This was the case that had initially led Kate to the morgue's records office. The typed words detailing the autopsy, despite the pathologist's technical language, were fairly easy to understand. Removing the steno notebook from her purse, Kate wrote the name ANNA KINGSLEY on one side of a blank page and on the other CAUSE OF DEATH—

DROWNING. She checked Anna Kingsley's age and physical condition. She had been a young woman in perfect health. There were no other injuries listed. So why had she drowned?

Benny delivered her chili, set a frosted glass of draft beer on a coaster, and silverware wrapped in a linen napkin on the bar in front of her. From beneath the bar he removed a box of individually wrapped packages of Saltine crackers. Before walking away he asked, "Do you want hot sauce?"

"No thanks, Benny," she said inhaling the aromatic spices wafting from the steaming bowl. "I'm sure it's hot enough."

She crushed crackers and spooned them into the chili. She took a small mouthful of the bean and meat concoction, which forced her to snatch up the beer and take a healthy swallow to put out the fire that had ignited in her mouth. Slowly, she got used to the chili, but was forced to order a second beer before she was halfway through the bowl. Then she returned to the photographed autopsy reports.

The next one following Anna Kingsley's was that of a male named Kevin Quinn, who was found dead in the apartment where he lived with his mother. The police case report, accompanying the autopsy report, stated that Quinn was found dead in front of his television set. He'd been watching a Bulls-Pistons basketball game. The cause of death listed on the autopsy report was cardiac arrest. Kate reread the physical description of Kevin Quinn. He was under thirty and in ". . . excellent physical condition" according to this Dr. W. McGuire, who had performed both the autopsies of Anna Kingsley and Kevin Quinn.

Kate flipped through the remaining autopsy reports. Each of them was performed by Dr. W. McGuire. Coincidence?

She smelled a rat lurking within these photographed pages. There were enough to get her interested in snooping further, but she needed to talk to her anonymous informant first. And this she would never do from a public telephone in a bar.

Quickly, she gathered her documents and tossed down the

swallow of beer she had left before motioning for Benny to give her the check. He moved with infuriating slowness to collect her money and ring up a receipt, which she placed in her purse. She considered the repast she'd enjoyed in Sandy's a working lunch.

Out on the street it was still hot, but Kate didn't notice it so much now. It took her ten minutes to get to her town house. As she was approaching the entrance to the flower and evergreen tree-lined courtyard, a young man in a wheelchair came rolling from inside toward the front gate. Kate felt an instant wave of pity when she saw how young he was and that he had no legs.

As he passed he looked up at her, smiled, and said, "Good afternoon, ma'am."

"Good afternoon," she managed. She had closed the front gate behind her. As he moved toward it, she dashed past him and snatched the gate open. Again he smiled and said, "Thank you very much, ma'am, and have a nice day."

"You do the same," she responded before adding, "and God bless you."

She watched him roll off down the street and wondered who he'd been visiting in the town-house complex in which she lived. Of course, like most urban dwellers, she didn't know most of her neighbors. As she walked to her unit, she remarked to herself that it was indeed a tragedy that he'd lost his legs. She wondered how it had happened? She also knew that there were few agencies in government, at any level, to help him. She could only hope that he had a good, supportive family.

She unlocked the three locks securing the front door of her town house and stepped inside, feeling the cool air from her central air-conditioning unit. She picked up the mail, which had been dropped through the slot while she was out. Carrying it, she crossed to her study. She flipped through the letters and catalogues. Most of it was junk, interspersed with a couple of bills. She threw away the junk mail and placed the bills in the pending file on her desk. She also removed her luncheon receipt from Sandy's and placed it in a portfolio labeled TAXES—1999. She then removed the steno book from her purse and looked up the telephone number of her informant. An informant who was no longer anonymous.

Kate Ford had not become interested in the comings and goings at the Cook County Morgue on her own. She had been tipped off by a mysterious woman's voice on the telephone. The first call had come at one-thirty in the morning the previous Monday. Rousing herself from a sound sleep, the reporter had fumbled with the instrument and even hit herself in the head with the receiver when she tried to get it to her ear.

"Hello?"

"Is this Kate Ford, the woman who writes those exposé books?" Whoever was talking was masking her voice by having placed a handkerchief over the mouthpiece, which made the words barely audible. However, Kate was able to detect that the caller was outdoors and near an expressway. Kate's phone was also equipped with caller I.D., so she at least had the location of her caller's public phone. Kate would later discover the locations from which this first call and subsequent calls were placed.

"This is Kate Ford," she said waking up quickly. This could be a prank, but something in the caller's voice told Kate that this woman was not only very serious, but scared to death.

"I think some people have been killed and someone over at the Cook County Morgue is trying to cover it up."

Kate noticed that, despite the disguise attempt, the caller spoke with a lisp, as if she had a gap in her teeth or a missing front tooth.

"Who has been killed?"

There was a long pause from the other end. Then, "A woman named Anna Kingsley."

Kate switched on her night table lamp and picked up the pen

and notepad she always kept there. "That name sounds familiar. Who is she?"

Again there was a pause. "You should be able to find that out if you're as good as people say you are. But they're trying to make it look like she died accidentally. I'm certain she was murdered by someone named Jonathan Gault."

Now Kate was beginning to wonder seriously if this woman was legit. The way she was talking indicated that she was crazy, drunk, or doped up.

"Why would this Gault want to kill Anna Kingsley?" Kate wrote the name "Jonathan Gault" on her note pad.

"Because he was paid and paid well to do it. And he's killed others."

The informant gave Kate the name of Kevin Quinn and the information on the deaths of four criminals, two burglars and two auto thieves, who had also supposedly died under suspicious circumstances while committing crimes. This had started her investigating, which had led to her foray into the morgue that morning. Her snitch had called her back twice, each time from public telephones. The first call on Monday at one-thirty had come from a phone booth on Madison Street near the Dan Ryan Expressway. The next two had come from the lobby of the Municipal Administration Building at 180 North LaSalle Street in the Chicago Loop, the same building that housed the offices of the director of public safety, who Kate knew was Tommy Kingsley, the husband of the dead Anna Kingsley. It hadn't taken Kate long to discover that her anonymous informant worked for Tommy Kingsley. Now the journalist was about to startle the snitch with the rude awakening that she'd been unmasked.

Kate was picking up the phone to dial the number of the executive secretary to the City of Chicago Director of Public Safety when she caught a brief glimpse of something moving across the floor of her study a short distance from where she stood. Turning to investigate made her freeze with terror. Her brain kept telling her that the image that her eyes were transmitting to it was wrong. That the enormous rattlesnake gliding toward her simply could not be in the study of her Hyde Park town house.

Then, as the snake coiled to strike, Kate Ford screamed.

14

July 7, 1999
1:58 P.M.

Larry Cole had arrived at police headquarters shortly after eleven and was forced to rush to a meeting in Superintendent Jack Govich's office. There all the division heads were assembled for a meeting concerning the cost overruns in the police budget so far this year. The Detective Division was second only to the much larger Patrol Division in having so far exceeded the money allotted to them. Two days before, Cole had his staff assemble the documents necessary to support the cost overruns. As a former chief of detectives himself, Govich was sure to understand what the investigative arm of the CPD was up against.

But when Cole entered the superintendent's office with the chiefs of the Patrol and Organized Crime Divisions, he noticed a definite tension in the air. When he saw Herb Donaldson seated at the conference table next to the superintendent, Cole instantly recognized the reason for the tension.

Donaldson was the official auditor of the Department of Public Safety and reported directly to Tommy Kingsley. The auditor had a completely bald skull and wore thick, horn-rimmed glasses over a face that could only be described as pinched. However, this was where the resemblance between the auditor and the stereotypical bookkeeper ended. From the neck down, Herb Donaldson was a mass of bulging muscle.

Once, Cole had watched the auditor work out in the police gym's weight room. He had no training partner and discouraged any contact with the cops using the gym with either evil stares or brutish grunts. Then he had loaded fifty-pound plate after fifty-pound plate onto a barbell with which he proceeded to do squats, bench presses, and dead lifts with an ease that amazed the cops present. Later Cole talked to Jimmy Stevenson, one of the weight room veterans, about the muscle-bound auditor.

"Chief," Stevenson said, "in order for that guy to lift that kind of iron and develop his body that way, he's got to be popping steroids like they were M & M's."

After that Cole kept the weight-lifting Herb Donaldson under a remote surveillance and, except for a little periodic wildness in his eyes and a stiff gait caused by a rapid deterioration of his knee joints and spine, the auditor seemed almost normal. And if he was on anabolic steroids, which played havoc on the body in so many different ways, Cole never saw any indication of it, especially when he had a spreadsheet in one hand and a calculator in the other.

Now, in Govich's office, the only thing in front of the auditor was a laptop computer. The three Chicago Police Department division chiefs took their seats and waited.

Donaldson started with Jim Caine, the chief of the Patrol Division. "We have made an extensive examination of the budget overages in your division, Chief Caine, and it all comes down to one thing: overtime."

Caine was a man of medium height and build with penetrating eyes and thinning hair. He was considered something of an academic within the department and ran the Patrol Division as if it were a Fortune 500 company with balance sheets keeping tabs on expenditures versus production; arrests, citations issued, and investigations initiated. Caine had a folder in front of him, which contained all the information he felt was necessary to defend himself and his division from attack by the Department of Public Safety's auditor.

"Counting the number of felony arrests we made last year and including the citations written along with the other activities engaged in by the patrol force," Caine said looking directly at Donaldson, "the overtime comes out to less than one hour per officer per month."

Donaldson waved a hand through the air, which caused the muscles of his massive forearm to ripple. "Let's not confuse the issue with superfluous and totally unrelated statistics, Chief Caine. Your division was given a set budget for overtime for the fiscal year commencing on one January 1998 and concluding on thirty June 1999. You exceeded that budget by over ten percent and the productivity you mentioned has nothing to do with it."

The auditor punched keys on his laptop. "Instead of looking at the overtime averaged out over your entire eight thousand plus strong division, let's look at it specifically. In fact, ninety percent of the overtime in the patrol division is being eaten up by twenty-five percent of your officers."

"That's not hard to understand or explain," Govich interrupted. "Our tactical, gang, and rapid-response cars handle the majority of the hot calls and therefore make the majority of the arrests."

Donaldson gave the superintendent a look of barely concealed contempt. Cole noticed it and was shocked that the auditor would dare behave in such a fashion in Govich's office. That is unless Donaldson had something in his computer that was pure dynamite.

"Begging the superintendent's pardon," Donaldson said with an irritating condescension, "but that lame excuse simply won't wash. The overtime, at least the vast majority of it, comes from cops milking the system. They extend their time in court, make bullshit arrests toward the end of their tours of duty, and pad whatever legitimate overtime they do make to the point that it's costing this city millions of dollars a year."

Although Donaldson had not raised his voice, his words had the effect of a bomb going off.

The three chiefs waited for their boss's retort. In response to the auditor's allegation Govich chuckled. "Can you prove all of what you just said or is it information you've dug up from the files of some of our local anticop organizations?"

Donaldson tensed, which caused his muscles to bulge to the point of being seemingly capable of bursting out of his clothing. "I don't make groundless allegations, Superintendent. I can provide you with proof of everything I've said."

With an ease that Cole found impressive, Govich said, "I'll be looking forward to seeing it. Now, if you don't mind, could we continue the audit?"

"Shall we turn our attention to the Organized Crime Division?" Donaldson said, punching more keys on his computer.

Mary Delgado, a portly woman who resembled a grade-school teacher, was the chief of Organized Crime. Belying her appearance, her nickname in the department was "Iron Maiden the Second," after the first female superintendent of police. Mary was not a woman to be trifled with. Cole had worked for her two years ago during the brief period he'd been assigned to the Organized Crime Division. He considered her a friend.

Chief Delgado had nothing in front of her. She had an awesome memory, which some claimed was photographic. Actually, she possessed total recall and could read a report or review a column of numbers and recite them verbatim. She appeared quite confident in the face of the auditor's planned assault. That is until he addressed himself to her division.

"I say this only after very careful research into the productivity of the Organized Crime Division as compared to the yearly expenditures of the other divisions," Donaldson said looking from Govich to Delgado, "and what I've discovered simply does not justify Organized Crime's continued existence."

This statement stunned all the cops in the office.

"You can't be serious," Mary Delgado said, leaning toward the auditor, her eyes flaring. "We spearhead the enforcement efforts for the department's investigations into not only violations of narcotics, gambling, and prostitution laws, but also all organized criminal activity in the city. To do away with us would be pure insanity."

Donaldson shook his head and returned Chief Delgado's gaze. He punched more computer keys. "In the past three years your division has been responsible for a mere fraction of the narcotics confiscations and arrests, and only a smattering of the prostitution and gambling arrests. The vast majority of this work was done by the Patrol Division and the largest drug confiscation ever made by the CPD was conducted by Chief Cole."

Donaldson was talking about the Barksdale Manufacturing Company formerly located in the 7200 block of South Chicago, which was the largest narcotics processing plant in the world. Cole and Blackie had singlehandedly busted it the year before.

Mary Delgado reddened. "Your statistics show no more, Mr. Donaldson, than your lack of knowledge of what the Chicago Police Department's mission and responsibility is."

"That comment, Chief Delgado," Donaldson shot back, "reveals that you have no concept of the fiscal realities in the age in which we live. The bottom line is that your division costs money and if my audit shows that the work you do can be done by another division in the department, then that is what I'm going to recommend."

Delgado started to respond, but Govich held up his hand. "Chief, I think we should keep in mind that Mr. Donaldson's recommendations are just that. Recommendations. I'm certain that we'll have our day in court with the mayor and the City

Council Finance Committee prior to any decisions being made concerning changes in this department." Then Govich turned to Donaldson and said, "Why don't we move on to the Detective Division?"

Donaldson leaned forward and shut off his computer. Closing the lid he said, "All the expenditures for the Detective Division seem in order at this time, Superintendent. I have no comment on Chief Cole's operation right now."

Cole and Govich exchanged questioning frowns. Then Cole looked at the auditor, who refused to return his gaze.

Cole was in a contemplative mood when he got back to his office. Blackie and Judy were waiting for him. Judy was bursting with excitement.

Before they could say anything, Cole said, "Give me a minute, guys." Then he walked into his office and shut the door behind him.

He sat down behind his desk and stared out the window at the South Side of the city, which was sweltering in the ninety-degree heat. However, he wasn't seeing anything that was out there.

Donaldson's actions had puzzled not only Cole, but also Govich. The auditor was a nitpicker, who would have attempted to find fault with Jesus Christ himself. And although Cole was very proud of the Detective Division, he didn't think for a moment that there was nothing Donaldson could find wrong with the operation. Then why the positive report?

Alone, he and Govich had discussed it briefly after the meeting broke up.

"What's going on, boss?" Cole asked.

Govich shook his head. "I don't know, Larry. Donaldson was obviously playing the auditor's game in here today with those comments about Patrol and his threat to recommend disbanding Organized Crime. That justifies his pitiful existence.

But saying he didn't find anything wrong with the Detective Division is ridiculous. One thing is definitely for certain, Herb Donaldson and his boss, Tommy Kingsley, are no friends of the Chicago Police Department."

Cole agreed.

Now, back in his office, Cole examined the situation more carefully.

The police department was a public service for the citizens of Chicago. As such, under the democratic form of government, it was subject to the checks and balances imposed by elected officials. This made the cops subordinate to the whims of politicians, up to a point. Crime and public safety were major problems in contemporary American society. Such issues were attractive to voters and, invariably, politicians either supported or attacked the police according to the way the winds of public sympathy were blowing at the moment.

Cole had been a Chicago police officer for over half his life. During that time he'd done his best to avoid politics. He wasn't always successful in this regard, especially after he became a command officer, and on more than one occasion he'd had run-ins with politicians. The former director of public safety E. G. Luckett had tried to destroy Cole's career and his life.

Herb Donaldson was a political animal by nature of his position with the office of the current director of public safety. Failing to find anything wrong with the Detective Division audit could only mean that some how, some way, Donaldson and his boss, Kingsley, had a secret political agenda up their sleeves. A political agenda which Cole was certain would not only be damaging to the Detective Division, but the entire department.

His intercom buzzed.

"Yes." Cole's voice indicated that he was less than enthused by the interruption.

"Boss," Blackie said, "I'm sorry to disturb you, but Judy has something important she needs to show you."

For just an instant he started to tell Blackie he was busy and that he'd see Judy later. But he really wasn't busy. He was simply sitting here staring out the window and brooding. Enough of this nonsense.

"Send her in, Blackie."

"But why are we going to see the reporter, Chief?" Judy said as they cruised down Lake Shore Drive in Cole's car. "Shouldn't we be contacting Soupy McGuire and finding out what went wrong with the autopsies?"

Cole, who was driving, responded, "I was in the morgue this morning while Kate Ford was there impersonating you. If I'm not mistaken, she got into the records office and took a look at some autopsy files. Me and Soupy almost walked in on her, but she managed to slip out through an autopsy room next to the records office. We heard a noise in there, but when I checked it out she was gone. However, what was really strange was Soupy McGuire's reaction to her being there."

"I don't understand?" Judy said.

Cole turned the police car onto Fifty-third Street in Hyde Park and cruised past Sandy's jazz club. "Soupy was extremely nervous and when we got to the records office it was obvious that he was trying to hide something."

"Hide something, like what?"

"I don't know, but I'd be willing to bet that Kate Ford does." He made a left onto the street where the reporter's town house was located. "I got her address from Barbara Zorin. Barbara also told me that Kate Ford works out of her home."

They pulled up to a stop sign and Judy said, "Oh, boss, isn't that pitiful."

Cole followed her gaze to a young man in a wheelchair. One of the wheels had run off the pavement and was stuck in the parkway grass. His face was flushed with the effort he was expending to free himself. He didn't appear to be making any progress.

Cole pulled the car over to the curb. "I'll be right back," he said to Judy as he got out.

The young man stopped struggling when he saw Cole approaching.

"Let me give you a hand," the cop said, stepping around in back of the chair.

"Thank you, sir," he said, twisting around to look up at his rescuer. "I wasn't watching where I was going. It's kind of you to help me."

Cole grabbed the handles at the back of the chair and began maneuvering it back onto the sidewalk. He had just gotten it onto the pavement when he felt a vibration through the chair's frame as if something in the housing of the chair had shifted violently. Cole studied the wheelchair's construction. It looked like any other such device Cole had ever seen; however, the area beneath the seat was enclosed with black wooden panels. He was distracted from his scrutiny by the young man saying, "Thank you very much, sir." He extended his hand.

Smiling, Cole took the hand noticing the young man's extraordinarily strong grip, which had undoubtedly been developed from his operating the wheelchair.

"My name is Christian."

"Nice to meet you, Christian. I'm Larry Cole."

Christian looked over at the car. "Are you a policeman, Larry?"

Although the black Chevy had whitewall tires, Christian had made it as a cop car.

"Yes, I am," Cole said.

Christian smiled making his face light up. "Can I use your name if I ever get stopped for speeding in my chair?"

Cole laughed. "I don't think you're in any danger of going that fast, but if you want to use my name, feel free."

A muffled scream carried to them from down the block. Cole tensed and looked in that direction. Christian paid the sound no attention as he spun his wheelchair around and began rolling away. "Good-bye, Larry. I'll be seeing you."

Then the scream came again and Cole sprinted off down the block toward its point of origin.

15

July 7, 1999
2:13 P.M.

Kate Ford didn't know anything about snakes, other than the fact that she didn't like them. Her exposure to the slithering, legless creatures on TV gave her enough information to realize that the one confronting her now was a rattlesnake. She could tell this because of the distinctive rattling noise it was making, a noise that possessed a decidedly hostile tone.

After her initial scream, adrenaline flooded into her system and she managed to snatch herself from the paralyzing shock that held her frozen in place. Now was the time to vacate the premises. Once safely away from the thing on her study floor, she'd get the cops to deal with it.

Kate devised an instant strategy to effect her escape. The brown-and-gray patterned snake was moving toward her from the entrance to the living room. This eliminated escape by way of the front door. But behind her was the entrance to the dining room. By crossing the dining room she could make it to the kitchen and out the back door into the alley. She was glad that she had on flat, open-toed sandals, which would make running easier than if she was wearing heels. She was getting ready to make her break when an idle thought occurred to her. She wondered how fast the snake could move in pursuit of her? She forced this from her mind. If it did catch her that would be disastrous, but she was sure as hell going to make a run for it.

The rattlesnake had again coiled and the rattling noise seemed to echo through the entire house. The snake's evil, unblinking eyes glared at her and she knew at any moment it would strike. Slowly, she backed away without taking her eyes off the snake. She felt her buttocks bump the edge of the desk. Now she was in position. All she'd have to do was spin to the left and make a break for the back door.

She tensed and was just about to launch herself into headlong flight when she heard a second angry rattle. With terror raging through her, Kate looked over her shoulder and spied another rattlesnake. It was gliding toward her from the dining room, blocking her escape route.

Now she was trapped between them. Again she screamed as they converged on her.

16

July 7, 1999
2:14 P.M.

Cole followed the sound of the screams to the courtyard surrounded by town houses. He realized that Kate Ford lived in this complex in Unit F, which was on the end down on the left. The screams he heard came from her place.

He reached the wrought-iron front door. It was locked. He banged on the door and pressed the buzzer. There was no response. A man's head poked out of a unit on the other side of the courtyard. He was an elderly Asian man with enormous bags under his eyes. In unaccented English he said, "I heard Ms. Ford screaming. I called nine one one."

"I'm a police officer," Cole said. "Call them back and tell them I'm here and dressed as a civilian."

"Yes, sir," he said, ducking back inside.

Cole looked around the exterior of the town house for a way to get in. There was a large plate-glass window on the adjacent wall. Running to it, Cole found that the inside of the window was covered with vertical blinds. However, he was able to peer through them at the inside of the house.

He saw the reporter first. Then he spied the two snakes converging on her. He banged his fist against the glass, but it was at least half-an-inch thick and barely vibrated from the blow. He stepped back and looked around for something to use to break the glass. A earthenware flowerpot with a sixteen-inch base stood on the grass beneath the window. Reaching down Cole snatched the flowers out and dumped them on the ground. Then, with difficulty, he lifted the dirt-filled pot over his head. He felt his back and shoulder muscles shriek as he braced himself and, using his legs for leverage, hurled the pot through the window. The glass imploded into a million shards and the blinds were knocked from their mounts. Cole leaped into the town house through the space where the window had been.

The noise of the glass breaking distracted Kate Ford and the deadly reptiles. The two rattlesnakes, who were less than a foot away from her, suddenly turned from their intended prey and started toward him. Cole drew his Beretta and took aim at the first messenger of slithering death. Three shots smashed its head into a bloody mass. He set his sights on the other one. This snake was a great deal harder to kill. Cole didn't know whether it was his aim or the fact that the snake moved toward him with a relentless speed. He knew he'd hit it with at least three of the first five bullets fired, but it kept coming. Now he was beginning to worry about running out of ammunition.

The snake left a trail of blood in its wake, giving Cole some encouragement, but it had not slowed down. He watched its head come up and its jaws open wide. As it swung forward with fangs bared, Cole pulled the trigger and kept pulling it until the slide locked back on empty. The remains of the snake collapsed to the floor.

The room stunk of cordite and fear, but Cole felt a sudden giddy relief. He looked across the room at Kate Ford, who still stood with her back against the wall. Her eyes bulged with terror.

"Are you okay?" he asked.

She took a deep breath, which suddenly caught in her throat. She coughed, choked, coughed again, and then started to cry.

Avoiding the carnage on the floor, Cole crossed the living room. Before he got to her he'd removed the empty clip from his gun and replaced it with a full one. Snakes could come in groups of threes and fours, as well as pairs, for all he knew.

"C'mon, sit down," he said, taking her gently by the shoulders.

She resisted him. "No! I don't want to sit anywhere in here until we're sure there are no more of those . . . !" She pointed at the two bloody piles on the floor, but refused to give them a name.

"Okay. Let's get out of here." With his arm around her, Cole began leading her to the front door. They detoured sharply to avoid the dead reptiles.

They stepped into the courtyard, which was now filling rapidly with curious neighbors. Judy Daniels pushed her way through the crowd to get to them.

"Are you okay, boss?" she asked.

"We're fine, Judy. Ms. Ford's neighbor put in a call to nine one one, so . . ." His words stopped suddenly and he cocked his head to the side. There was a frown of intense concentration on his face.

"What's wrong?" Kate asked.

Then Judy heard it too. "Somebody's playing a flute."

The music came from the alley behind the town-house courtyard.

"I don't understand what that's got to do with what we just went through," the reporter argued.

"I don't either," Cole responded, "but it needs to be checked out. Maybe our flute player doubles as a snake charmer. I'm going to have a little talk with this street musician."

Leaving Kate with Judy, Cole ran to the rear of the courtyard.

The gate exited onto an alley, which was devoid of excessive garbage, clean and well maintained. Now, outside the walls of the courtyard, which had partially blocked the transmission of sound, Cole heard the flute music with crystal clarity. And there, a short distance from the rear entrance, was Christian in his wheelchair. He was playing a silver flute.

Cole didn't recognize the tune. The only thing he could compare it to was a bleak funeral dirge.

When Cole approached him, Christian stopped playing, looked up at the cop and smiled. "Hello again, Larry."

Cole stood over him. "Hi, Christian. What are you doing?"

Christian's smile remained in place. "Playing my flute."

"What was that tune?"

Christian shrugged. "Oh, just something I made up."

"You know it sounded like a piece I once heard on a National Geographic television special. The topic was dangerous snakes. In one segment they showed this Indian, who called himself a snake charmer. He played an eerie melody that sounded a lot like yours and he was able to make this big cobra come out of a basket and even dance for him."

Something changed in Christian's face. The angelic quality vanished to be replaced by hardness. "There are no snakes around here, Larry."

Cole never took his eyes off the young man in the wheelchair. "At least not any live ones. I want you to come with me, Christian. There are some questions I'd like to ask you."

Christian made a show of dismantling his flute and placing its three sections into a compartment on one side of his chair beneath the right handle. Cole remarked to himself that this wheelchair seemed to have a great deal of room inside it.

"Am I in trouble?" Christian asked softly.

"I don't know. I just want to ask you—"

Christian's hand came out of the compartment holding a short rod that Cole first thought was a metal truncheon or a smaller version of a cop's nightstick. The boy's hand fit around a rubber handle at its base from which a length of cable led back into the wheelchair compartment. The exposed section was six inches long.

Christian moved so fast that Cole barely had time for his mind to register what he was doing. The double amputee leaned forward in his chair and extended the metal rod to touch the center of Cole's chest. The cop spasmed rigid as twenty thousand volts of electricity coursed through him. Cole's eyes locked with Christian's. The cop saw a cruelty there he'd only seen before in the orbs of the bestially cruel or the criminally insane. And Cole could tell that Christian was deriving immense enjoyment from the pain he was inflicting.

Finally, Christian jerked the rod back releasing Cole from the electrical charge's grip. As Christian turned his wheelchair around and began rolling away, Cole fell to the ground. The cop's heart had stopped.

17

July 7, 1999
4:05 p.m.

News travels fast. Bad news travels even faster. Each of the daily media outlets in the city, both print and electronic, monitored transmissions over the 911 Emergency radio network. When a frantic female voice came over the citywide frequency used by the detective division, the ears of the media listeners perked up.

"Car Fifty, emergency! I've got a police officer down in the west alley of the Fifty-four hundred block of South Kenwood! Send me an ambulance right away!"

The dispatcher answered with a cool, controlled, "Ten-four, Car Fifty."

Some of the eavesdroppers knew that Car Fifty was the beat designation for the chief of detectives. A few of the less informed had to use their CPD reference guides to tell them not only what Car Fifty was, but also the identity of the chief of detectives. Then things really started to pop.

In newsrooms and television studios across the city, orders were given to find out what had happened in that alley. Reporters were dispatched to University Hospital, where the injured officer was being taken. The more veteran scribes, who had been on the police beat for a number of years, were able to pick up the phone and call cops whom they knew personally or who owed them favors. And slowly the story began being pieced together.

The injured cop had been removed from the scene in a CFD ambulance. Before the ambulance left the west alley of the 5400 block of South Kenwood the attendants had worked on him for over fifteen minutes. What had happened to the cop was still a mystery, but the reporters used their imaginations to fill in the blanks. He'd probably been shot. But what was he doing there and, again, the question was asked, who was assigned to Car Fifty?

A veteran reporter in the pressroom at police headquarters filled in a few more of the blanks. The only member of the Chicago Police Department authorized to use the Car Fifty designation was Chief Larry Cole.

The first contingent of reporters arrived at the University Hospital emergency room. The ambulance attendants and emergency room medical personnel refused to comment on the injured officer. Then the staffer from the *Chicago Times-Herald* saw Kate Ford inside the treatment area. He shared this piece of information with his fellow reporters.

Phone calls were made and more reporters dispatched to the west alley of the 5400 block of South Kenwood. Although the excitement was over, there were still people milling around in the courtyard surrounded by town houses. Kate Ford's elderly Asian neighbor was discovered and convinced to give an on-camera interview. His image and words were broadcast live throughout the city.

Reporters were camped out in the lobby of police headquarters waiting for Jack Govich to leave for the hospital. The superintendent had always been good copy, because he was not only intelligent, but very witty. He also made it a habit of being quite candid with the press. However, when the center elevator door opened and they got one look at his face, they were certain that Govich was not about to be his usual jovial self. He did stop to give them a brief statement.

"I don't have all the facts right now," Govich began, "and I will not disclose the identify of the injured officer pending notification of his next of kin."

The reporters erupted with questions.

"Is the officer dead, Superintendent?"

"I don't know."

"What happened to him? Was he shot?"

"I'll have more information on that when I get to University Hospital and talk to his doctor."

"We understand the injured officer was working a beat designated as Car Fifty. Would that injured officer be Chief of Detectives Larry Cole?"

With a tired expression, Govich shook his head in the negative and replied, "I already told you I am withholding the identity of the injured officer pending notification of his family. Right now I need to get to the hospital. Please excuse me."

As he headed for the headquarter's entrance more questions were shouted at him, but he ignored them.

Larry Cole was seated in a canoe. He was floating on the lake in Michigan where he'd gone often as a child. The water possessed a stillness that almost made the surface resemble an immense pane of glass. The trees surrounding the lake were lush with summer greenery. Cole had been in this spot many times before. His father had brought him here. His father, Hugh, was in the boat with him now. Hubert "Hugh" Cole had been dead for twenty-seven years.

"You catching anything, son?"

Cole looked from his father down into the clear water. "They don't seem to be biting today, Dad."

"Maybe you should change your bait." Hugh Cole flipped his line to a spot farther away from the boat.

Larry reeled in his own line. There was no bait on the hook. He looked around him. Something wasn't right.

"Dad?" he asked.

"Yes, son." His father never took his eyes from the water.

"I don't think I belong here."

The elder Cole sighed. "You've been close to being with me many times before and I really miss you."

Cole felt a lump form in his throat. "I miss you too, but this isn't the time for us to be together again."

Hugh Cole continued to stare out at the water. "If you're aware of that, you truly don't belong here. You'd better start back."

Larry looked around. "How do I do that?"

"Someone's coming for you."

"Who?"

Then Larry Cole was no longer in the boat.

Judy Daniels and Kate Ford followed Cole to the alley exit from the courtyard. They arrived there just as the young man in the wheelchair spun away and Cole fell to the ground. They ran toward him.

Judy pulled a Smith and Wesson .45 pistol and aimed it at the rapidly retreating wheelchair. She shouted, "Stop!"

The young man kept spinning the wheels as fast as he could and was quickly reaching the end of the alley.

Judy was aiming a shot at one of the wheels to dismantle the chair when Kate called to her, "We've got to help him!"

The policewoman turned to see the reporter kneeling beside Cole. She had her hand on his chest. Cole wasn't moving. Alarm surged through Judy and she ran back to them.

"He's not breathing," Kate said, positioning herself over Cole's head, "and his heart has stopped."

Judy got down on her knees beside Cole and placed her hands over his sternum. Without another word spoken between them, they began applying cardiopulmonary resuscitation to the injured cop.

Kate Ford blew air into Cole's lungs while Judy kept up a rhythmic chest pressure. The seconds stretched into minutes, which seemed as long as eternity. Then, as the wail of approaching sirens pierced the atmosphere of the quiet summer afternoon, Cole coughed, took in a deep, ragged breath, and opened his eyes.

18

July 7, 1999
5:40 P.M.

Jonathan Gault was watching the TV news in the basement of the Kow Loon Restaurant. After the destruction of Astrolab a year ago, he had moved into Chicago and found a couple of secure hiding places. Although what had happened out in the Indiana countryside had been classified as a mysterious explosion of unknown origin, the United States government was still looking for him. The military wanted Gault's research papers, which they felt belonged to them. In a way, the scientist was forced to concede, they were right, as he had developed everything while he was in the army's employ. But Gault vowed that they would never get them. He would die first and, if it came to that, he would take a number of them with him. He turned his attention back to the television.

The broadcasts on all the major networks carried stories about the attempted murder of Larry Cole. Additional information was added to each account until Gault was certain that Christian was responsible for the attack and the police were looking for him.

The scientist switched off the set and headed for the alley entrance, which Christian had used earlier. Once outside he walked two blocks to a warehouse located in a depleted industrial area on the outskirts of Chinatown. En route he passed few people and those he did encounter paid him no attention.

The warehouse took up a quarter of a square block and could only be accessed from a front entrance on a narrow, one-way side street, which was devoid of parked vehicles. The only other structures on the block were two other warehouses, which had long ago been abandoned and were now windowless and rat infested.

Gault used a key to unlock a metal case embedded in the wall to the left of the entrance. Inside the case was a numbered keypad. He tapped in a four-digit combination and the door snapped open. He entered.

The interior was dark, as all the windows had been bricked over. He needed no lights to find his way and he was aware of movement around him. Anyone gaining unauthorized entry to this place would be dead within minutes. However, none of the slithering sentries of death approached him. In fact, they maintained a pronounced distance.

He came to a large room, which led off the main corridor. Stepping across the threshold caused him to trip an infrared sensor beam and the lights blinked on.

The room was furnished as a near replica of his laboratory back at Astrolab. There was a metal storage cabinet against the wall. Gault went to it and worked the combination lock securing the doors.

He removed a number of items from the cabinet to include a flesh-covered plastic mask mounted on a mannequin's head and a makeup kit. The mask had perforations for the eyes, nose, mouth, and ears. The plastic was of a soft pliable material, which the scientist had developed at Astrolab. Once it went over the head, the heat of the body caused the material to adhere to the contours of the face. Now the scientist placed the mannequin head on the lab table, opened the makeup kit, and went to work.

When he finished working on the mask, Gault stepped in front of a floor-to-ceiling mirror. He studied his reflection. What stared back at him was not pleasing even to his mismatched eyes. In fact, the sight could easily be termed ugly. But what was there in an appearance? Why was one person called beautiful and another hideous to begin with? Was it because of the way their features were arranged or their body structure constituted? Did it have anything to do with the color of their skin or the texture of their hair, which racists often touted? Or was it the inner self, or the spirit, that had the greatest influence on the appearance.

The scientist detected movement in the room behind him. His eyes flicked in that direction to see a large cobra crawl across the floor and curl itself around one of the legs of the cot. Through unblinking eyes the snake watched him.

The scientist began the transformation. The plastic mask completely covered his head. A pair of contact lenses and a wig were added. Then he changed his clothes.

A short time later he stepped in front of the mirror once more. What appeared there now was the image of a muscular Native American with thick, jet black, shoulder-length hair. The eyes were dark brown and had an exotic look. The overall appearance could be called "handsome"; however, there were a few who would sense that there was something evil about this beautiful male creature. The matinee idol figure was clad in a black Giorgio Armani suit, a black band-collar silk shirt and black boots with a mirror sheen. However, concealed behind this disguise, Jonathan Gault remained.

Turning from the mirror he looked at the cobra curled around the bedpost. His smile had a decidedly demonic cast. Gault spoke to the snake. "Christian tried to kill the chief of detectives today, Satan. My young friend was supposed to place

Napoleon and Marshal Ney inside Kate Ford's apartment, wait for them to kill her, and then retrieve them. But something went wrong. The journalist is not dead and Cole also survived. If the police haven't caught Christian yet he's gone to his old hiding place beneath the railroad tracks. I've got to get to him before they do."

Gault picked up a cloth pouch from the lab table and checked its contents before placing it in his pocket. A black cane with a gold head in the shape of a snake was in a rack beside the table. Gault removed it and crossed the room toward the door leading out into the entrance hall. Before exiting he stopped and looked back at the cobra named Satan. "Christian will have to be rescued and Kate Ford must still die, but first things first." As an afterthought he added, "And then we must do something about Mr. Cole."

With that he let himself out. The automatic sensor shut off the lights and Satan hissed into the darkness.

19

JULY 7, 1999
5:45 P.M.

Blackie Silvestri stood behind Manny Sherlock, who was seated at the computerized communications console in detective division headquarters. By way of LED readouts, fax, and telephone lines, Manny was linked to the Office of Emergency Communications on West Madison Street, operations command on the sixth floor of police headquarters, and each of the twenty-five patrol districts and five detective areas across the city. Silvestri and Sherlock were in charge of a manhunt for a white male in his late teens or early twenties with sandy brown hair and hazel eyes. He was described as being of medium weight; however, there was no estimated height given in the general description they'd issued. This was because they didn't have one. And this fact led to the most significant identifying factor about their wanted perpetrator of all. He was a double amputee confined to a wheelchair.

Blackie had an unlit, twisted cigar stuck in the corner of his mouth. He'd chewed the tip to a soggy mess. His dark eyes under thick brows scanned the data that Manny Sherlock retrieved. Sherlock was tall, in his early thirties, wore horn-rimmed glasses, and was beginning to develop shoulders as broad as Chief Cole's. Blackie didn't know all of the intricacies of Manny's manipulation of the keys and the dials on the communications console, but he did know how to interpret the data.

Every cop in the city had been alerted to be on the lookout for the man in the wheelchair. Patrol officers were to check their beats, while teams of detectives fanned out across the city checking hospitals and clinics specializing in the treatment of amputees and paraplegics. Blackie felt a nervous impatience, but he controlled it. He'd been a cop too long not to realize that this was going to take time. And he wanted that kid in the wheelchair. Blackie wanted him bad, because he'd come closer to doing something that any number of criminals had tried during the past twenty-six years, but failed to accomplish. That something was to kill Larry Cole.

Blackie thought back over the many near misses with death Cole'd had since they'd first teamed up together back in the old Nineteenth District over twenty years ago. Their first case had involved rapist and murderer Steven Zalkin, who had taken them fifteen years to catch. It was Zalkin who'd nailed Larry's hand to the floor of a chapel inside Our Lady of Peace Catholic

Church's rectory. Then they'd gotten on the case of notorious mobster Antonio "Tuxedo" Tony DeLisa and the complications caused by the involvement of FBI agent Reggie Stanton with Senator Harvey Banks. Next had come Neil and Margo DeWitt, a pair of murderers, who had revised every theory on serial killers ever devised. The DeWitt case was followed closely by the strange events at the National Science and Space Museum, where once more Cole had come very close to death when a one-hundred-year-old booby trap had come close to severing his head. And despite the dangers and the numerous close calls, Larry Cole had never come as close to dying as he had earlier today.

At the hospital, Blackie learned from Judy Daniels that Cole had stopped breathing and his heart had stopped. Although it had only been for a few seconds, that was sufficient time for Cole to go on a journey from which there was no return. In the past, Cole had been lucky, but Blackie knew that luck only went so far, and perhaps this was the Grim Reaper's way of sending the chief of detectives a final warning that another brush with death would cause the curtain on his life to come down for the last time. Blackie only hoped that Cole would heed the warning.

"I think we've got something," Manny said, as letters began marching across the screen to form a message from the Twenty-first Police District. "According to the beat cop working Chinatown, there's a kid in a wheelchair named Christian, who lost both his legs in a train accident a few years ago. The beat cop also thinks he knows where this Christian hides out."

"Where?" Blackie said, leaning forward and squinting at the screen.

Manny frowned. "It says here, in the caves beneath the Conrail Railroad tracks across the expressway from White Sox Park."

"Let's go, Manny," Blackie said, heading for the door.

20

July 7, 1999
6:01 p.m.

Larry Cole awoke in a hospital room. At first he didn't know where he was. Then it all came back to him; Christian jabbing him with the electric rod, waking up in the alley with Kate Ford and Judy hovering over him, and even the dream he'd had about being in a rowboat on a Michigan lake with his father. The last part lingered and left him uneasy. Now he wondered if it had actually been a dream.

The blinds were shut, but, there was enough daylight left to illuminate the room. There were people present: a nurse, who was seated beside his bed, Jack Govich standing by the door, Judy Daniels, who stood beside Govich, and Kate Ford seated in a chair a few feet from Judy. Cole's eyes stopped on the reporter and he managed a weak smile.

"You had chili and beer for lunch," he said.

The reporter blushed and smiled back. "I'll have to remember to pop a breath mint the next time I give mouth-to-mouth."

"Hey," Govich said, "if you're saving a cop's life, Kate, you can chew garlic cloves beforehand."

"That's easy for you to say," Cole said.

The exchange galvanized the nurse. Although she looked to be barely out of college, she said a stern, "Doctor's orders. The three of you can't stay for more than five minutes while the patient is awake. He's going to be under observation for the next forty-eight hours."

"What?!" Cole said, managing to rise slightly before collapsing back on the bed.

Govich stepped forward. "We and your patient will follow the doctor's orders to the letter, miss."

Judy walked over to the side of the bed and took Cole's hand. Tears glistened in her eyes. "How are you feeling, boss?"

He squeezed her hand gently. "Like a rookie right out of the academy who got careless and almost got himself killed."

Kate Ford stood at the foot of the bed. "From what I hear, you're too tough to kill. And when you get out of the hospital we need to discuss what you did to my plate-glass window."

"Okay," the nurse barked, "that's enough. The patient needs to rest. You can come back tomorrow during visiting hours, which are from two in the afternoon until seven in the evening."

As she moved to usher them out the door, Cole called to Govich, "Superintendent?"

Govich stopped and turned around. "Yeah, Larry."

"Did you get him?"

"Not yet." Then the superintendent's face turned hard. "But we will. I promise you, we will."

21

July 7, 1999
6:12 p.m.

The Conrail Railroad surface tracks ran from one end of Chicago to the other. Before there had been roads and then paved streets, and, finally, high-speed expressway networks crisscrossing the city, trains had ferried passengers and goods from the Windy City across the country. The railroad's sloping embankments, on which the dual set of tracks was constructed, were set approximately fifteen feet above street level. On the city's South Side at Thirty-sixth Street this embankment faced west and overlooked the Dan Ryan Expressway, a stone's throw from White Sox Park. On the east side of the embankment loomed the Stateway Gardens public-housing development.

The original railroad tracks had been laid on this site in 1869 when the surrounding area was mostly farmland and the city that would become Chicago was composed of a number of small villages. Over the years, repairs, new construction surrounding the tracks, and landfill had resulted in the right-of-way changing significantly. As such, in 1890 large cement drainage tunnels were built beneath the embankment to accomodate rainwater runoff. These tunnels were fairly well maintained until after the First World War. By the beginning of the Depression, flooding in the surrounding area was becoming severe and in the mid-1930s a WPA Project temporarily alleviated the excess water problem with the installation of new stone pipes, which were five feet in diameter. By 1960 the Dan Ryan Expressway and Stateway Gardens public-housing development were under construction and new sewer lines were installed making the pre–World War II drainage tunnels beneath the railroad embankment obsolete. However, they were never removed, simply abandoned.

In 1975 a section of the old drainage system collapsed. As it did not threaten the railroad's operation, it was never repaired and remained untouched until weeds and crabgrass eventually grew to obscure the hole left by the cave-in. In 1992 the spot where the cave-in occurred was discovered by a twelve-year-old runaway from a state-supported orphanage. The runaway's name was Christian Dodd. On September 2, 1993, Christian Dodd was playing on the railroad tracks above the hidden entrance to the drainage tunnels, running beneath the embankment, when he was struck by a southbound train. He survived, but lost both his legs.

Police Officer David Banahan of the Twenty-first District had handled this tragedy. He'd even searched the embankment until he found one of the child's legs and then rushed it to University Hospital in the hopes that it could be surgically reattached. But it was too late. Later, while Christian was recuperating, Banahan came to see him every day and found that his presence perked up the mutilated boy's spirits. Banahan even considered talking to his wife about adopting Christian. Then he was removed from University Hospital and placed into a state institution on the city's West Side. Banahan still came to see him, but with less frequency. And on these occasions he noticed that Christian was becoming increasingly sullen. The police officer did everything he could to cheer him up, but nothing worked. Then Banahan was forced to suspend his hospital visits because he got shot.

It was one of the duties that police officers perform routinely—the traffic stop. However, the late model van Officer Banahan stopped on that spring afternoon contained two wacked-out junkies, who had earlier stolen the van before robbing a convenience store and killing a clerk. They opened fire as soon as Banahan exited his squad car. His Kevlar vest saved his life and practice with his semiautomatic .45 caliber handgun enabled him to dispatch the junkies into the next world. The officer received a gunshot wound to his left thigh, which put him in the hospital for two weeks and placed him in a cast for a month and a half. As soon as he was ambulatory, he went to the state hospital to see Christian only to discover that the youth was no longer there. Banahan's investigation disclosed no more than the fact that Christian Dodd had simply vanished. It took three years but Dave Banahan discovered where Christian had disappeared to.

Now Banahan and his partner Jill Roberson sat in their squad car on Dearborn Street just south of Thirty-sixth. The sides of the railroad embankment were overgrown with weeds and bushes, but Banahan knew the location beneath the growth where the entrance to the abandoned drainage tunnels was located. Banahan also suspected that at this moment Christian Dodd was hiding there.

Banahan was a five-foot-ten-inch, forty-five-year-old redhead with a fireplug build. He walked with a slight limp due to his gunshot wound and above the right pocket of his uniform shirt there were two rows of ribbons denoting awards received for exceptional valor in the line of duty. Jill Roberson was an exquisitely built, ebony-skinned African American, who was an inch taller and twelve years younger than her partner. One of her lingering regrets was that she'd been off the day Banahan had been shot. She also knew about his interest in Christian and, prior to today, had admired him for it. Now that interest had assumed a completely different aspect.

"Dave, why do you think the kid will come back here?"

"I got a hunch," he answered, never taking his eyes from the bushes concealing the entrance to the drainage tunnels. "He hid here after he ran away and I bet he's here now."

Roberson stared down the street at the embankment. Her partner's hunches were generally on target and if he was right this time they were going to bag the attempted murderer of Larry Cole, the legendary chief of detectives. Placing her uniformed cap squarely on her head and picking up her flashlight, Officer Jill Roberson said, "Well, let's go check it out."

They got out of the marked squad car and walked slowly toward the railroad embankment down the street. Twilight was approaching and the sky was overcast, threatening rain. The hum of traffic was audible from the Dan Ryan Expressway, but the officers paid it little attention, as it was simply the background music of the urban jungle in which they worked.

Below the location on the embankment, where the entrance

to the drainage tunnels was located, they stopped. Banahan looked down at the ground and said, "Christian's here."

"How do you know?" Roberson said, dropping her voice to an urgent whisper.

Her partner pointed to the track marks. Her eyes followed his finger to the spot where narrow wheel prints were visible leading from the street up the embankment's incline.

"But he couldn't have rolled his chair up there," she protested.

Banahan squinted at the heavy brush covering the surface of the incline. "He wasn't in the chair when he went up there, Jill. He got out of the chair and dragged it behind him."

Roberson's eyes widened slightly. "Then's he got to be extremely strong."

"He is, and he's also got a device that can give you a twenty thousand volt shock, so watch yourself." With that he began climbing the embankment. After a second-long hesitation, she followed him.

Halfway up the incline Banahan stopped. He switched on his multicell flashlight despite there still being enough light to see by. He pointed the beam at a clump of bushes. "The entrance is right there."

All Roberson could do was take his word for it, because she could see nothing but the dense foliage.

Banahan reached down and tugged at the brush. He was able to pull most of it away to reveal a tunnel lying underneath. The edges of what was left of a jagged stone pipe surrounded the hole. What lay beyond this makeshift entrance was immersed in darkness.

"Now what?" Roberson asked.

"We go inside."

"C'mon, Dave," she protested, "that place isn't safe. We need to call our sergeant and get . . ."

The words stuck in her throat, as something moved at the bottom of the drainage tunnel entrance. Automatically, Banahan trained his light on it.

The large pit viper reacted to the light by coiling, glaring up at them with unblinking eyes, and hissing. Roberson took a step backward, lost her balance, fell, and rolled down the embankment. When she came to a stop she scrambled to her feet and looked up to find her partner still standing over the tunnel entrance. She didn't realize it at the time, but she'd torn her uniform trousers and cut her arm on a sliver of broken glass during the fall.

"Dave," she shouted, "get away from there!"

She watched him draw his gun, as he continued staring into the tunnel.

"Dave, please!"

Finally, he began backing away slowly and almost lost his balance and fell.

When he reached the street she said, "What are we going to do now? That snake is the meanest, ugliest thing I've ever seen."

Banahan looked back up the embankment. "That's not all of it. There's more than one of them."

"What?!"

"I counted at least three and Christian's in there with them."

22

July 7, 1999
6:30 p.m.

The sky darkened rapidly as thunderclouds rolled across the city. A tornado watch was issued on the local six o'clock news programs for the Cook County area until 11:00 p.m. Before seven o'clock this watch would be upgraded to a warning as violent thunderstorms swept across Chicago.

Blackie Silvestri looked up at the menacing sky as he trotted back to Superintendent Govich's command car, which was parked in the middle of the 3700 block of South Dearborn. This was approximately one block from the entrance to the drainage tunnels in which Christian Dodd was believed to be hiding. As a sixty mile an hour wind kicked up dirt and debris, Blackie climbed into the backseat.

Govich was seated in the passenger side front seat. Behind the wheel was his pretty blonde secretary, Detective Patsy Huels. The superintendent turned to hear Blackie's report.

"Officer Banahan from the Twenty-first District says that it's a good chance the kid with no legs is somewhere inside the tunnels, boss, but him and his partner, Roberson, said the place is infested with poisonous snakes."

Govich frowned. "There are no poisonous snakes in Chicago, except what they have in the zoo."

"Begging your pardon, Superintendent," Huels said, "but Chief Cole killed two snakes at Kate Ford's place and our double amputee apparently planted them there."

A lightning bolt lit up the back window of the car.

Govich glanced from his driver back to Blackie. "So how do you suggest we deal with these poisonous snakes."

The lieutenant shrugged. "We could do it the Larry Cole way, boss."

Govich waited.

"We could shoot them."

Govich shook his head in the negative. "No, we can't kill them. If it got out, we could have the Anticruelty Society down on us."

"We could call the zoo and see if they could recommend something," Huels said.

Govich nodded to the dashboard telephone. "Call them."

23

July 7, 1999
6:35 P.M.

A black Mercedes sedan with tinted windows exited the southbound lanes of the Dan Ryan Expressway and made a left turn to cross the Pershing Road overpass. At the center of the overpass the car pulled to a halt. Its headlights were extinguished, although the engine remained on. Behind the wheel of the luxury car sat Jonathan Gault, disguised as a handsome young Native American. Through the windshield he could see a marked police car, its mars lights flashing, blocking access to Dearborn at Thirty-ninth Street. By now the police would have blocked all access routes to the area where Christian was hiding.

The heavy Mercedes rocked from the force of the oncoming storm. The menacing sky had turned black and lightning bolts illuminated the heavens across the horizon. As there was nothing else he could do, Gault turned the car around and drove away.

A few moments later he pulled up in front of Comiskey Park at Thirty-fifth and Shields on the opposite side of the Dan Ryan Expressway from the location where the search for Christian was taking place. From there he watched the search for his young friend progress. If they did find him then Gault would have to engineer an escape for his young assistant. The thought of abandoning him never crossed the renegade scientist's mind.

As Gault watched and waited, the ferocity of the storm increased.

24

July 7, 1999
6:37 P.M.

Jack Govich had sixteen police officers, six detectives, Sergeant Manny Sherlock, and Lieutenant Blackie Silvestri with him, as he commanded the search for the man who'd attempted to kill Cole. Most of them had been born and raised in Chicago, where there was an old saying, "If you don't like the weather just stick around and it will change." This was a humorous way of saying that not only was the weather unpredictable, but could also be very violent. However, none of the cops out on Dearborn had ever experienced anything like the violent thunderstorm that struck the area in which they were conducting their manhunt.

The wind-driven rain fell with such density that visibility was reduced to zero. The officers caught outside their squad cars barely made it inside managing to slam the doors, as the wind nearly snatched them off their feet. The cars themselves were buffeted back and forth as if they were toys in the hands of a gigantic, angry child.

In his command car Govich held on to the dashboard and watched the rain run off the windshield in torrents. He had never experienced anything like this and being caught in it was truly frightening. He glanced at Blackie Silvestri in the backseat to see the lieutenant's usually hard-boiled exterior glazed over with fear. He looked over at Detective Huels. She had gone pale with terror.

A lightning bolt struck very close to the car. Actually, too close, as the flash and the deafening thunderclap were virtually simultaneous. The lightning bolt made contact with the railroad embankment near the entrance to the drainage tunnel. Then, as the terrified occupants of the police cars looked on, a second and third lightning bolt streaked from the heavens. Suddenly, the rain slackened, flames leaped into the sky from the entrance to the drainage tunnels and what seemed like the amplified sound of a slow-moving freight train engulfed them. And the veterans of the changing Chicago weather realized that what they were hearing was not a train, but the deadly noise of a tornado that had touched down nearby. A tornado which was rapidly approaching the 3600 block of South Dearborn.

25

July 7, 1999
6:40 p.m.

In the tunnels beneath the embankment, Christian crawled using one arm to propel himself along at a fairly rapid pace. He dragged his wheelchair behind him. The tunnels were pitch-black, but he knew every square inch of space, because for a number of years before Dr. Gault had come into his life, this place had been his home. Beside him a pair of pit vipers crawled, using their acute tracking sense to keep their distance from the mutilated human, as well as navigate in the dark tunnel. The snakes were Christian's friends. He took care of them and they protected him. Not one of them had ever bitten him. This was because Dr. Gault told them not to. However, with others it was different and these snakes were far more deadly than their species was in nature. Dr. Gault had also made this so.

Christian was headed for his secret exit from the drainage tunnels, which came out on the west side of the embankment approximately one hundred feet from the Thirty-fifth and Federal Streets intersection. Suddenly, the tunnel shook violently. Frightened, Christian stopped. Many times before he'd been in the tunnel when trains had rumbled across the tracks above. However, he had never experienced anything like this last jolt. Then there came another and still a third.

The tunnel brightened and became noticeably warmer. The

pit vipers accompanying him began to crawl more quickly and Christian could sense their panic. He began trying to move faster. Then the tunnel walls began to glow. Christian abandoned the chair and crawled as fast as he could.

26

July 7, 1999
6:50 P.M.

The freak storm vanished as quickly as it had formed. Weather stations around the Chicago area tracked it and those manning the radar scopes expressed unbridled amazement when in a matter of seconds their screens had become virtually clear of any turbulence.

Motorists on the Dan Ryan Expressway and residents of the buildings flanking the South Side high-speed thoroughfare were equally surprised when the sky went from an almost midnight overcast to a clear evening twilight, in just a matter of minutes. The ground was soaked and water ran with the force of rivers through the gutters; however, other than that, there was little remaining evidence that there had been any storm at all. Despite meteorological evidence that indeed a tornado of truly violent proportions had touched down in one of the most densely populated cities in America, there were no apparent injuries, nor was there any obvious damage. Except in the 3600 to 3900 blocks of South Dearborn.

The Office of Emergency Communications command console dispatcher, located in the new complex on West Madison, was the first to notice that something was wrong. A twenty-year veteran of the department, she had spent six years in Communications. She was good enough at what she did to be assigned to the frequency the superintendent of police was using to command an operation in the field. Now she hadn't heard from Car Four, the superintendent's vehicle call number, nor any of the other vehicles at the 3600 to 3900 South Dearborn manhunt site, for over ten minutes.

Depressing the transmit pedal beneath her console, she said into the microphone of her headset, "Car Four." She listened. Nothing. "Car Four, come in." No response. She tried it twice more with the same negative results. She hit the red button to summon her supervisor. The OEC's watch commander, aware that this dispatcher was on the command frequency, was at her station in less than thirty seconds.

She explained the situation to him.

Plugging into her console with his own headset, he repeated the hail to Car Four and "any other unit assigned to the 3600 to 3900 block of South Dearborn." Still nothing. He looked at her CADS board, which showed the location of the units on a geographic overhead map above the dispatcher's station. Although the superintendent's vehicle did not broadcast a signal, which allowed them to trace its location on the board, the other units did. The display told them that all the cars were still in the original search area.

"We'd better send another unit over there to check them out," the supervisor said, walking away. "Maybe the storm caused their radios to fail."

27

July 7, 1999
7:00 P.M.

The Second District field operations lieutenant was dispatched to check on the superintendent. When she was still two blocks from the Thirty-ninth and South Dearborn intersection she realized that something had gone seriously wrong here. A marked police car, which looked as if it had been picked up by a giant hand and dropped from a great height, was lying upside down in the middle of the street. Pulling up to this car, the lieutenant was just about to order emergency assistance on her radio, when she became aware of what had happened to the rest of Govich's search party. She opened her mouth to scream and then caught herself. She was a professional law-enforcement officer and she was damn sure going to act like one.

She took a deep breath and said into her microphone, "This is two-ninety. I have thirteen wrecked police vehicles with injured occupants in the thirty-six to thirty-nine hundred blocks of South Dearborn. One of the officers in need of assistance is Superintendent Govich. From all indications there are a number of officers trapped in their cars. I'll need four Second District units for traffic control, the Chicago Fire Department's Emergency Rescue Squad, and the Second District watch commander to respond to this location." She unkeyed her mike, then as an afterthought added, "That's just for starters."

* * *

Each of the police cars had been severely damaged by the tornado. A couple of them—the superintendent's command car and Officers Banahan's and Roberson's marked squad car—also bore lightning-bolt scorch marks. All of the eight marked cars were totaled. Officers were trapped inside five of them when the storm's force crushed the metal shells and jammed the doors shut. Of the remaining three vehicles, two were flipped over a number of times, which had caused all four of the doors to be ripped off at the hinges. Miraculously, none of the officers in these vehicles were seriously injured. The occupants of the remaining marked vehicle, which had been assigned to traffic control at the intersection of Thirty-ninth and Dearborn, were not so lucky.

Officers McDonnell and Maragoi were in the unit farthest from the tornado's center when it touched down. However, they were caught in the storm's backlash, which hurled them against the brick wall of the Conrail Railroad's Thirty-ninth Street overpass, yanked them back, as if by the will of some malevolent intelligence, and then hurled them into the wall again. The car was whipped back and forth before landing upside down in the center of the intersection.

McDonnell and Maragoi were both veteran officers and could sense unseen danger on the city streets they worked. But this sixth cop sense did not prepare them for the ferocity of the storm they were caught in. When it hit, they were sitting inside their squad car drinking coffee. As they were stationary they'd unbuckled their seat belts. They never knew what hit them.

Two Chicago Fire Department Emergency Rescue Units arrived within minutes of the field operations lieutenant's request. When they saw what they were up against, the ERU captain in charge quickly got on his radio and requested additional rescue units to respond. Then the available personnel fanned out to begin giving what assistance they could to the trapped and injured police officers.

The captain and one of the ERU technicians ran to the superintendent's smashed command car. The roof had collapsed and the tires flattened. There was a strong smell of gasoline, which indicated that the fuel tank had ruptured. The technician used a fire extinguisher to spray the car and the ground around it with foam. They were turning their attention to extricating the occupants when a loud banging noise came from the driver's side backdoor. As the ERU personnel watched, the door shuddered, opened a crack, shuddered again, and finally flew open. A man's legs protruded through the opening from inside the car. The firemen grabbed them and pulled him from the vehicle. A bruised and battered Blackie Silvestri came out of the car.

For a moment the lieutenant seemed dazed, but he quickly snapped out of it and barked, "The superintendent and his aide are trapped in the front seat."

Together the cop and the two firemen began working to rescue Govich and Detective Huels.

It took nearly an hour to free them from the wreckage. Despite the air bags deploying, the dashboard had been pushed into the passenger compartment when the front end of the car was demolished during the storm. Huels sustained cracked ribs, a punctured lung, and a few minor facial contusions. Both of Jack Govich's legs were broken. This was quite a devastating injury for the superintendent of police; he was an avid jogger. As he was whisked away in an ambulance, Blackie started looking for Manny Sherlock, who had been in one of the detective cars.

By now, Dearborn from Thirty-fifth to Thirty-ninth streets was crammed with emergency vehicles. The lieutenant was approaching the fire department captain, who had rescued him, when a familiar voice called, "Blackie!"

The lieutenant turned to see Manny walking toward him. Blackie frowned. The sergeant not only didn't have a scratch on him, his clothes weren't even rumpled. When he asked Manny about his pristine condition, he explained, "The car I was in got buffeted around a bit and even flipped over. I guess I was just lucky."

"Yeah," Blackie said, reaching for a cigar in his inside coat pocket. He scowled when he pulled out a mass of crushed tobacco, which he dropped on the ground. Then he said, "I guess most of us were lucky today." His voice dropped an octave in memory of the two dead cops.

They stood in silence for a moment before Manny asked, "Blackie, what in the hell happened here?"

"Hell if I know, kid. Hell if I know."

28

July 7, 1999
7:07 P.M.

In the confusion caused by the massive rescue operation, the hunt for Christian Dodd was temporarily suspended. As frenetic activity continued on Dearborn, which was located on the west side of the Conrail tracks, Gault's black Mercedes sedan cruised down Federal Street located on the east side of the tracks.

As a rule, Federal, which was lined on one side by the massive, sixteen-story structures of the Stateway Gardens public-housing development, was a place that most people avoided, if they could. As urban jungles go, this was one of the worst. Even now a group of young men sporting gang colors and wearing baseball caps cocked to the side to signal their individual affiliation, were loitering around the rear of the 3544 South Federal building. Their idleness and the hostility they exuded indicated they were looking for trouble. If necessary, in a matter of minutes, one of the gang members could be dispatched into the building where their secret weapons cache was located. And the gang members were as well armed as the police.

The Black Gangster Disciples watched the black Mercedes with the tinted windows pull up next to the railroad embankment and stop. The gang members were aware of what had happened on the other side of the tracks during the storm. They were glad there were a lot of cops injured, but also realized that what had occurred over there would disrupt normal police operations in this area for some time. That meant the Mercedes and its driver were at their mercy. The looks they exchanged transmitted a silent signal. They would wait to see what the driver did. If he was stupid enough to get out of the car, his ass would belong to them. The car door opened and the lone occupant got out. The BGDs uncoiled from their casual positions against the graffiti-scarred wall of the housing development building and advanced.

Gault walked around the Mercedes carrying the gold-headed cane in his hand. This was a device that he had also designed at Astrolab, but had only recently perfected. A twist of the serpent's head caused a pair of metal rods to protrude from the cane's tip. It was based on the same principle as the rod Christian had used in attempting to kill Larry Cole. However, Gault's cane could produce thirty thousand volts of electricity. The scientist looked down at the wet ground. Water was an excellent conductor. Gault's boots were insulated so he would be protected. The young men approaching him would not be so fortunate. Standing in front of the Mercedes he waited. A sadistic smile made the corners of his mouth twitch, as he slowly twisted the gold serpent's head.

The six gang members spread out to form a semicircle around the Mercedes. The leader, who'd been given the rank of war chieftain in the hierarchy of the BGDs, said a menacing, "What are you doing here, man?"

Gault didn't respond.

The gang members began looking around the ghetto street for weapons. One found a brick, another a broken bottle, and a third a rusty length of pipe. One of the remaining BGDs pulled a five-inch-blade folding knife from his back pocket. The fifth one slipped on a pair of brass knuckles. The last wore steel-tipped combat boots. They tensed preparing to attack the man in black. Gault lowered the cane to make contact with the wet ground.

Each of the gang members spasmed rigid, as the multivoltage electrical current began coursing through them. They were unable to move and Gault kept the cane in place until they began to burn. With a near childlike fascination, the renegade scientist studied his victims. He wished that he'd had the foresight to bring along a video camera to record what was happening here. Finally, he broke the connection and the six dead gang members collapsed to the ground.

They were smoldering when Gault turned and walked over to the railroad embankment. He cast a glance back at the burning Black Gangster Disciples. Then he found the entrance from Federal Street into the abandoned drainage tunnels beneath the railroad tracks. He vanished inside.

The tunnel was dark and filled with smoke. Gault used a powerful pocket flashlight to illuminate the tunnel in front of him. He was forced to crouch down to negotiate the low ceiling.

He found the badly scorched remains of the pit vipers first. These slithering creatures had been Christian's pets and the handicapped youth had raised them from the instant they emerged from their mothers' eggs. The snakes had been trained to be completely obedient to the scientist and Christian. Now they were nothing but overdone meat.

A noise came from farther down the tunnel. Gault moved toward it. There he found a large break in the old stone wall. He examined the hole. The dirt was warm, but not as hot as the stone surface surrounding it. The scientist looked up and down the tunnel. There was no place else that Christian could have gone. Using his bare hands, Gault began to dig.

It took him a full minute to find the handicapped youth. Christian had nearly suffocated after he'd burrowed beneath the soil to protect himself from the flames, but he was alive.

Jonathan Gault unearthed the young man finding that his face was blackened and his hair was encrusted with the black soil. However, his eyes shone brightly.

The scientist felt his own eyes fill with tears. It wasn't until this moment that he realized how much Christian meant to him. And then Jonathan Gault remembered "The Man Who Walked in Blood." A man whom he hadn't thought about in a very long time. A man whom Gault had no way of knowing he would be seeing very soon.

Now, with tears streaming down his cheeks, the evil scientist picked Christian up and carried him out of the abandoned drainage tunnel.

When he stepped outside with his burden, three of the BGDs were burning with the intensity of small bonfires and the others were on the verge of erupting into flame. Gault placed Christian onto the cushioned leather backseat of the Mercedes, started the engine, put the car in gear, and floored the accelerator. He ran over two of the burning Black Gangster Disciples as he rocketed off Federal Street.

PART 2

"Christian, help me!!!"
—Jonathan Gault

29

July 9, 1999
9:02 A.M.

The medical staff at University Hospital decided to release Larry Cole early after he'd only been under observation for thirty-six hours. Their reasons were twofold. They had consulted with the Chicago Police Department Medical Director, Dr. Dean Drake, who agreed with them that the patient was in excellent physical shape. This was confirmed by tests revealing no abnormalities in Cole's heart rate or blood pressure. The second reason behind the early discharge was Cole's high level of agitation at being kept inactive with so much happening in Chicago.

Superintendent Jack Govich was in guarded condition in another wing of the hospital. At 2:00 A.M. on the morning of July 8, the night duty nurse heard voices coming from the top cop's private room. Going to investigate, she found Cole in pajamas and robe conferring with the superintendent on what was explained to the nurse as urgent police business. She'd been forced to threaten to call security if the chief of detectives didn't leave.

Cole's doctor restricted the patient to his room and this slowed him down, to an extent. The patient was almost continuously on the room phone conferring with officers he referred to as Blackie, Manny, and Judy. That is when these same officers, in violation of hospital visiting hours, weren't in Cole's room. And late the previous evening, when a nurse had attempted to eject a scowling Lieutenant Blackie Silvestri, she'd been threatened with arrest.

Finally, it was decided, for the good of all parties concerned, that the chief of detectives should be discharged with the admonition that he take it easy for at least a week. Then they watched him charge off as if he'd been shot from a gun. So much for cooperative patients.

Cole's first stop was Govich's hospital room. Both of the superintendent's legs were encased in knee-to-toe casts. The casts were suspended from pulleys above the bed. Despite being flat on his back, Govich was clean shaven and his hair was perfectly combed.

Cole closed the door behind him and pulled a chair up beside the bed.

Govich got down to cases immediately. "This is a bad time for me to be laid up, Larry, but I'm only as far away as the telephone. First Deputy Bishop will be running things, but I want you to give him as much help as you can."

"Whatever he needs I'll make sure he gets, boss."

"Ray's a good man," Govich said, referring to the first deputy, "but he's a straight arrow. Plays everything honest and aboveboard. Some of our friends over on LaSalle Street will try to take advantage of him."

"Friends like Tommy Kingsley and Alderman Sherman Ellison Edwards?" Cole said. Edwards was the chairman of the City Council Police and Fire Committee and a close political ally of Kingsley.

"The same. They're always looking for a way to get their patronage hooks into the department and over the past few years they've come close to succeeding, so watch them closely."

"Don't worry," Cole said. "I'll handle them just like all the others."

"What others?"

Cole smiled. "The other crooks."

They both laughed.

"Now for this other thing," Govich said. "Tell me what you're going to do."

Cole checked to make sure the door was still closed before leaning closer to the superintendent and lowering his voice.

30

July 9, 1999
9:15 A.M.

Tommy Kingsley was deep in thought. He was in his LaSalle Street private office with the door closed. He'd told his secretary to hold his calls. The director of public safety was tense; however, the politician in him recognized the fact that no matter how bad the situation might appear at the moment, there was always something that could be salvaged. At least he hoped so.

He hadn't liked the idea of getting involved in this thing with Jonathan Gault to begin with. Of course, at the time he'd had no choice, because the man, who kept his office in the basement of the Kow Loon Restaurant, definitely had Tommy by the proverbial balls.

Tommy couldn't recall whether it had been his idea or Gault's to kill Anna and her lover. Yes, at the time he'd been quite angry when Gault had verified for him that indeed his unfaithful wife and Kevin Quinn were plotting and had even made a down payment on his assassination. As Kingsley recalled, he hadn't actually told Gault that he wanted them dead. He'd said something more along the lines that he wanted them taken care of. Tommy quickly corrected this to have this thing taken care of. That would sound better in case he was ever dragged before a grand jury. And as a veteran Chicago politico, he knew exactly how to play this game. It wasn't so much what he said; it was what he meant. At the time he was getting over pneumonia. He'd been weak. Gault had taken advantage of him. At least that's the way he'd play it.

"But what about the others, Director Kingsley?"

The unbidden thought stopped him. Well, he had put Gault in touch with certain people who were interested in upgrading the security of their property to what could be called the fail-safe point. The clients actually hadn't known how Gault was securing their homes and autos, and the owner of the Jaguar freaked when he found a dead thief in his car. The cost for the service was high, but the desired objective was obtained. Professional burglars and auto thieves were not only becoming rare in Chicago, they were reaching the point of virtual extinction.

But Tommy Kingsley didn't give a hoot about the crime rate. Gault was giving him a third for each referral. Tommy's end also covered making sure any of the dead autopsied thieves had their causes of death listed as undetermined. This would keep any nosey cops . . . or reporters, from snooping around. But now that wasn't working either. And it was all because of Larry Cole and Kate Ford.

Tommy had not heard or attempted to contact Gault since their meeting at the Kow Loon Restaurant two days ago. In fact, at one point, after he'd heard about the attempts on Kate Ford's and Larry Cole's lives, Kingsley was certain that the jig was up. He was expecting the cops to come knocking at his door. But nothing happened, which had given him the time to regroup. Now he almost had it pieced together.

If the cops did find out about Gault and his unique antitheft measures, then Tommy would be prepared to drop all the weight on the ugly old man. Soupy McGuire would have to be dealt with, which he would leave to Gault. Then there were Cole and Kate Ford. He'd have to figure out something for the reporter as he went along, but Gault had given him an idea how best to handle Cole. After all he was indeed Cole's boss, as Gault had reminded him.

He picked up the phone, punched the intercom button for his secretary and said, "Get Herb Donaldson for me."

31

July 9, 1999
1:55 P.M.

The fire department, assisted by crews from Streets and Sanitation, excavated the tunnels beneath the railroad embankment at Thirty-sixth and Dearborn. They were accompanied by Chicago Police Sergeant Manny Sherlock and Detective Judy Daniels, who donned hard hats and protective coveralls for the expedition. Although the acrid smoke had cleared, the stench from the fire was still quite pronounced. They found what remained of Christian's wheelchair. Everything else had been turned to ashes. The entrance to the tunnels was of particular interest to them, as this was where three lightning bolts had struck. The scoring on the tunnel walls was more pronounced here than at any other place and they were actually able to see where the repeated electrical discharges from the storm made the tunnels so hot that the walls had begun to melt.

Their faces streaked with soot and grime, Judy and Manny came out of the tunnel on Federal Street. Cole's car was parked a short distance away. They headed for it.

The presence of the police and so many official vehicles had brought out a number of the residents of the Stateway Gardens housing development. They stood by watching the employees of the so-called City that Works perform their duties. However, seldom had they ever seen this level of service generated on their behalf. Their silent, hostile stares transmitted the resentment they felt. Some of them were also either related to or had known the six BGDs who'd been mysteriously incinerated on this narrow street. But death in the public-housing developments was such a daily occurrence that few of them gave the violently brutal murders more than a passing thought. In a very short period of time—perhaps too short a period—the young men would be completely forgotten. This was what was known as life and death in the Windy City.

But one of the officials present at the scene was particularly interested in the deaths of the six Black Gangster Disciples. He was interested because their deaths made no sense, which, coupled with everything else that had happened out here, enveloped this case in a cloud of mystery. The interested city official was Chief of Detectives Larry Cole.

Cole listened to Judy and Manny's report concerning what had been found in the tunnel. Cole hadn't expected the remains of Christian Dodd to be found. That would have been a predictable event in a series of totally unpredictable ones. When their report was concluded Cole said, "Okay, let's head over to the hospital. I want to talk to the superintendent."

When they got in the car with Manny behind the wheel and Judy in the backseat, Cole detected the strong smell of smoke coming off them. He made a mental note to let them go home early. They had always been loyal to him and he prized that loyalty very highly. Now as they drove to University Hospital he contrasted his professional relationships with his personal ones. And the personal did not come out looking very good.

Larry Cole was divorced. His wife, Lisa, had left him for a combination of reasons. Primary among these was that she felt their son, Butch, could be in danger from the numerous dangerous enemies his father made. One such enemy was Margo DeWitt, who had kidnapped Butch with the intention of murdering him in a rather horrible fashion. However, the main reason Lisa left Cole was because of his devotion to the job. A devotion that she felt bordered on the fanatic.

It was true that Cole enjoyed his work. The Chicago Police Department defined him as a man. Had he chosen another line of work, such as doctor, lawyer, author, or mechanic, he would have brought just as much enthusiasm and all-encompassing energy to those occupations as he did to police work. And Cole had never neglected his family. It was true he wasn't there all the time, but what father was? And he didn't have a simple nine-to-five job like most other men. He'd been rewarded for his dedication to the department by being promoted to the rank of chief of detectives. Perhaps, he mused, the fault was with Lisa and what had occurred with Margo DeWitt was merely an excuse. Yes, he knew it had frightened Lisa badly. Hell, what had happened to Butch scared Cole, too, but he'd realized a long time ago that you couldn't go through life running from problems.

Then there was Edna Gray, his current significant other, whom he hadn't seen or talked to since that morning behind the National Science and Space Museum. She didn't even come to see him while he was in the hospital.

They pulled up to the emergency room entrance to the hospital. He was in with Jack Govich for fifteen minutes. When Cole returned to the car he was deep in thought.

"Do you want to go back to headquarters, boss?" Manny asked.

Cole didn't answer right away. Finally, he said, "No, but

I'm going to drop you two there. After you check in with Blackie you can have the rest of the day off."

"Thanks, boss," they said as one.

Cole merely smiled in return. He'd decided on a more direct approach to a pressing problem.

32

July 9, 1999
2:20 P.M.

Larry Cole tried Edna Gray's number from his car phone. He was puzzled when a recorded message said, "The number you have dialed has been disconnected at the owner's request." A few minutes later he pulled up in front of her apartment building on the north end of Jackson Park overlooking the National Science and Space Museum. For a moment he sat behind the wheel staring at the entrance. Edna had pulled disappearing acts on him before. At times she could be extremely reclusive, due to things she'd experienced in her past life. However, each time she did this it worried him. Finally, he made a decision and got out of the car.

There was a doorman in the lobby. Although he'd been here many times, Cole had never seen this guy before. Cole remarked to himself that the doorman's thick build and patently cynical expression made him look like an ex-cop. The "Can I help you, sir?" came out with a forced cordiality.

"I'd like to see Edna Gray in apartment twelve oh three."

The doorman consulted a directory in front of him. Looking

up from it at Cole, he said, "There's no one living here by that name and apartment twelve oh three is vacant."

Cole laughed. *Oh, was this guy wrong.* "I think your records are in error, pal. Miss Gray has lived here for some time."

The doorman affixed Cole with a hostile stare. He looked ready to throw Cole out. To keep him from making a critical mistake the chief of detectives flashed his badge. "I want to see the building manager."

The manager was a sixtyish, officious woman with snow white hair. She gave Cole's badge as much scrutiny and respect as she would had it been the prize from the bottom of a Cracker Jack box.

"Are you investigating Ms. Gray, Officer?"

"No," Cole said. "She's a coworker and I'm concerned because I haven't heard from her for some time."

"A coworker?" the manager said with a mocking grin.

Cole managed a chilly smile. "That's right."

The manager's grin did not alter. "Then I assume Ms. Gray has not been to work."

Cole's patience was wearing thin. "She's currently on a two-week vacation."

"I see," the manager said, dropping her eyes to a stack of papers resting on the surface of the desk in front of her. "Actually, I shouldn't disclose this information to you or anyone else without some form of official inquiry being mounted; however, I don't think you can do any real harm with it."

Unable to figure out what she was talking about, Cole waited.

"As the doorman told you, Edna Gray no longer resides in this building. She moved out two days ago." Before he could ask the question, she added, "And she left no forwarding address."

* * *

"Have a nice day, sir," the doorman said when Cole crossed the lobby on his way out the door.

The chief of detectives merely waved.

The doorman watched Cole trot down the front steps and get in his car. Then the man with the looks of the veteran ex-cop picked up a telephone, dialed a number, and said, "He's on the way."

33

July 9, 1999
3:17 p.m.

Larry Cole parked in an "emergency vehicles only" spot and entered the emergency room of University Hospital. He'd been inside the hospital so much lately that he felt like a permanent resident. This time he hadn't returned to see Govich, but was instead going to the northeast wing of the hospital where the Dillion Psychiatric Annex was located. There Edna Gray's sister, Josie Gray (aka Eurydice Vaughn), was a patient.

Access to this wing was restricted and a security guard was stationed at a desk in front of a pair of metal double doors. The doors could only be opened with a key from the outside. There was another guard stationed inside. The entrance to the wing, the guard stations, and each of the corridors were monitored via closed-circuit TV hookups leading to a room in the basement of the medical complex. The Dillon Psychiatric Annex was for the treatment of the violent and criminally insane.

Cole walked up to the guard's station and flashed his badge.

He saw the guard's eyes widen when he read the inscription CHIEF OF DETECTIVES.

"I'd like to get some information on one of your patients," Cole said.

The guard came on in a very similar fashion to that of the doorman back at Edna's building. He had the cynicism and hardness of the veteran cop about him. But he said a respectful, "You'll have to speak to Dr. Vargas for that, Chief."

Cole had hoped to avoid going through official channels for what he wanted, but if he had to see this Dr. Vargas then so be it. "Where can I find him?"

The guard gave Cole a weak smile and picked up the telephone. He dialed a four-digit number and waited. Then, "Chief Larry Cole of the Chicago Police Department is here to see the doctor." The guard paused a moment. "Sure thing." Then he hung up.

The door behind the guard snapped open. "Dr. Vargas's office is through the third door down the corridor on the left. You can't miss it. He's expecting you."

Cole didn't move nor did he take his eyes off the guard. "How did you know my name?"

The guard's smile twisted into a cynical sneer. He said a sarcastic, "Everybody knows who you are, Chief."

Still, to Cole, something didn't seem right. Then, slowly he walked through the door into the hospital for the criminally insane.

The uneasy feeling gripping Cole intensified the instant he stepped across the threshold of the bland, antiseptically clean Dillon Psychiatric Annex. There was another guard seated at a desk just inside the door. He could have been a clone of the one outside and he watched Cole with a careful wariness as the policeman walked past him. There was no one else in evidence and Cole found the third office on the left side of the corridor without difficulty.

The closed door to the office did not have a name or a number on it. Cole knocked. There was no answer. He looked down the hall at the guard, whose expression had not altered. Cole tried the knob. The door was unlocked. He walked inside.

The interior was indeed an office, but a barren one. There was a desk, a couple of straight-back chairs, and a barred window, which provided a view of a brick wall ten feet away. However, there was nothing on the desk; not even a blotter, a telephone or even a stray paper clip; there were no file cabinets or paintings on the walls. To Cole it looked more like an interrogation room in a police station than a doctor's office. This only served to reinforce his feeling that there was something seriously wrong here.

He was about to step back into the corridor when the door sighed shut behind him with an audible click. A brief wave of panic swept over him as he grabbed the handle and found that the door was locked.

Cole forced himself to calm down and assess the situation. None of this made any sense. But then he was, in fact, locked in a room in one of the largest medical complexes in Chicago. He'd been a patient in another wing of this same hospital only a few hours ago. This was a responsible, state-supported, federally licensed institution. It was also an insane asylum.

Cole began rationalizing the door locking behind him and the absence of the normal accoutrements one would expect to find in a doctor's office. It was obviously for security reasons. The criminally insane could be dangerous. It would be best to lock them in places where they couldn't get out and where there was nothing they could use to hurt themselves or anyone else. Then an alarmingly contradictory thought occurred to him. If the administrators of this facility were so concerned about security, why hadn't they made a closer check of his ID?

He recalled the guard recognizing him. Flattering, but Cole

wasn't the type to succumb easily to ego-boosting comments. And, if these guys were so lax with their security, then they should constantly be losing patients. On top of that the two guards he'd encountered so far didn't look like your garden-variety rent-a-cops. There was too much hardness and professionalism about them. The feeling that he was somehow in trouble was becoming stronger with each passing second.

Cole crossed the office and looked out the window at the brick wall, which extended as far as he could see in all directions. The glass was at least an inch thick and then there were the bars. He had just decided to wait a bit longer before coming up with a plan to break out when the door opened and two men walked in. Cole was stunned speechless when he saw them.

One was white, the other black. The white one, who leaned heavily on a cane, had straight, blond, shoulder-length hair. He was slender and had pretty, rather than handsome, features and startling blue-gray eyes. The black man was tall and possessed the build of an exceptionally strong man. He had a head of tightly curled, sandy-colored hair and a light complexion. His eyes were of the same exceptional blue-gray color as those of his white companion's.

Cole knew that the reason for this sameness in eye coloring was because they were brothers. The white one was Ernest Steiger, an assassin who had been responsible for the murder of Senator Harvey Banks of Illinois six years ago. The black man was ex-FBI agent Reggie Stanton, whom Cole had shot when Stanton attempted to kill mobster Antonio "Tuxedo Tony" DeLisa on the same day that the senator had died. Cole had believed that both of these men were dead. Now they stood before him.

Sensing Cole's surprise, Stanton said, "Sit down, Larry. We've got a couple of things to discuss."

34

JULY 9, 1999
3:32 P.M.

Cole pulled his gun and said, "I want both of you to turn around and face the wall."

Steiger shot Stanton a questioning glance. The muscular black man initially appeared amused. "Are you placing us under arrest, Cole?"

"You're damn right I am."

"For what?" Steiger asked.

"You for the murder of Senator Harvey Banks six years ago and your brother here for a number of crimes to include murder and kidnapping. Now turn around!"

Slowly, the two men did as they were told. Carefully, Cole stepped up behind them. He snatched Steiger's cane away and threw it behind him. It bounced off the desk before rolling onto the floor. The crippled man almost fell, but Stanton caught him. The big man glared at the cop, as he supported his brother.

"This isn't necessary, Cole," Stanton protested.

"Sure it is," Cole shot back. "You should know that. Frisking suspects is standard procedure when making arrests. Now lean forward and touch the wall. You won't need his help to assume the position, Steiger."

Again, the two men did as they were told.

Ernest Steiger placed all his weight on his good leg as Cole frisked first him and then his brother. They were unarmed.

When he was finished, Stanton said, "I think we should discuss this before you make a big mistake, Larry."

"I think the mistakes have already been made by the two of you, Reggie."

"Have you given any thought to how you're going to get out of here?" Steiger threatened.

"If you haven't noticed, my friend," Cole said, "I'm holding the gun. And I'm not only going to get out of here, but I'm taking the two of you with me."

"What did I tell you, Ernie," Stanton said. "This guy is all cop. Always has been."

"Knock off the bullshit, Stanton," Cole said.

"Okay, then let's get down to business. Do you think we could take our hands off the wall?"

"Sure," Cole said, stepping back and continuing to cover them. "But don't turn around."

The two men stood up straight, with Steiger awkwardly keeping his weight on one foot. Cole shoved a desk chair over to him. He sat down hard.

Stanton squared his shoulders under the tailor-made suit he wore. He was even broader than Cole remembered him being six years ago. "We carry the official identification of a United States government law-enforcement agency. Identification which you can check out with Special Agent-in-Charge Dave Franklin of the Chicago office of the FBI."

Cole studied his two prisoners for a moment. The last time he'd had any dealings with them had been during a period when there was a great deal of covert, black operations, government involvement in events happening in Chicago. However, he still couldn't imagine these two being let off after what'd they'd done both in Chicago and Washington, D.C.

"Where is your ID?" Cole said.

"In my back pocket," Stanton responded. "Do you want me to take it out?"

Cole hesitated a moment before responding, "Okay, but do it very slowly and carefully, Reggie."

And he did.

They had all taken seats in the office. Cole was behind the desk, Ernest Steiger sat across from him with his back to the door, and Reggie Stanton was perched on the edge of the desk. They had said little since Cole, utilizing a telephone, which was concealed in one of the bottom drawers of the desk, had called Dave Franklin of the FBI. Franklin had confirmed not only the bona fides of Stanton and Steiger, but had also faxed Blackie, at detective division headquarters, a copy of a federal court order absolving the two brothers of any wrongdoing, as their actions were deemed, ". . . in the interests of national security." Cole figured that to be a crock of bull, but there was nothing that he could do about it.

Cole looked down at the sheet of paper on which he'd written the name of Stanton's and Steiger's law-enforcement agency, which Blackie had given him over the phone. THE NATIONAL SECURITY AGENCY—SCIENTIFIC RESEARCH DIVISION. It didn't sound like a law-enforcement agency and Cole had had dealings with it in the past. The people who worked for the NSA were not cops and they didn't enforce any laws. They rather did, as Jack Govich once said, "Whatever was necessary." The two men seated in the room with Cole now had been born to work for shadowy, mysterious government entities such as the NSA.

"Now that we've established who you are and that you're no longer wanted, why are you here?"

Stanton smiled. "We're in Chicago for a couple of reasons, Larry. We're looking for a scientist named Jonathan Gault, who destroyed a research facility in Indiana and made off with the plans for some very sophisticated weapons. But he has nothing to do with you."

"But the other investigation does," Steiger added.

Cole looked from one to the other and waited. They would tell him in their own good time and he didn't want to appear too eager to hear it, although as a cop he was.

"Let me explain a little about what the NSA's Scientific Research Division is responsible for," Stanton said. "We are charged with initiating and following through on investigations having anything to do with scientific advancements which could affect the safety and security of the United States."

"So that's why you're looking for the scientist named Gault?" Cole said.

"That's right," Steiger said.

"Tell me," Cole said, unable to hide the sarcasm in his voice, "what are you going to do when you find him?"

"I don't think that is any concern of yours, Cole," Steiger said, angrily.

"But I thought you said that I was involved in one of your investigations. I wonder what kind of risk I'm in right now?"

Stanton laughed. "You're not in any danger from us, Larry. We're simply looking into one of your old cases."

"Which old case?" Cole asked, not liking the way this was going.

"We're investigating what happened inside the National Science and Space Museum a couple of years ago," Steiger said. "Specifically, the experiments of the late Katherine Rotheimer."

It was Cole's turn to laugh. "I think you boys are wasting your time. Katherine Rotheimer's dead, and even when she was alive, her experiments were failures.

"Not all of them," Stanton said.

Steiger added, "Do you remember a construction boss named William McElroy?"

Cole nodded. "Homer and Eurydice Vaughn kidnapped him from the lakefront site he was attempting to develop across from the National Science and Space Museum."

"And Katherine Rotheimer infected him with leukemia."

"Or so she said," Cole quipped. "The lady was one hundred sixteen years old and really not all there." He tapped the side of his head with an index finger.

"Oh, he did have an advanced state of leukemia, Cole," Steiger said, "and Katherine Rotheimer gave it to him. She also gave him an injection that cured the disease. McElroy's been under study for the past two years and a platoon of cancer specialists have been trying to reproduce the vaccine, but they haven't had any luck."

"So they called us in," Stanton added.

"Called you in to do what, kill him?"

Steiger bristled at the insult, but before his brother could reply, Stanton said, "We're here to find out what Katherine Rotheimer's stepdaughter, Eurydice Vaughn, or as she's known on the admittance form here at the hospital, Josie Gray, knows about the experiments."

Cole shook his head. "Eurydice was kidnapped at the age of four and brainwashed by Katherine Rotheimer. With all the psychological trauma she's been through I doubt if she will be able to tell you very much."

The two brothers exchanged knowing looks. "The therapy she's been getting here from Dr. Vargas, with the help of her sister Edna, has been quite beneficial."

"I don't understand what you mean," Cole said with a frown. "How could Edna help her sister's therapy?"

Again the brothers exchanged glances. "You're a very lucky man, Larry," Stanton said. "A very lucky man."

35

July 9, 1999
3:42 p.m.

Jonathan Gault watched Christian sleep. He had confined the boy to bed after his ordeal in the tunnel beneath the Conrail Railroad tracks. Gault had served all Christian's meals to him in bed and forced him to rest. He did not appear to have sustained any injuries during his ordeal other than a few minor burns.

They were in the warehouse near Chinatown. There were sleeping rooms equipped with washrooms outfitted to accommodate Christian's handicap. Now, the scientist left his slumbering charge and returned to his lab.

Gault was working on a replacement for Christian's wheelchair. A replacement which would be a great deal different from the one that had been destroyed in the tunnel. The new model would be motorized, enabling Christian to travel much faster than he ever had before. The scientist had carefully considered the size of the solar-powered engine he installed in the housing of the new device. Actually, what he was putting together for Christian was more of a go-cart than a wheelchair—a very sophisticated go-cart that could travel at speeds in excess of forty miles an hour, that would be equipped with four-wheel drive, sectioned tires, and a balancing rod. This go-cart would enable Christian to climb stairs or go over obstacles with relative ease. Then there were some additional accessories that would enable him to do things beyond his wildest imagination.

The work on the device was Gault's way of atoning to

Christian for almost getting him killed. Indeed, Jonathan Gault was a brilliant man, a genius who was a bit crazy and had a criminal mind. He was also very lonely, and Christian was one of the few people in his life that he had ever been able to call a friend. As the scientist worked, he remembered.

Jonathan Gault had been born on an Indian reservation in New Mexico not far from Santa Fe. The reservation was a haphazard arrangement of adobe huts on the desert floor surrounded by mountains. The Native Americans who lived on this miserable little patch of land were poor, disenfranchised, and unable to rise above the oppression of the white man's society. Gault was of the Navajo Nation and was given the name of Red Sky at birth. His father was named Night Walker and he was the reservation shaman, the traditional tribal magician or medicine man. When his son was born with one black eye and one blue eye, the shaman had proclaimed this a blessing from the gods. All his life Gault had thought of the deformity as a curse.

The ringing phone snatched Gault from his work and his memories. However, he made no move to answer it. The instrument was connected to an answering machine. Gault waited for it to click on. There was no message on the machine. It merely emitted a beep signaling that the caller could leave a message.

It was Tommy Kingsley.

"I am keeping tabs on Cole's movements through a contact I have in the police department. We need to take care of this situation with him and Kate Ford. Please contact me as soon as you can."

The call ended.

Jonathan Gault shook his head. He no more trusted Kingsley than the director of public safety trusted him. Gault could also anticipate the politician attempting to cover himself by turning Gault in. This was something that the scientist would not allow him to do. But Gault did plan to deal with Larry Cole and Kate Ford. Then he would see to Tommy Kingsley.

Night Walker, the Navajo shaman, had attempted to teach his son the art of the Indian magician. But even as a child, Red Sky had shown no interest in following in his father's footsteps. As he progressed into adolescence, Red Sky dropped his Indian name and adopted that of his maternal grandfather, Jonathan Gault. He attended white schools in Albuquerque and concealed his eyes behind dark glasses. He began dressing and acting like the white man, which greatly disappointed his father. However, the young Jonathan Gault didn't care, as he viewed Night Walker's incantations, chants, and spells as nothing but a lot of superstitious mumbo-jumbo. He excelled in school and earned a science scholarship to the University of Arizona. Then The Man Who Walked in Blood came into his life and changed it forever.

The phone rang again. As he had done before, Gault waited for the machine to answer it. The director of public safety was on the line.

"Right now my sources tell me that Cole is at University Hospital. When he leaves, his movement will be monitored. This will give you an opportunity to deal with him. We still need to talk. Call me."

Gault was annoyed with Kingsley badgering him in this fashion, but perhaps dealing with Mr. Cole was what he needed to do. Gault owed Cole for what had happened to Christian and the evil scientist believed in always paying his debts. Putting his past and The Man Who Walked in Blood back in the memory file of his mind, Gault went to wake Christian. Tonight the scientist planned to kill Larry Cole.

36

July 9, 1999
4:10 p.m.

Larry Cole was operating on emotional automatic pilot as he entered the cathedral-like lobby of University Hospital. There was a complimentary coffee service in the waiting room area. He crossed to it and poured himself a cup from a sterling silver urn. He added a dab of sugar before sitting down in one of the cushioned chairs. Without tasting it, he placed the coffee down on the table in front of him. He hadn't wanted coffee in the first place. Pouring it had simply been something to do.

Stanton and Steiger of the NSA had finally called in Dr. Mitchell Vargas, the psychiatrist. Cole had only seen the doctor once before when Cole had accompanied Edna on a visit to see her sister. And on that occasion Vargas had prohibited Cole from visiting Josie Gray. Now, as Cole sat in the hospital lobby with an unwanted cup of coffee in front of him, he understood the reason behind the doctor's ban.

Vargas was a handsome man with dark features and a winning smile. When he came into the barren office, Ernest Steiger excused himself and limped out. Reggie Stanton remained.

The doctor stood in silence waiting to be told the reason he'd been summoned. Cole surmised that he'd already been indoctrinated into compliance with the wishes of the NSA agents.

"Dr. Vargas," Stanton said, "we've come to the clinical aspects of Josie Gray's treatment here. My brother and I thought that you'd be the best one to explain them to Chief Cole."

The doctor looked from one man to the other. For a moment Mitchell Vargas appeared uncomfortable. Then he sat down in the chair Steiger had just vacated, clasped his hands in front of him on top the desk, and leaned toward Cole.

"You've been rather close to Edna Gray since her sister was admitted here, Mr. Cole." The doctor's words came out a statement, making Cole feel even more apprehensive than he had when he first walked through the door.

"What has that got to do with Josie's therapy?" Cole asked.

The doctor's quiet, controlled bedside manner did not alter. "We adopted a somewhat radical approach with Ms. Gray's treatment. We attempted to find something in our world, or shall we say the *real* world, to which she could relate. Perhaps something that she could anchor herself to and begin to build a new life on. Of course, we couldn't force anything on her, but instead attempted to find a situation in her life that she felt a strong attachment to. Because of the complications caused by her relationship to Katherine Rotheimer and the deformed giant Homer, we decided that affection for a human being would provide the best anchor and perhaps repair some of the damage that had been done to her by the Eurydice Vaughn personality."

Vargas paused for a moment. A brief flash of uncertainty, or possibly even fear, shone through his professional facade. But he quickly shoved it away and became the cool, detached psychiatrist once more.

"We began by developing an attachment in her with her sister, Edna, but this caused complications. You see, although she remembered Edna from the time before she was kidnapped at the age of four, Josie had a tenuous emotional relationship with her at best. She even considered Edna something of a rival."

Cole looked away from Vargas over to the closed door to

this room. Now the chief of detectives was quite certain that he was in a bona fide insane asylum.

"Then," Dr. Vargas said, slowly, "there was you."

Cole picked up the Styrofoam cup and took a sip of the tepid liquid. He put it down again. What Vargas had told him was almost ludicrous, but actually not funny at all. Cole had been part of Josie Gray/Eurydice Vaughn's therapy. A form of emotional and physical rehabilitation. Once, during his investigation into the disappearances that had occurred in and around the National Science and Space Museum, Eurydice used a hallucinogenic aphrodisiac to seduce Cole. The word *seduced* stopped him. Actually, she had raped him; however, a strict interpretation of the law made it impossible for a woman to rape a man. But Cole had not consciously consented to what had happened between them, so what else could it be termed but a sexual assault. But this was far from the most bizarre aspect of what Dr. Vargas had revealed to him.

In April 1998, Josie Gray managed to reproduce a mind-altering aromatic inside the psychiatric hospital. Using a teddy-bear-shaped pin, in which a small spray nozzle was concealed, she'd drugged Edna and escaped from the hospital. She then proceeded to Cole's house where she had dinner with him while posing as Edna. After dinner they had sex. The next morning, of her own volition, Josie Gray had returned to the hospital. Vargas had been stunned when the deception was revealed, but he also noticed that upon her return, Josie was happier and behaved in a more normal fashion than at any time during her prior confinement.

Following Edna's recovery from the drugged stupor, the doctor and sister had discussed the patient's future treatment and a decision was made. Josie, posing as Edna Gray, would be allowed to leave the hospital from time to time. During these brief furloughs they would have to be very careful, as one slip could ruin everything. Initially, they'd even considered keeping her away from Cole, because they believed him to be too smart a cop to fall for the deception. Then they realized that such a prohibition would never work. Josie Gray was in love with Cole and during her absences from the hospital she would be alone. There would be no way that they could keep her away from him. However, they were able to impose some restrictions on her activities, which she accepted voluntarily.

Disguised as Edna, Josie could only visit Cole at night. She would also provide accounts of her contacts not only with him, but about everything else she did on the outside. These accounts, which were first given verbally and later in writing, revealed that during each contact with Cole, over a period of a year and a half, they'd had sexual relations. Vargas studied everything with the eye of a scientist and found Josie's progress to be remarkable. He was considering writing a paper about his prized patient. Everything was going splendidly. Then Edna began developing problems.

Although Josie Gray, in her identity as Eurydice Vaughn—National Science and Space Museum curator, fell in love with Cole, it was Edna Gray who had developed a relationship with him along traditional "boy meets girl" lines. The search for her missing sister had been a twenty-five year nightmare for Edna. When her objective was realized, after she and Cole almost drowned during a flood in a hidden cavern beneath the museum, she was elated. At least initially. Then her own phobias began to emerge.

After Josie Gray vanished inside the museum on August 7, 1972, Edna's life became a nightmare. Blaming the older girl for Josie's disappearance, their mother, Jane Margaret Gray, treated Edna with a cold indifference that badly scarred the child. When Edna reached adulthood she still bore these scars, which prevented her from sustaining any meaningful personal relationships. Then she met Cole, whom she was certain was her soul mate. Eurydice/Josie came between them.

It was almost as if what had occurred before, with the alienation of her mother's affection after Josie disappeared, was happening all over again. Edna's younger sister was once more taking something that Edna felt belonged exclusively to her. And despite her love for her sister, Josie's psychological problems, and Cole being totally unaware of what was happening, Edna's affection for both her sister and Cole began turning to hatred.

Following each episode between Josie and Cole, Edna would go into a shell in which she would refuse to see or have any contact with either one of them for days, weeks, and sometimes even months. Dr. Vargas noticed the changes in Edna and was just about to approach her with a recommendation of how to deal with her problems when the NSA, in the persons of Ernest Steiger and Reggie Stanton, showed up.

Still seated in the lobby of University Hospital, Cole felt a hollow ache begin growing inside him. An hour ago he'd been unaware that he had two lovers. Now he had none. Yes, he was surprised Josie and Edna had been able to pull off such a deception, but the two women did have a remarkable resemblance to each other and there was no reason for him to suspect that the woman with him was not Edna Gray. Now both of them were gone.

"Where?" Cole had asked Stanton.

The ex-FBI agent shrugged his massive shoulders. "Someplace where they'll be safe and we can help Josie remember whatever she can about Katherine Rotheimer's experiments."

"And how are you going to *help her* memory?" Cole asked with a hard edge.

Stanton's reply was equally hard. "That's our business, Cole."

"And Edna?"

"She's going along to take care of her sister. I guess you could say she wants to get away from you for a while."

A cold fury began building inside the cop. "Did she ask you to be her messenger boy or did you volunteer for the task?"

Stanton smiled and shook his head. "I'm surprised at you, Larry. I didn't think a guy like you would let a woman get to him so easily." He reached into his inside pocket and removed a folded sheet of paper, which he handed to Cole.

The policeman took it, unfolded it and read the words typed on a form. It was a Chicago Police Department Personnel Action Request. It was used to initiate interdepartmental actions and it had been filled out by Detective Edna Gray, star number 12038. It announced her resignation from the Chicago Police Department effective July 10, 1999.

"I guess you could say that amounts to a 'Dear John' letter," Stanton said.

"Larry?"

His name being spoken snapped Cole out of the trance he'd been in. He looked up to find Kate Ford standing a few feet away. She was carrying a bouquet of roses and a couple of books.

"Hi," he managed, finding that he was hoarse. He stood up and noisily cleared his throat. "What brings you here?"

"I came to see you, but they told me you'd already been discharged."

Everything had a strange unreality. Cole felt as if he was under water. He rubbed his temples and said a halting, "They released me earlier today. I'm fine."

The reporter studied him carefully. "You don't look fine, Larry."

He attempted a smile that failed. "Really. I'm okay."

She shrugged. "If you say so." She thrust the flowers and books at him. "These are for you."

"Oh, thanks." He looked at the book jackets. Their titles were *Keys to the City* and *Witch Hunt* by Katherine Anne Ford. They'd both received excellent reviews.

"You're not obligated to read them, if you don't have the time," she said. "I know you're a busy man."

"Oh, I'll definitely read them," Cole said, feeling awkward. "I've heard you're a very good writer and a better than average investigator."

She smiled. "Coming from the Chicago Police Chief of Detectives I take that as quite a compliment."

They stood in silence for a moment. She looked down at the floor then up at him. "Would you mind if I make a personal comment?"

After the day he'd had, he started to say that he would object, but then she had given him flowers and, more important, had saved his life. "Go ahead."

"You look like you could use a drink and I'm buying."

He started to beg off, but then he looked from the roses to her book jackets and then back at the reporter. Maybe she was right. A drink was exactly what he needed. He also noticed that Kate Ford was a very attractive young woman. He was in a hospital and this looked like exactly what the doctor ordered.

"Okay," Cole said, "you're on."

37

July 9, 1999
5:25 p.m.

Christian could barely control his excitement as Dr. Gault helped him into his new personal transport vehicle. He refused to refer to the four-wheel, solar-powered, motorized machine as a wheelchair. It was painted bright red and was, as the doctor had told him when he began constructing it, capable of performing tasks that Christian could only dream of before. Now the physically challenged youth would not only be capable of moving very fast, but he had also become extremely powerful.

Gault took his time explaining each of the controls to Christian. As the scientist explained the operations of the motorized device he had created, Christian's eyes gleamed with excitement. Then Gault said, "I want you to take it for a spin around the factory, but don't go faster than ten miles an hour inside the building. Later, when we go outside, I'll let you go faster."

"Yes, sir," he said, taking the control yoke, which served the dual purpose of steering and accelerating the vehicle.

Adhering religiously to Gault's dictates, Christian took the fire-engine red vehicle for a test drive around the main floor of the Chinatown warehouse. As he rolled through the dark corridors, the legion of snakes infesting the structure scurried out of his way. At this moment Christian felt a newfound sense of power, a power that he planned to exercise and enjoy.

Back in the lab, he gushed, "This is great, Dr. Gault. It's like magic."

"Don't ever say that!" Gault exploded. "Magic has nothing to do with it. I made this machine with my own hands using computer chips, electrical relays, wires, metal, and rubber. I used my brains, which I developed through education and these two hands to make it work. There were no spells, incantations, or spirits, either good or evil involved. Do you understand me, Christian?"

Shocked at the scientist's violent outburst, all Christian could do was say a wide-eyed, open-mouthed, "Yes, Doctor."

Then as quickly as his anger had flared at white hot intensity, it vanished. For a moment he stared off vacantly across the lab. In a quiet voice, Gault said, "What do you want to name it?"

It took Christian a moment to find his voice. Finally, he managed to swallow and say, "Red Lightning, if that's okay with you."

Slowly, a smile spread across the scientist's face. Then he responded, "That is very fitting, Christian. Now it is time for us to go in search of your friend Larry Cole. Are you ready?"

"Yes, Doctor."

38

JULY 9, 1999
6:01 P.M.

The cocktail hour was concluding at Sandy's jazz club on Fifty-third Street in Hyde Park and the place was packed. The front window curtains were drawn and the lights inside dimmed. A sextet took the stage and began warming up. The noise level of the club, which was filling to capacity rapidly, and would stay that way until 2:00 A.M., dropped from the happy hour din to a rumbling murmur.

Larry Cole and Kate Ford were escorted to a table at the left of the twelve-foot-square dance floor in front of the stage. They had been shown there by the maître d', a rapier thin, elegantly dressed black man wearing a white dinner jacket. When they had walked in the door, the reporter had called the maître d' Bob. In turn, he kissed her on the cheek and referred to her as Katie. When she introduced Cole, Bob bowed and said, "Good evening, sir, and welcome to Sandy's."

Cole detected the slightest trace of a French accent in his voice. After they were seated, Kate said, "Bob's originally from Haiti."

"Oh," was Cole's only comment.

The band began playing a soft instrumental. A waiter, attired in a waist-length white jacket, came over to take their order. Both of them requested bourbon and water. Another waiter placed a bowl containing peanuts and pretzels down on the table. Cole took a handful of the snack mix and munched on it as he looked around the club.

"Nice place. You come here often?"

"If I came here any more than I already do, Sandy would probably start charging me rent."

The waiter brought their drinks. As he was placing the glasses on coasters in front of them, Kate asked, "Are you hungry?"

"I haven't eaten since this morning, so I could stand a bite."

She instructed the waiter to bring them menus.

They ordered fried chicken with corn on the cob, collard greens, cole slaw, and corn-bread muffins. They were both stuffed by the time they were finished. The waiter served coffee and recommended a dessert of either apple cobbler or rum cake topped with whipped cream. They declined dessert and ordered another round of drinks.

"You know I really needed that," Cole said.

Kate smiled. Then said, "Do you mind if I ask you a question, off the record?"

"After all we've been through, I guess I can trust you with an 'off the record' response."

She chose her words carefully. "When I saw you in the hospital lobby earlier, you looked as if you'd just lost your best friend."

Cole studied the table surface. The meal and the relaxing ambiance of Sandy's had made the earlier events of the day a bit more bearable, but the anguish they had caused him was still there. He looked up at her and said, "I just had some things on my mind that I need to sort out."

"Can I help?" she asked, sincerely. But he noticed something else in her voice. He didn't want to speculate as to what that might be at this stage in their relationship.

"Maybe you can," he said. "But first, tell me what you were doing in the morgue the other day."

She looked away from him and suppressed a guilty smile. "So you know about that."

"I was there, remember?"

Before she could answer, the lights dimmed and a spotlight focused a bright halo of light on the stage. A tall, exquisitely built woman in an iridescent black gown with a white corsage pinned over her left breast, walked from the wings. The spotlight illuminated her café au lait complexion and jet black hair, which was piled high on top of her head. Applause rippled through the club, as one of the musicians stepped forward and handed her a microphone. The band struck up "Just in Time" and after waiting a beat the woman began to sing.

Her voice was strong and had just the slightest trace of a Southern accent. Her delivery and the way she moved sensually across the stage reminded Cole of Lena Horne.

Noticing his absorption with the vocalist, Kate leaned forward and said, "That's Sandra Devereaux. She owns this place."

Cole nodded.

Sandy stopped singing and the band continued playing softly. "Good evening, ladies and gentlemen and welcome to Sandy's." Now her Southern, or more specifically Louisiana, accent was a great deal more evident. "We've got a great lineup of entertainment for you tonight and maybe a song or two from a guest vocalist, who is seated in the audience. So enjoy and remember . . ." She sang the final verse of "Just in Time."

Sandy Devereaux finished to resounding applause. After bowing, she handed the mike back to the musician and came off the stage. As the band went into another jazz instrumental, she began stopping at tables, shaking hands with patrons, and inquiring about the service. Slowly, she made her way over to Cole and Kate Ford. When she approached, Cole stood up.

"Katie," Sandy said, "why you stay away so long, girl?"

"I was just here the other day, Sandy. I had lunch at the bar. Benny served me."

"That man don't tell me nothing," the woman said angrily. "Maybe one of these days Benny will find himself out of a job." Then Sandra Devereaux turned to look at Cole. "What have we got here? What you trying to do, Katie, bring some class into this gin mill?"

Cole extended his hand, as Kate made the introductions. "Sandra Veronica Devereaux, this is Chief of Detectives Larry Cole of the Chicago Police Department."

Sandy glanced at Cole's hand before stepping forward, embracing him, and rubbing her cheek against his. She also pressed her voluptuous body against him. "You too fine a man for a woman to say hello to with a handshake, honey."

Cole could feel the heat of her body and smelled the aroma

of her perfume. Although she had a few years on him, she was still a very sexy, vibrant woman.

"You better watch yourself, Katie, or Mama Devereaux is gonna take this man away from you."

Kate surprised Cole when she adopted an accent very close to Sandy's and said, "You better keep your hands off my man, Mama, or Katie'll pull out some of that hair."

The two women laughed and Cole smiled sheepishly.

"So what you gonna do, girl?" Sandy asked.

Kate smiled and gave Cole a glance that he could only classify as nervous.

"Buy me and Larry another drink and I'll see what I can do for you after the band takes a break."

Sandy squeezed Cole's arm. "I'm going to buy him a drink anyway. I want to keep this handsome policeman around as long as I can. Maybe you'll slip up and I can steal him from you later."

"You mess with mine, girl, and you'll be sorry," Kate said with a grin.

"Okay," Sandy said, "I'll send you a round. Then you know what I want."

"Yes, ma'am," Kate said.

When Sandy was gone, Cole said, "So you're a jazz singer along with being a journalist."

Her eyes widened. "How did you know that?"

"Well, Sandy wants you to do something and I would bet that it's up on that stage. She also mentioned that there was a guest vocalist in the audience."

Kate smiled. "You know you really are a very good detective. You're also right."

"I'm looking forward to hearing you sing."

"How do you know I'm any good?"

Cole wiped the condensation off his cocktail glass. "Looking around this place and having met Madam Devereaux, I'd be willing to bet that just not anybody is allowed up on that stage."

Kate merely nodded, because Larry Cole was absolutely right.

39

July 9, 1999
6:35 P.M.

Detective Lula Love was sitting in an unmarked gray Ford police car across the street from Sandy's jazz club. She was a short black woman with cornrowed hair. She generally dressed in colorful, traditional African garb as often as she could. She could have been considered attractive except for two things. She was forty pounds overweight and her face was etched into a perpetual frown. This was because Detective Love was a very unhappy woman. She felt that the reason for this unhappiness was caused by the man whom she had followed from University Hospital to Sandy's jazz club on East Fifty-third Street in Hyde Park. This man was Larry Cole.

Lula Love, although she didn't know him well, had a great deal in common with Tommy Kingsley. Both the detective and the director of public safety were firm believers in the principle that advancement within the public sector in Chicago was based on who as opposed to what you know.

By way of the manipulations of her local alderman, Lula had managed to obtain a cushy assignment right out of the police academy to the Preventive Programs Division, where she performed the duties of a file clerk, as opposed to that of a police officer. She maintained this position, because her alderman or clout was Sherman Ellison Edwards—the Chairman of the Police and Fire Committee of the fifty member Chicago City Council. She could have remained in this well-paid, minimal-labor position for some time, but she made a critical mistake. Officer Lula Love became ambitious. She wanted to be a detective.

There was a process to be followed to obtain the position. For most of the applicants, it was necessary to take a competitive examination and withstand a review of their prior performance with the department. A small percentage of promotions to detective were based on merit and reserved for police officers who had distinguished themselves far and beyond the call of duty. Although Officer Love had never done anything ". . . above and beyond the call . . .," with the nefarious manipulations of Alderman Sherman Ellison Edwards, arranged by Tommy Kingsley, she was given a meritorious promotion to detective. Then her problems began.

Newly promoted Detective Love had made arrangements to remain at her administrative post in Preventive Programs even though she was now charged with conducting follow-up investigations of crimes committed in the city. And the grease was applied by her Edwards-Kingsley connection. Then Chief of Detectives Larry Cole intervened.

When Cole took over as the chief of detectives, he had ordered all personnel assigned to his division to work as criminal investigators. Detective Love didn't think that this edict applied to her. She was wrong.

Now Lula Love hated Larry Cole and would do anything that she could to destroy him. When she had been offered the task of following Cole, she had jumped at it. She had waited until Cole left the hospital with a woman. Then she had tailed him to the jazz club. After Cole and the woman had gone inside, Detective Love used her car phone and dialed the number Alderman Edwards had given her.

"Hello."

She recognized the slight Southern drawl of Tommy Kingsley. "I have some information for you, sir."

"Go ahead."

And she did.

A new motor home pulled onto a side street a half a block from Sandy's. Jonathan Gault, disguised again as the handsome Native American, was behind the wheel. Christian, seated in his Red Lightning vehicle, was in the rear.

"Can I go with you, Doctor?"

Gault turned around. "I wish that you could accompany me, Christian, but I have to do this alone."

Christian lowered his head in disappointment.

"Tell you what," the scientist said, "we'll turn on our comlinks so you'll be able to hear everything."

Gault reached into the glove compartment and removed two small microphones that were an inch and a half in length. They were bullet-shaped and equipped with clips. Gault attached his to his shirt and gave the other comlink to Christian. "With this you'll be able to hear everything."

Then Gault, carrying his black cane with the gold serpent's head, got out of the truck, locked the door behind him, and walked toward the entrance to Sandy's.

40

July 9, 1999
6:40 p.m.

Bob, the maître d' at Sandy's, was pleased. For a weekday night, the club was doing extremely well. Of course, this was the way things went nearly every night. Now that it was summer, the trade had been particularly brisk. A number of tourists visiting Chicago had called to make reservations. For years Sandy's had been one of the most popular entertainment spots in the Windy City. Bob intended to make sure that it stayed that way.

From his post by the front door, Bob saw Sandy Devereaux go over to the table where Katie was sitting with the cop. Bob hoped that Katie would sing tonight. She had the voice of an angel and, if she wasn't so dedicated to writing, could have joined the ranks of blues and jazz legends such as Billie Holiday, Johnny Hartman, Gloria Lynn, Nancy Wilson, and Anita Baker. However, the maître d' didn't think too much of her choice in men.

It wasn't that Bob had anything against Cole. In fact, he instinctively liked the tall, handsome cop. The only problem was that Cole looked very much like all the others. Good-looking men who'd come into Katie's life, made a mess of it, and then left her. Somehow Cole did seem different. Maybe he would even be good for her.

The front door opened behind him. Bob turned, as a tall,

broad-shouldered man in black walked in. Quickly, the maître d' assessed the new patron. The guy had money, which his clothing and the expensive cane he carried indicated. He was also strong and confident, which was evident by the way he carried himself. But the maître d' at Sandy's jazz club could tell that this guy was wrong.

Establishments that offer entertainment and sell booze are also magnets for the wrong type of people. A few years ago a local street gang had attempted to muscle in on Sandy's. The gang wanted sixty percent of the profits to allow the club to continue operating. But Bob, Benny the bartender, and Madam Devereaux had taken care of that and they hadn't needed Larry Cole's police department to do it.

Now the broad-shouldered, well-dressed man in black looked like trouble of the same ilk. Bob considered the possibility that this guy could be okay. Maybe all he wanted was a drink and to listen to some good jazz. If he had come to Sandy's for anything else, then he was going to have big problems.

But the more Bob studied the newcomer the more uneasy he became. There was something just a bit too smooth about his face. Something which the maître d' sensed was artificial.

Bob locked eyes with the newcomer for a moment and then the man in black began twisting the head of the snake-headed cane. With a sudden, almost imperceptible movement, he extended the tip of the barrel and touched the maître d's arm. Bob jerked violently as the electricity coursed through him.

The man quickly pulled the cane away and said, "I'll just take a seat at the bar and watch the show," as he walked past Bob.

A couple entered the club and stepped up to Bob's station just as the maître d' exhaled sharply, looked at them through unfocused eyes, and collapsed.

41

July 9, 1999
6:42 P.M.

Kate and Cole were enjoying the music when the commotion started by the front door. As they both looked on, Benny the bartender, a heavier man wearing an apron identical to Benny's and, finally, Sandra Devereaux began hurrying toward the maître d's station.

"I wonder what's going on?" Kate said.

"Beats me," Cole said, staring off across the club.

Then Kate got up and pushed her way through the crowd. Curious, Cole got up and followed her.

They made it to the spot where Madam Devereaux was kneeling over the prone maître d'. Cole could see Bob's face over the jazz club owner's shoulder. He was unconscious and his face was drenched with sweat. After a moment he opened his eyes, recognized Madam Devereaux, and whispered something to her. Alarm registered on her face and she stood up. "Take him up to my office," she instructed the two bartenders.

"I could call an ambulance for him on my police car radio," Cole volunteered.

"Bob don't need no ambulance," she said, looking around as if searching for something. "He needs protection from whatever did that to him."

Cole frowned. "Did what to him?"

But she was already following the men carrying the maître d'.

"What do you think that was all about?" Kate asked Cole.

The cop shrugged. "I don't know."

42

July 9, 1999
6:43 p.m.

Jonathan Gault sat at the far end of the bar in an area that cast him in shadow. He watched the confusion at the maître d's station with interest. He expected them to summon an ambulance for the man whom he had just given a powerful electrical shock. The scientist had not used the megavoltage he had employed against the gang members on Federal Street. Turning the curious maître d' into an instant human torch would have directed too much attention at Gault. But the charge that he did use was indeed powerful. If the maître d' had a weak heart or some other cardiopulmonary ailment then he would not survive.

But instead of an ambulance, two men carried the maître d' to the rear of the club with the tall woman following them.

A bartender approached. "Can I help you?"

Before replying, Gault watched Kate Ford and Larry Cole return to their table. Turning back to the bartender he said, "Give me a bottle of your best champagne."

The scientist didn't often drink alcohol, but tonight was an occasion. Now he would have to decide on a way to dispose of the journalist and the cop. They would be dispatched into the next world either by lightning or the venom of a serpent.

Sandra Devereaux's office was on the second floor of the club. To get to it they had to pass through a locked door marked PRIVATE and go down a corridor with walls lined with paintings, sculptures, and odd talismans from all over the world. Although a few of the privileged, who had been allowed to see this collection, thought that what she'd assembled was art, the more informed knew that each of these items served a purpose. This purpose was to ward off evil. That is uninvited evil.

Sandy unlocked the door and held it open as the two men carried Bob into the corridor. The bearers had been around long enough to know better than to look too long or too hard at any of the things hanging on the walls. Obediently, with heads lowered, they carried the injured man into Madam Devereaux's office and placed him down gently on a leather couch. Without having to be told, they left.

The office was modern and had been furnished in leather and chrome. There was a bookshelf against one wall containing printed volumes that were all in French. The other books were handwritten and there were few people still alive who could decipher the words written in them.

Behind the glass-topped desk on the far wall hung a painting of a stately looking black man wearing a magnificent robe of royal purple with a black fur collar. Beneath the robe was a black tuxedo. This man was Sandy's father. He was well over a hundred years old now and still lived in Louisiana. It was to her father's portrait that the club owner went now.

She had not come to admire the old man's handsome visage. In fact, she didn't even notice the painting itself for what it was. Instead she reached out her right hand and grasped the lower corner where a small trigger was secreted. Activating this trigger caused the oil painting to swing away from the wall on hinges. A safe was concealed behind it.

She worked the combination quickly and opened the door. From inside the steel-lined vault she removed a cloth bundle, which she carried over to the desk.

She set it down carefully, as if it contained precious crystal or something equally fragile. Before opening the bundle she took a deep breath. She was sweating despite the air-conditioning unit keeping the temperature at a comfortable seventy degrees. Then she looked over at Bob, who had again lapsed into unconsciousness. Sandra Devereaux realized that she had no choice. There was something wrong down in the club. Something that was strange and equally dangerous. Something that she knew how to deal with.

43

July 9, 1999
6:45 p.m.

Gault was enjoying the champagne. It was cold and dry. The club's atmosphere was okay, but he had never been much for socializing. The music he did find interesting, but he wasn't much of a music lover either. As he sipped his drink, his mind again returned to that time an eternity ago in the New Mexico desert.

By the time Jonathan Gault earned a masters degree in Engineering from the University of Arizona, he was being recruited to work for every scientific research organization in the country from Dow Chemical to the Pentagon. He decided to forego any of the lucrative offers and return to the reservation. And the young scientist had a plan. A plan to drag the Navajo out of the age of superstition and bogus magic into the world of prosperity through technology.

His father, the tribal shaman, was quite old by the time Gault returned, but still practiced his art on gullible members of the tribe. Gault contemptuously watched the old man attempt to summon rain from the sky during the dry season, cure disease by sprinkling magic dust around the beds of the sick, and cast spells to ward off demons. Jonathan Gault also worked to help the tribe. When there was a drought, the young scientist constructed an electrically powered pumping system to transport purified well water to the village and surrounding crops. To prevent disease, he introduced updated hygienic practices among tribal members and strongly urged the sick to seek treatment at the free white man's clinics in Albuquerque. As far as demons went, Gault didn't believe that such things existed.

Then one night the shaman gathered the tribe around the campfire. Even Gault joined the throng, although he remained at the edge of the group, snorting derisively as the shaman began telling the tale of "The Man Who Walked in Blood." A tale that was going to effect Jonathan Gault for the rest of his life. Later the shaman and "The Man Who Walked in Blood" forced Gault onto a mountain and forced him to endure a night of terror, which had made him what he was now.

Now seated at the bar in Sandy's jazz club forty years later, Gault felt a chill caused by the memory. Pushing the past away once more, he noticed a woman seated a few stools away from him. She was a tall, well-built young black woman with thick black hair, and a voluptuous mouth highlighted by a slash of blood red lipstick. She was clad in a black dress that would have gone on easier with spray paint rather than cloth. There was a strand of cultured pearls around her neck and a large diamond ring on her finger, which occasionally sparkled brightly in the overhead lights. She was a looker, but Gault had never been interested in women. But he could think of something that he could do with this one. Idly, he wondered how she'd react to being live prey for his slithering friends in Chinatown.

The woman had looked in his direction three times since he sat down. He knew she couldn't see him clearly because of the shadow in which he was partially concealed. However, she was able to sense him and he could tell that what she was feeling intrigued her.

He motioned to the bartender.

"Yes, sir," the white-aproned man said.

"I'd like to buy that young lady a drink."

When the bartender informed her that she had been offered a drink, she flashed an inviting smile in Gault's direction. He watched her slide off the stool and saunter toward him. He glanced back at Cole and Kate Ford. The cop was now alone. Gault decided to use the approaching woman as a diversion while he decided how he was going to dispatch the reporter and Cole.

Kate Ford had excused herself and gone backstage. Cole was intrigued by the idea of a journalist also being a jazz singer. He'd never met an entertainer. He did like music and even had a collection of classical jazz and blues numbers on CDs. And Cole could tell by the high quality of the music played so far, that Madam Devereaux was expecting something quite spectacular from his dinner companion.

Slowly, Cole became aware of the change he was experiencing. He now felt completely relaxed. In fact, he hadn't thought about the earlier problems of the day since he walked into this night club. He figured that the dinner and drinks were contributing factors, but he couldn't ignore the company. He chuckled softly to himself when he thought about the contradiction of a cop and an investigative journalist keeping company. Well, he thought, maybe times were indeed changing.

The band came back out on the stage and picked up their instruments. Then Kate Ford stepped from the wings into the spotlight. She was dressed in the same sleeveless blouse and dark skirt she'd had on before; however, Cole noticed that something about her was different. Now she looked more vibrant, somehow more alive. Cole noticed that under the illumination from the spotlight she was exceptionally beautiful.

An offstage, deep-voiced male announcer said, "Ladies and gentlemen, our guest vocalist of the evening, Kate Ford."

The club exploded with applause. Cole was stunned by the enthusiastic reception she received. Up on the stage, Kate merely gave them a slight curtsy and waited, her hands at her sides, for the noise to subside. She didn't appear nervous or ill at ease in the slightest. Finally, things quieted down. Waiting a tick, she lifted the microphone to her lips and began to sing.

The first song was, "Can't Take My Eyes Off of You," followed by "Storm Warning." Her voice possessed a sultry quality reminiscent of Anita Baker, but the way that Kate handled certain verses and notes also reminded him a bit of Chanté Moore and Gloria Lynn. And the most amazing thing was that this young blonde lady was belting out songs with as much soul as any singer Cole had ever heard.

He was getting a great deal of enjoyment out of Kate's singing when he happened to look up and see Madam Devereaux standing on the balcony above the stage. He noticed that the club owner had something clutched in both hands. Cole merely gave her a glance and went back to the music.

The woman sitting with Jonathan Gault was a recent divorcée. For ten years she had remained in a psychologically abusive relationship with a man who did everything he could to make her feel worthless. Her life had been so restricted that she promised herself that the instant she was free she was going to go out and kick up her heels. Tonight was her first night out on the town.

She had flirted with the man at the end of the bar primarily because he was different. Yes, she could sense something dangerous about him, but she wanted something dangerous and different in her life.

When she slid onto the bar stool beside him, she still couldn't see him very well, which made him even more intriguing to her. But she could tell that he was handsome and the gold-headed cane he carried was exotic, perhaps even a bit scary. She couldn't define exactly what it was about him that attracted her and could only compare the strange attraction she was feeling to the time when she was in college and a friend had talked her into going skydiving. It had been terrifying and exhilarating all at the same time. Now, in Sandy's jazz club, she was having that same sensation.

"You a music lover?" she asked, taking a sip of her martini. It was her second and she was beginning to feel it.

"Not really," he said in a deep voice. "I'm more interested in the singer."

"Do you know Kate Ford?" She put a cigarette in her mouth and waited for him to pick up the cigarette lighter she had placed on top the bar.

He ignored it. "No, but I know of her."

Finally, she picked up the lighter and did the honors herself. "She's got one helluva singing voice, but I heard she spends all her time doing these elaborate investigations and writing books."

"She's a very curious lady," he said. "And you know what they say about curiosity."

She gave him a questioning frown. "It killed the cat?"

He flashed her a bright, toothy smile. "You're a smart girl."

On the balcony above the stage Sandra Devereaux shook her bundle three times and felt it starting to get hot.

44

JULY 9, 1999
6:55 P.M.

The club lights blinked a couple of times, but no one gave this more than a passing thought. No one that is with the exception of Gault and the woman seated next to him. Suddenly, the scientist experienced a terrible weakness. It was as if an icy cold hand was squeezing his heart. Bracing himself against the edge of the bar he struggled to his feet. As he did so he knocked over his champagne glass.

"What's the matter, honey?" the woman said.

He didn't acknowledge her, because he had to get out of here. He was having trouble breathing and reaching up he tore the front of the mask off exposing the aged face lying beneath it. He started for the entrance.

The woman watched him go with a horror that turned her to stone. Getting off her stool, she staggered back toward the ladies' room.

Gault made it to the double-glass doors leading from Sandy's out onto Fifty-third Street. He reached for the handle, but his hand was stopped by some unseen force. Now he knew what was happening. Someone was using black magic on him. Frightened for the first time in many years, he raised the comlink and managed to say a raspy, barely audible, "Christian, help me."

The message galvanized Christian. He activated the remote-control backdoor of the motor home, pushed the yoke of Red Lightning forward, and exploded onto the street. He raced toward the jazz club to rescue the doctor.

Larry Cole was completely enthralled by Kate Ford. She had a voice with such range and strength that with each song she sounded like an almost completely different vocalist. But there was something else that he noticed. This woman had experienced a great deal of pain in her life.

When she sang she did so from a heart that had been repeatedly broken, and she was capable of transmitting every bit of that pain into the words of each song. Her eyes remained dry, but with each phrase her face contorted with emotion. It was at once compelling and fascinating.

She concluded a song and bowed as the audience applauded. She managed a shy smile and pushed a wisp of hair out of her face. Sweat glistened on her forehead and cheeks. "Like a lot of people nowadays, I was raised in a one-parent household. My father . . . ," she paused a heartbeat, ". . . was a musician who spent most of his time on the road. My mother was a freelance writer and a poet of some renown in the Chicago area." Again a pause. "I've never been a parent, but if the problems my mother had with me are any indication, then being one is a damned hard job. For my final number of the night I'd like to sing a song made popular a few years ago by a group called TLC. It's called 'Don't Go Chasing Waterfalls.' "

The band began playing and she picked up the chorus that

soulfully told the tale of a mother worrying about her child, who had grown to adulthood. As Kate sang, the pain and the mother's concern came through quite clearly with each verse.

Cole was listening to the song when he happened to look up and see Sandra Devereaux still standing on the balcony above the stage. He squinted to see her better, as she was standing in shadow, but he was certain that whatever the club owner was holding in her hands had begun to emit smoke.

He was still studying Madam Devereaux when Kate began the second chorus of "Don't Go Chasing Waterfalls." Then a resounding crash came from the entrance to the club.

45

July 9, 1999
7:06 P.M.

Everyone turned in the direction of the noise. Cole was able to see that the glass front doors had been smashed in. The cop's initial thought was that an out-of-control car had done the damage and the front end of a red vehicle was visible, but it was too small and low to the ground to be a car. Everyone else was frozen into immobility by what had just happened and it took Cole a moment to snap out of his own trance, get up, and head toward the front door.

From the stage, Kate was able to see a great deal better than Cole. She also noticed the red vehicle and was able to see a man struggling toward it, moving as if he were either ill or injured.

She saw him climb into the vehicle, then it reversed itself and backed out of the club taking portions of the damaged doors with it. Larry Cole was headed in that direction and her curiosity raged as she jumped from the stage and started after him.

Detective Lula Love was still parked across the street from Sandy's when the low-slung cart zipped down the sidewalk. She was glad that there were no pedestrians on the street, as the sandy-haired kid driving the thing would have killed somebody. Then, she watched in horror, as the vehicle executed a hard ninety-degree turn and smashed through the front doors of the jazz club.

Although Love was more of a file clerk than a cop, she did carry a gun and, to some degree, felt a certain responsibility as a law-enforcement officer. She also considered the possibility that she could take advantage of this situation, as she would be the first cop on the scene, which might even succeed in impressing the high and mighty Larry Cole.

She got out of the police car and started across the street.

When Christian crashed Red Lightning through the double-glass doors, the spell that Madam Devereaux had cast over Jonathan Gault was broken. With the front end of the cart protruding inside and covered with glass, Gault was able to see Christian hunched down over the steering yoke. Shards of glass glistened in his hair, but he didn't appear hurt. The scientist struggled forward and climbed into the narrow space behind Christian.

Wrapping his arms around the young man's waist, he said, "Take me away from this place, Christian."

Christian began backing Red Lightning out of the club when they both looked up to see Cole approaching. The policeman was thirty feet away when he recognized Christian. He couldn't see the man behind him clearly, but Cole noticed that he was dressed in black and there was something wrong with his face. It appeared that his flesh had been shredded, but there was no blood. Then, as the cop reached for his gun, they vanished onto Fifty-third Street.

Detective Love reached the sidewalk just as the cart turned around. She held up her badge and shouted, "Hold it!"

Gault reached around Christian and flicked a switch beneath a red button on the dashboard. When he pressed the button a thin stream of flame shot from the front of Red Lightning and enveloped the detective. Catching fire, she screamed. Christian drove around the human torch.

When Cole reached the destroyed entrance to Sandy's and leaped out onto the street, the cart was nowhere in sight, but the horror of what had occurred here was obvious. The only way that Cole could tell the burning figure was a woman was because of her shrill screams. He looked for some way to extinguish the fire consuming her, but realized with a sinking heart that there was nothing that he could do.

The burning figure collapsed to the sidewalk, just as Kate Ford rushed out of the club. When she saw the burning human figure she screamed and would have also fallen to the concrete if Cole hadn't caught her.

46

July 9, 1999
8:20 p.m.

Fifty-third Street was clogged with emergency vehicles and hundreds of curious spectators, who had come out to see what had happened outside of Sandy's. The Second District evidence technician assigned to the case had examined and photographed the pile of ash and bone that had once been Detective Lula Love, before moving on to collect what evidence she could from the remains. The E.T., Officer Phyllis Humphries, also took photos and collected evidence from the smashed front doors. On the pieces of broken glass, which would be replaced by a glass-company crew standing by until the cops finished, Officer Humphries discovered traces of red paint. When she was finished she conferred with Detective Judy Daniels, who was the liaison between the chief of detectives' office and the detectives charged with investigating what had occurred here. It was the evidence technician's understanding that Chief Cole had been on the scene when the woman had been incinerated.

The Mistress of Disguise/High Priestess of Mayhem was standing in front of Sandy's when Humphries approached. "I've collected everything I could, Judy, but other than a few paint chips we don't have much. Then there's this."

Judy took the object. Tonight the Mistress of Disguise was wearing a Whoopie Goldberg dreadlock wig, a Superman T-shirt, and skin-tight black jeans with a gun belt bearing a nine-millimeter semiautomatic handgun, handcuffs, a canister of pepper spray, and two extra bullet clips. The E.T. had handed Judy a Chicago police detective's badge. The number in raised brass was 22145.

"I ran the number," the E.T. said, "and it comes back to a Detective Lula Love, who is assigned to Area Four Property Crimes." Humphries pointed across the street. "See that gray Ford over there?"

Judy noticed that it had "cop car" written all over it.

The E.T. continued, "It's registered to Area Four Detectives and I bet Detective Love was on duty when she ran in to whoever did this to her."

Judy had heard of Lula Love. She planned to call Area Four and find out what the deceased detective was working on when she was incinerated, but first Judy would share what she had learned so far with Cole.

Before entering Sandy's Judy idly asked Humphries, "What do you think could have done something like that to her?" She indicated the remains of Detective Love, which were covered with a rubber sheet provided by the Chicago Fire Department.

The evidence technician shrugged. "I don't know, Judy. Maybe a flamethrower."

The reference to the military weapon struck a chord in Judy's memory. It was one of Cole's and Blackie's old cases involving a murderer named Steven Zalkin, who had used stolen military hardware on his victims. Military hardware stolen from a place called Astrolab.

47

July 9, 1999
9:02 p.m.

Cole and Kate Ford were in Sandra Devereaux's office above the club. Kate sat in the chair behind the desk and Madam Devereaux hovered over her, holding a glass of water from which the reporter sipped slowly. Cole was on the other side of the desk facing them.

The policeman looked around Madam Devereaux's office as he pondered what had occurred. Only a few minutes ago he had talked to Judy and it was obvious that Detective Love had been killed with a flamethrower. Then there was the strange vehicle that had smashed through the front glass doors of the club. Christian Dodd had been driving that vehicle, and from the accounts of witnesses inside the club, the man Cole had seen with Christian had been in the club prior to the crash. So, the cop asked himself, was there a connection between the red vehicle and the death of Detective Love? One thing was certain, he intended to find out.

Cole's eyes stopped at Madam Devereaux's safe, which was still open. Sandy noticed his scrutiny and closed the oil portrait over it. She managed a smile for the policeman, as she said, "I trust you, Larry, but there are some things that shouldn't be advertised."

He smiled back. The wall safe didn't look large or secure enough to hold a lot of money, so the question he asked himself was what did it contain? He recalled Madam Devereaux holding something in her hands when she'd stood out on the balcony, something that had appeared to be emitting smoke.

"Thank you, Sandy," Kate said, pushing the glass away. "I'm feeling better now."

"You need to lie down for a bit, Kate," Sandy said. "Then this nice policeman will drive you home."

Kate looked about to argue, but finally her shoulders sagged and she allowed Sandy to lead her to the couch, which not too long before had been vacated by Bob, the maître d'. The moment her head touched the cushions her eyes closed. She was instantly asleep.

"Can I offer you a brandy, Larry?"

"That would be nice," he replied.

She went to a bar in the corner of the room. At least, when Cole initially saw it, he thought it was a bar. Actually, it was a shelf covered with a lace cloth, which looked more like an altar than a bar. On it were four candles in various colors, a crucifix, a statue of the Blessed Virgin, and a pair of crystal decanters. Sandy picked up one of the decanters and carried it back to the desk. On top of the desk was a tray containing a silver water pitcher and three stemmed glasses. Kate Ford had drunk from one of the glasses of this set. Sandra Devereaux half-filled two of the remaining goblets with liquor from the decanter. She handed one of the glasses to Cole.

He noticed the rich aroma instantly. As he savored it, she said, "That's original Napoleon brandy, Larry. Very rare."

"This must cost a fortune."

"For my friends, cost is unimportant." Sandy toasted him and took a sip. Cole did likewise.

They sat in silence for a moment before Cole said, "What happened down there tonight?"

For the first time he became aware that Sandra Devereaux was frightened, but was making a valiant effort to hide it. Cole decided to use an old cop strategy for conducting interviews: he lapsed into silence. He had asked his question, now he would see if he got a response.

The silence stretched on for some minutes, but the time wore more heavily on Madam Devereaux, who had gone pale. During the wait, she had not looked at the policeman, but instead concentrated on the contents of her brandy glass. Finally, she did look up. She stared across the office at the sleeping Kate Ford, then her eyes swung to Larry Cole. The fear he'd noticed before had vanished to be replaced by something else. He wasn't quite certain what that something was, but it succeeded in making him uneasy.

"To answer your question, Larry," she said in a voice, which was thick with her Louisiana accent, "we have to start with something called a Voodooienne, which is the name for a practitioner of Voodoo. After what happened to Bob, I thought there was one down in the club tonight. I was wrong. There was an evil entity there, but not one whose power comes from Voodoo. I believe that everything that occurred, including my doors being smashed and that detective being killed, was caused by the same entity. An entity using a power unlike mine. I was able to use my own magic as a Voodooienne to defeat it, whatever it was, but I doubt if Voodoo will work against it twice."

"Could you tell me something about Voodoo?" he asked.

She hesitated a moment before saying, "Voodoo is as much an art as it is a science, which some have perceived as witchcraft, while others see it as a religion just as that which is practiced by Catholics, Jews, or Moslems. Of course, that depends on your point of view.

"It is believed that Voodoo came to America with the slave trade. Its origins in Africa are not known, but the followers of the god Vodu were snake worshippers."

Cole's memory flashed back to the two snakes he killed in

Kate Ford's town house. He wondered if the story Madam Devereaux was telling him had anything to do with what had happened there.

"In the late eighteenth century, slaves who practiced Voodoo were barred from being sold in Louisiana, because it was believed that such slaves were capable of taking control of their masters. As far as the religious basis for Voodoo goes, there are certain parallels between the snake worshipers of Africa and Judeo-Christian tradition. For example, in the Book of Genesis, Adam and Eve were tempted by Satan in the guise of a snake to eat the fruit that gave them the knowledge of good and evil. In Voodoo it is believed that the first man and woman came into the world blind and it was the snake who gave them sight."

"Variations on the same theme, so to speak," Cole said.

She nodded, got up from her chair, and picked up the brandy decanter. Cole attempted to decline the offer of a refill, but she scolded him with, "You got to drink with Sandy, because she's gonna tell you some things you really need to know."

After refilling their glasses she returned to her chair. "Voodoo has been associated with all kinds of mischief over the years from people being cursed and losing all their money and possessions, to the spreading of a little dust around a person's bed and sending them away from this world."

"You mean killing them, don't you?" Cole asked.

She pointed a bright, red-nail-tipped index finger at him. "Voodoo is powerful magic, Larry. Very powerful magic."

"For those who believe in it," Cole said.

Madam Devereaux's eyes narrowed. "It don't matter none if you believe in it or not. The power of Voodoo can affect anyone it is used against."

"But you said that whatever was in the club tonight didn't practice Voodoo."

"No, but it used the same methods that are used in Voodoo, only through an application of the science of your world."

"And these methods are?"

She frowned, displaying impatience. "I don't have the time to go into all of the intricacies of the dark arts. For that I will send you to an expert. But what all such applications do is channel energy, whether it be physical or spiritual. Some practitioners use objects to focus the energy, others are capable of using talismans or even their own will."

"You were holding something in your hands tonight when I saw you out on the balcony," Cole said. "I thought I saw it emitting smoke."

She held up her palms for him to see. The skin was covered with ugly red blisters.

"Shouldn't you see a doctor for that?"

"I got ways of healing myself better and cheaper than any of your doctors," she said. Lowering her hands she added, "My works did this to me when I went after the thing that attacked Bob."

"Your works?"

She shrugged. "It was a small burlap sack containing some odds and ends. A few strands of Madame Marie Laveau's hair, the skull of a black cat, and a tooth from a mad dog."

Cole didn't know what to say. He took a sip of brandy.

"The magic I used was very powerful and I've used it many times before. But this time that thing in here drained everything I had."

"Can you make more?" Cole asked.

"I don't know, but even if I could, I wouldn't have enough power to protect you and Katie."

"Why do you think we need protection?"

She affixed Cole with a disarming stare. "Because I am a Voodooienne and Voodooiennes know things. Whatever is after you uses a different form of magic from mine, so you're going to have to employ a very powerful magician to help you. You'll have to go to Dr. Silvernail Smith."

48

JULY 9, 1999
10:04 P.M.

Kate Ford sat beside Cole in the front seat of his police car. She was lying back against the headrest and her eyes were closed. A steady rain was falling making the streets shine like panes of glass. Driving from Sandy's to the reporter's house, Cole occasionally glanced at his passenger. She appeared to be asleep.

The Hyde Park neighborhood is one of the oldest and most exclusive in Chicago. It had been its own township before being incorporated into Greater Chicago. The streets were lined with stately mansions and well-maintained apartment buildings. It had an almost suburban look along with a great many trees. Now darkness, added to the stately ambiance, gave the venerable old neighborhood a sinister feel.

Cole found a parking place under a tree, which cast the car in shadow. The nearest streetlight was not working. He got out of the car and came around to open the door for his passenger. He checked the deserted street carefully. When Kate Ford came out of the car, she grabbed his arm and held on to it tightly as they made their way to her courtyard.

They reached the front entrance of her town house without incident. Her hands trembled badly when she unlocked the two locks securing the front door. Cole noticed that the front window and blinds he'd smashed in had been replaced.

They entered the dark living room. Kate reached out her hand and flipped a wall light switch. Lamps blinked on all over the house.

"Well, you're home safe and sound, so I guess—" Cole began.

"No!" she said, frantically, stepping forward and again grabbing his arm. "Don't go yet." She managed to bring herself under control. "Let me fix you a drink."

Stifling a yawn he shook his head. "No thank you. I've reached my limit for the night. All I want to do now is go home and go to bed. But I really had a nice time and we must do it again soon."

She still refused to release his arm. "Please don't leave yet. I'm afraid after what happened to that policewoman earlier. And I saw that boy, who tried to kill you. He was driving that red cart. He's the same one who planted the snakes here and he's still out there with that ugly old man."

Cole didn't know how to comfort her. "Do you want me to check the house?"

"Would you please?"

He checked the main floor, the upstairs rooms, and the basement. He found nothing threatening, but he did notice that the pretty reporter had a great deal of space in her expensively furnished town house. She had not moved from the living room when he returned.

"All secure," he said. He noticed that her terror had not abated.

"Why don't you go stay with friends until you feel more comfortable here?" he suggested.

"I couldn't," she said in a small voice. "I have to sleep in my own house."

Cole was again about to say good night when she said, "But you could stay here with me."

The offer shocked him.

"I mean," she explained quickly, "you could sleep in the guest room. It's clean and has its own private bathroom."

Cole was about to tell her that what she proposed was out of the question when he noticed the terror in her eyes. Then he remembered that this woman had saved his life.

"Okay," he relented, "I'll stay."

She squeezed his arm and said a very sincere, "Thank you."

The guest room was as big as the master bedroom where Kate slept, which was down the hall on the second level of the town house. It did have its own bathroom with a new toothbrush in the medicine cabinet. Cole washed up and got in bed. The last thought he had before dozing off was that he hadn't slept in his own apartment very much lately.

Some hours later, as the sky began brightening over the eastern horizon, he awakened. He noticed instantly that something now was different about the room in which he slept. It took him only a matter of scant seconds to recognize what that something was. He was not alone.

There was a soft noise coming from the floor. His gun was in its holster hanging from the back of a chair six feet from the bed. It was too far away for him to reach without getting up and exposing himself to whatever was making that sound.

Slowly, he raised his head until he could see over the edge of the bed. He saw her head of blonde curls first. Kate was asleep on the floor. The sound he'd heard had been her softly inhaling and exhaling. She had covered herself with a pink blanket. He had no idea how long she'd been there or how she'd managed to get into the room without awakening him. He collapsed back on the bed, looked up at the ceiling and whispered, "Damn."

PART 3

"You survived the first time we met, Larry.
You won't be so lucky now."
—Christian Dodd

49

July 10, 1999
9:05 a.m.

The meeting was held in the ninth-floor offices of the Chicago branch of the Federal Bureau of Investigation at 219 South Dearborn. Present were the agent in charge Dave Franklin, Donald Hildebrand, the deputy director of Region Six of the National Security Agency—Scientific Research Division, Carolyn Falk from the U.S. Attorney's Office, and NSA Special Agents Reggie Stanton and Ernest Steiger. Under discussion was the hunt for mad scientist and murderer Jonathan Gault.

Dave Franklin was hosting the meeting because he was the chief federal law-enforcement officer for the Chicago and northern Indiana area and this was a case involving murder on a federal reserve, theft of government property, and sabotage of a U.S. government facility, but the special agent in charge didn't want anything to do with this case. That was because of Stanton and Steiger. Franklin didn't consider these men law-enforcement officers, but instead criminals. Assassins, who didn't have any business being in the employ of the United States government no matter how good they were at what they did.

For the most part, since this meeting had been convened at 9:00 a.m., the assistant U.S. Attorney had done most of the talking. Carolyn Falk was a pretty brunette who, despite her maintaining an extremely severe professional manner, was still quite attractive. Now her brown eyes were spewing ice daggers around the office.

"We've had this file open on Jonathan Gault and the boy Christian Dodd," she tapped the manila folder lying on the surface of Franklin's varnished conference table, "for over a year now. We have obtained fairly reliable information that they are in Chicago and yet, despite all the resources of the federal government's law-enforcement apparatus, you have been unable to apprehend them."

Hildebrand, a heavyset man sporting a thick mustache, glanced at his agents, who sat in stony silence. When they didn't defend themselves, he cleared his throat and said apologetically, "I think we've, uh, turned up a lead or two in the past few days, Counselor." He again glanced at Stanton and Steiger, who still didn't respond.

The United States Attorney looked from Hildebrand to the two shadow agents. Carolyn Falk had heard stories about them. Primarily, she understood that they were assassins, who had roots going back to World War II and Hitler's SS. Despite their differences in appearance, they were brothers and as deadly as any pair of siblings in history. However, they were the NSA operatives assigned to hunt for Gault and Dodd.

After a moment of protracted silence, the attorney glared down the table at Stanton and Steiger. The two agents unflinchingly returned her gaze with such menace that she looked away. Again, Deputy Director Hildebrand cleared his throat and said, "Would you gentlemen please share with us what you've discovered in connection with the Gault case?" Franklin and Falk exchanged furious glances because of the deputy director's pleading tone.

Finally, Stanton's cheeks swelled slightly in what could have passed for a smile and said, "From everything my brother and I have been able to find out, Jonathan Gault is not only in Chicago, but is responsible for a series of murders and attempted murders here."

Steiger took over from his brother, as if they'd rehearsed it. "To date, it looks like our mad scientist from Astrolab has killed six criminals and a police detective."

Stanton resumed. "The murders were carried out with electrocutions, snake venom injections, and a flamethrower."

Again, Steiger interjected, "With the exception of the police detective, who was incinerated, there hasn't been much of an official investigation mounted by the CPD. However, we can anticipate that situation altering radically after what happened last night."

Stanton concluded, "We expect this because Gault is obviously after Larry Cole, the Chicago Police Department's chief of detectives. Now all we have to do is wait for the scientist to make a move on Cole and we'll have him and his little crippled friend."

All of the federal agents in the room sincerely hoped that Stanton was right.

50

July 10, 1999
10:12 A.M.

Tommy Kingsley was at his desk plotting against the Chicago Police Department. The opportunity presenting itself was too great. Govich being in the hospital after that debacle out on South Dearborn a few days ago, freed Kingsley to make his moves and one of the moves he planned to make was getting rid of Larry Cole.

His intercom buzzed. He flipped the switch. "Yes?"

"Mr. Donaldson is here, sir," his secretary said with her characteristic lisp.

"Send him in."

A few moments later the hulking auditor walked into the office and took a seat across the desk from Kingsley.

"What have you got for me?" the director of public safety demanded.

Donaldson opened his laptop computer on top of Kingsley's desk. After turning it on, he booted up a program and said, "In my initial examination of the detective division, which was in conjunction with the audit you wanted on the entire CPD, it came out looking pretty good. It's less than twenty percent of the force, but they have some impressive stats."

Kingsley became irritated. "I didn't call you in to hear accolades about Cole's operation. I want to know what's *wrong* with the Chicago Police Detective Division."

Donaldson wasn't the least bit intimidated by the director's outburst. The auditor knew how to play the game and also was aware that Kingsley needed him. His tone betrayed this as he responded, "Why don't we deal with the real reason you're so interested in the detective division and cut through the other bullshit?"

Kingsley became very still. "You want to explain to me what you're talking about?"

"You're after Larry Cole. I know you've got a thing for the rest of the police department, but I've also noticed that you have a particular animosity for the chief of detectives."

Kingsley swelled with outrage, but his tone of voice remained normal. "How dare you make such an outrageous and insulting statement to me?"

Donaldson laughed. "Take it easy, Tommy. Your secret is safe with me. I'll even give you the way to get Cole."

Kingsley continued glaring at Donaldson, but remained silent.

"Okay, the detective division is an excellent law-enforcement operation, which has some impressive statistics, but that's not because Larry Cole is such a great resource manager. The detectives staffing the division are the real reason. Now Cole is one helluva leader and he has an impressive track record as a cop. But do we want heroes like him running our police departments in this age of rising crime and equally high costs, or do we want good managers who are capable of directing resources efficiently instead of crashing through windows and killing snakes?"

Kingsley's features altered to reveal an open interest in what the auditor was saying. "Tell me more."

As Donaldson continued, the director of public safety gave the auditor his undivided attention. That's why he failed to notice that he'd left his intercom on.

51

July 10, 1999
10:15 A.M.

Kate Ford fixed scrambled eggs, slices of honey-baked ham, and biscuits for breakfast. Cole smelled the food while he was dressing. When he awakened, the reporter was no longer on the floor of the guest bedroom. After taking a shower, he was forced to put on the same clothing that he'd worn the day before and a heavy growth of beard covered his chin and cheeks.

When he arrived in the kitchen. Kate was standing at the stove. She wore a full-length quilted robe and had just poured the eggs into a hot skillet.

"Good morning," he said.

She turned. "Good morning to you. I hope you slept well."

He wondered if he should mention anything about her sleeping on the floor of the guest room. He decided to let her bring it up.

"Why don't you sit down and let me pour you a cup of coffee?" she said.

"Sounds good."

As she set the cup down in front of him she said, "I like you with that rugged, unshaven, he-man look."

He rubbed the stubble on his chin. "Well don't get used to it, because as soon as I get to a razor it will be gone."

A few minutes later they were consuming the ham and egg breakfast she'd prepared.

"Larry," she said between bites, "I want to thank you for staying here last night. I would not have been able to sleep and would have also spent most of the night jumping out of my skin at every noise I heard."

They ate in silence for a time. Then Cole said, "While you were lying down last night at the club, Madam Devereaux and I had a talk about black magic."

"Do you believe in stuff like that?" There was incredulity in her voice.

"I've found over the years that I've been a cop that it's best to keep an open mind when you don't have all the facts."

"So what did Sandy say?"

"She explained a few things to me about magic and energy. She mentioned someone called Dr. Silvernail Smith and told me that someone she initially thought was a practitioner of Voodoo attacked the maître d'. She managed to drive it away. While you were singing I saw her standing on the balcony above the stage holding something in her hands. Whatever it was began emitting smoke. Later in her office, she showed me her palms. They were badly burned."

"How did she do that?" Kate was awestruck.

"I know what she says she did and it would be pretty extreme to burn the palms of her hands to carry off an illusion."

"I've heard stories about Madam Devereaux and those that have the nerve to talk about it say she's a bona fide Voodooiene."

"Okay, why don't we talk about something we have a bit more information about than Voodoo?"

"Such as?" she asked.

"What you were doing in the morgue the other day?"

Kate hesitated a moment before shrugging. She told him about her anonymous caller. She left out the caller's identity, as well as the names of the victims.

"So what did you find out?" he asked.

"That recently a number of normal, healthy people have died suddenly under what could be called suspicious circumstances. Then this Dr. McGuire classifies the deaths as either due to natural or undetermined causes when there are definite indications that they met with foul play."

"I assume you have documented proof to back up your theory?"

The reporter stiffened and her gaze assumed arctic coldness. Cole could see the brick wall of refusal going up, so he decided to make her an offer he hoped she would be unable to refuse.

"We've noticed a few so-called accidental deaths recently as well," Cole began, "which have involved career criminals we believe were in the act of either committing or fleeing from the scenes of crimes. If you give me what you have, I'll share what the department has so far with you."

Her chilliness remained, but he could tell she was weighing his proposal. Finally, she left the kitchen to return a few minutes later carrying a manila folder. She did not hand it over, but instead sat down across from him. She opened the folder on the table in front of her.

From Cole's vantage point he could see that the folder contained photostats of official forms. Now she was going to play "Let's make a deal."

"Okay, Larry, I know what I've got. Why don't you give me something that you have so I can be sure that I'm not being suckered?"

Cole smiled. She was one tough lady and he admired her for it. He had to consult his memory in order to recall the information Judy had given him. He figured he could remember enough to give Kate something tantalizing to bargain for.

"In those papers you have, there should be a few people who were professional criminals."

She frowned. "No one lists criminal specialties as occupations in official documents."

"The police department does," he argued. "On our case and arrest reports we do it all the time. Check box forty-seven of the CPD document attached to the autopsy reports."

She did and, without looking up from the reports, said, "The heading on box forty-seven reads 'Suspected Criminal Specialty.' "

"What's in the box?"

"On this one it's 'auto theft.' " Now she looked up at Cole.

He smiled at her and said, "Check the other reports."

She did. Each of them, with the exception of Anna Kingsley's and Kevin Quinn's, had box forty-seven listing their "Suspected Criminal Specialties" as either "burglary" or "auto theft." She checked the accompanying autopsy reports. Each of the criminals was worked on by Dr. W. McGuire, who classified the causes of death as either natural or undetermined.

She again looked up at Cole.

"Judy has a theory. We've found a couple of additional dead thieves since you compiled your files. And we believe that they were killed by deadly booby traps while they were in the act of committing crimes."

"But placing something deadly inside your house or car as protection from a thief is pure insanity," Kate said.

"I've given that some thought," Cole said, "and I agree with you. That is if the people whose property is being protected were aware the deadly devices were there."

"But how could they not know?"

"Maybe they weren't told. Just given a guarantee that their property would be secure. They could have been given a recommendation to apply for the deadly security service from someone who was fairly influential. Someone they trusted. We're obviously dealing with very powerful people if they're able to cover up deaths by altering autopsy reports.

"The property owners would be instructed to do certain things to protect themselves. The thieves, who are probably capable of circumventing your average alarm system, would be unaware of the trap until it was too late. Now the question remains to be answered, who and why, and I think you can answer them both for me."

He'd made his case. Now he waited for a reply.

She stared at her hands for a long time before she looked up and answered, "Everything I've been able to find out so far points to the director of public safety and someone named Jonathan Gault."

52

July 10, 1999
10:30 a.m.

Jonathan Gault awoke from a nightmare with a scream. Frantically, he looked around his spartan sleeping quarters in the Chinatown warehouse. Christian was sitting at the foot of the bed watching him. There was evident fear in the young man's face.

"You were having a bad dream, Doctor. I didn't know what to do." Tears welled in the amputee's eyes.

Gault reached out and patted his charge's shoulder. "I'm okay now, Christian. It's just a dream that I have from time to time about someone I knew a long time ago. Thank you for the concern."

The scientist got up and went into the bathroom. The cobra Satan was curled up in a corner. Gault ran cold water into the sink and splashed it liberally on his face, head, and neck. Dripping wet, he studied his reflection in the mirror. He looked like a drowned corpse. Gault recalled the events of the previous night. The woman in the nightclub had used black magic on him. He knew, because this had happened to him before.

He snatched a towel from a rack and vigorously rubbed his head and face. Walking back into the bedroom, he noticed that Christian had not moved.

Gault smiled. "I haven't had a chance to thank you for rescuing me last night. The Red Lightning vehicle performed up to expectations."

Christian ran the back of his hand across his tear-streaked cheeks and said, "It is the most wonderful thing I have ever owned, Dr. Gault. And that flamethrower was magnificent. Did you see what it did to that woman?"

Gault frowned. "I wasn't thinking clearly after what happened to me. We should have used it on Cole."

The Red Lightning vehicle was outside the bedroom in the lab. Using his powerful arms for support and propulsion, Christian got off the bed and crawled rapidly out of the bedroom to mount his new, deadly toy.

"Could you show me what else it is capable of doing?"

The scientist smiled. "I will show you everything, Christian, but first we have to make plans to vacate this place. We've stayed here too long and there will be more policeman looking for us after what happened last night."

"Where will we go, Doctor?"

Gault's odd-colored eyes glistened. "To take care of unfinished business."

Frances "Frankie" Bell was a homeless person who frequented Chinatown and the surrounding area. She could usually be observed between dawn and dusk pushing a rickety, rusting, wobbly-wheeled grocery cart, which contained any tin cans and other salable junk she could find on the streets and in the alleys. Occasionally, she'd go up on Cermak Road and attempt to hustle some loose change off tourists visiting Chinatown. But lately there'd been a lot of cops on the main drag, so Frankie stayed on the side streets and, of course, in the alleys.

On this July morning she was pushing her cart down a cracked sidewalk when she saw the new motor home parked outside the strange warehouse. She thought of it as strange because it was secured like a fortress, yet she'd never seen anyone going in or coming out of the building. But there was someone or something in there. She was certain of it. How she knew this she couldn't say. She just did.

Frankie Bell was a quarter of a block away when a man came out of the warehouse. She could tell that he was about her age and, by his appearance, looked like he could qualify for a position among the ranks of the homeless. Even though she was some distance away she could see that there was something wrong with his eyes. A moment later a strange red vehicle rolled up a ramp from the basement of the warehouse. There was a kid driving and she couldn't see much of him except his head and a portion of his upper body. To the bag lady they looked like an odd pair indeed. They met at the motor home and the older man opened a rear ramp and the kid drove the red vehicle inside. The man shut the door and was about to get behind the wheel of the motor home when he noticed her. She felt a chill as his eyes, which she could only term evil, swept over her.

Then he smiled and got into the motor home. She watched them drive off and was about to resume her scavenging when the Chinatown warehouse that the man with the evil eyes and the kid in the strange red vehicle had just exited blew up in a massive explosion that was heard for miles. Frankie Bell was knocked to the pavement by the concussion from the blast. She was still lying there when the first emergency vehicles arrived to investigate the explosion.

53

JULY 10, 1999
11:00 A.M.

The meeting in the FBI conference room on South Dearborn finally broke up. U.S. Attorney Carolyn Falk had stormed out after making some rather nasty threats to Deputy Director Hildebrand and Agents Stanton and Steiger that if Jonathan Gault and Christian Dodd weren't apprehended within the next forty-eight hours, the NSA operatives would be held responsible.

Hildebrand was pale as he exited the Federal Building onto Dearborn Street. Turning to his two agents he said, "What are you going to do next?"

"We already laid out our plan upstairs, Director," Stanton said icily. "And Ms. Falk's threats will not alter them. My brother and I are professionals, not a couple of broken-down cops she can scare with her threats because she went to law school."

"So you still plan to keep an eye on Cole?" Hildebrand asked.

"I'd say that would be our best bet, boss," Ernest Steiger quipped. "Unless you have a better idea?"

The NSA deputy director blanched and said a hurried, "No. You guys do what you think is right. Keep me posted." Then he rushed off down the street.

The brothers watched him go before turning and walking a block to a parking garage. There they retrieved Ernest's jet black

Porsche roadster. A few moments later, with the top down, they were literally flying south on Lake Shore Drive. Stanton glanced at the speedometer. His brother was traveling at over eighty miles an hour.

"Ernest, slow down," Reggie said. "This area is radar-patrolled."

"Lighten up, Reg," his brother said with a grin. "After all, we are cops."

But dutifully, as his older brother had instructed, he slowed his speed to seventy-five, which was thirty miles above the posted speed limit. They made it to the Forty-seventh Street exit without incident. Steiger raced from Lake Shore Drive to King Drive, a distance of approximately two miles, as if he was driving in the Indianapolis 500.

They skidded to a stop in front of a perfectly maintained brownstone in the 4500 block of South Martin Luther King Jr. Drive. As Steiger put the top up on the roadster, Stanton got out and crossed the sidewalk to a waist-high, wrought-iron fence. While he waited for his brother he looked up and down the broad, tree-lined boulevard. He had lived most of his life in this house and at one time had been terrorized by the neighborhood toughs when he was a boy. The two most important people in his life, his grandmother Ida Mae Stanton and his uncle Ernst von Steiger, had died in the brownstone. Now he and his brother occupied the old house and used it as a base of operations.

Reggie Stanton and Ernest Steiger were direct descendants of the von Steiger line of Prussian military officers that dated back to the Napoleonic Wars. A von Steiger was on the general staff of the German army in every generation through Hitler's rise to power. The last member of the German military was Hauptmann Ernst von Steiger, who had been on Oberst Otto Skorzeny's staff for the infiltration of commandos dressed as American soldiers behind Allied lines in December 1944. Because of von Steiger's involvement in the Battle of the Bulge, he was branded a war criminal. Ernst was forced to run after the war and this had brought him into Reggie Stanton's life.

Ernest joined his brother on the sidewalk and together they entered the brownstone. Since his grandmother had died, Reggie had had the interior remodeled. Now the place was brighter and equipped with modern furniture. The NSA agents went to the basement, which was different from the house above. If the area that Stanton and Steiger entered could be given a label it would best be described as a Bavarian hunting lodge, which it was built to resemble. The carpenter had been Ernst Steiger and the brothers had carefully preserved it in the exact condition it was the day Uncle Ernst, as he was called, died. There was also another reason why they preserved this place. It was because their father, Karl Steiger, had also died here.

The basement was L-shaped and spacious. Uncle Ernst had designed one leg of the L as a training area, which was equipped for practice with conventional firearms, daggers, and hand-to-hand combat training. However, for generations the von Steigers had preferred the thrown dagger and Ernest Steiger and Reggie Stanton were masters of the assassins' art of the Whistling Dagger of Death.

The only addition to Ernst von Steiger's hunting lodge replica in the basement of the Chicago brownstone was a computer workstation. Now Reggie Stanton removed his size fifty suit jacket, draped it over the back of a handcarved wood and leather chair that had been made in Germany, and sat down at the keyboard.

Ernest went to the practice range and picked up one of the daggers. All of the knives were of stainless steel with razor-sharp edges and black vulcanized-rubber grips. A silhouette target was fifteen meters downrange. There was a bull's-eye painted on the center of the chest. Hefting the dagger, Ernest sighted in on the target and with a fluid, overhand motion, hurled it. The projectile zipped across the distance and imbedded itself two inches below the center of the bull's-eye. Silently, Ernest scolded himself. He wasn't concentrating or he would have hit it dead center. He picked up another dagger but before throwing it turned to look at his brother.

Reggie Stanton was working busily at the computer. His broad back was turned to Steiger. The blond man stared at his brother for a long time. Had there been anyone present to observe Steiger, they would have noticed that his expression was inscrutable. Although he held the dagger loosely in his hand, Ernest's simple possession of it imbued him with a measure of silent menace. Stanton remained totally unaware of his brother's gaze.

Finally, Ernest looked away from his brother and over at a brown, scarred-with-age leather couch against the wall at the apex of the junction of the L. On that piece of ancient furniture both Uncle Ernst and Karl Steiger had died. Ernest shivered. There were ghosts in this old place. A great many ghosts.

"Ernest," Reggie called, "I think I've got something."

The blond man hesitated for a moment. Despite the fact that Reggie Stanton was an African American, he looked more like their father than Ernest ever had. And when Reggie spoke to him he sounded very much like Karl Steiger. At times the tone could be disapproving, just as their father's had been.

"Ernest," Reggie repeated before turning around to see where his brother was. When he saw the dagger, Stanton's eyes locked with Steiger's. For a long moment there was silence. Then Reggie said, "Are you coming over here to see what I've got?"

In one quick, fluid motion Ernest spun and hurled the dagger at the silhouette target. It pierced the bull's-eye dead center. Then Ernest Steiger walked over to join his brother.

54

July 10, 1999
11:32 A.M.

Cole heard the gunshots from police weapons before he turned off Cermak Road onto the street where the destroyed warehouse was located. There were a couple of fire trucks, four police cars, an ambulance, the police department's animal-control van, and three TV Minicam trucks parked on the street. A crowd had gathered to watch the spectacle. Cole found a spot behind one of the Minicam trucks and got out.

Under the supervision of a young, broad-shouldered sergeant, three uniformed police officers wielding semiautomatic handguns had formed a skirmish line and were shooting the snakes that were slithering from a hole in the debris. The carcasses of six of the creatures littered the street. Three more officers were assigned to keep the crowd, consisting mostly of Asians, from getting too close to the target area.

Cole flashed his badge at one of the officers on crowd control and walked over to the sergeant. The supervisor turned and recognized the chief. Touching his fingers to his cap, the sergeant muttered a terse, "This is the damnedest thing I ever saw, boss."

Cole looked on as a rattlesnake crawled from beneath the debris and hissed at the cops. A hail of bullets reduced it to a bloody pulp.

"Where are the animal-control people?" Cole asked.

The sergeant hooked a thumb back at the crowd. "They're

over there somewhere. Said that they're not equipped to deal with anything like this. Their area of expertise is restricted to stray dogs, cats, and raccoons. They won't go near the snakes."

Cole looked back at the rubble. "Do we know what happened to this place?"

"Looks like some type of explosive. The Bomb and Arson Unit is on the way to check it out. There's an old bag lady in the ambulance, who we found lying on the street. She's close to going into shock and was babbling something about a man with evil eyes and a kid in some kind of red vehicle coming out of the warehouse before it blew." The sergeant paused a moment before he asked, "These snakes being here don't make much sense. Didn't you have a run-in with a couple of rattlers a few days ago, Chief?"

"Yeah," Cole responded, studying the dead snakes. "Those ended up just like these." Then he forced the memory from his mind, turned to the sergeant, and said, "I'd like to talk to this woman."

"Sure thing." The sergeant accompanied Cole to the ambulance. Cameras were trained on them and reporters shouted questions, which both cops ignored.

Thirty minutes later, Cole stood on the street and watched the Cook County Dead Animal Removal unit picking up the remains of twelve snakes from the street. The trio of workers was clad in coveralls. They moved slowly and very carefully using long sticks to which pincers were attached to probe the snakes first to see if they were indeed dead and then picking them up to drop them in a plastic container.

Cole hadn't known a great deal about snakes until a few days ago. Now he was getting to be an expert on them. And they didn't belong in Chicago, unless they were in the zoo.

So someone had brought them here and could also control them. Considering what had happened at Kate Ford's place, in Sandra Devereaux's nightclub last night, and to the thieves who had been killed in Chicago, Cole strongly suspected that what had occurred here in Chinatown with the dead snakes was connected to everything else. He remembered the name Madam Devereux had given him last night. Dr. Silvernail Smith. Also, NSA Agents Reggie Stanton and Ernest Steiger were in Chicago looking for a renegade scientist named Jonathan Gault. A man whose name Kate Ford had also mentioned, as being in league with Tommy Kingsley in covering up murders in the Windy City. Cole headed for his car as the county workers continued to pick up dead snakes from the street.

55

July 10, 1999
11:45 A.M.

Mary Keenan, Tommy Kingsley's secretary, got off the elevator in the lobby of the Municipal Administration Building. She crossed to the LaSalle Street doors and stepped out into the bright sunlight. After the air-conditioned cool of the building she'd just left, the midsummer Chicago heat was oppressive.

She walked over to the curb, preparing to cross the street to the State of Illinois Building, when a woman wearing sunglasses and a wide-brimmed straw hat appeared at her side.

"Sure is a hot day," the woman said.

"You can say that again," the secretary agreed, speaking in such a manner so as not to show her missing teeth.

A gap in the traffic allowed the two women to cross the street. The secretary entered the revolving doors of the state building and noticed that her companion in the straw hat was right behind her. The secretary crossed the lobby to the escalator leading down to the lower level where the food court was located. As she descended, she glanced back to see the woman was three steps above. Curious more than alarmed, the secretary got off the escalator and stopped before heading to the Good Dog hot dog and lemonade stand where she planned to purchase her lunch. She watched the woman in the strawhat walk over to the line serving Geno's pizza.

The secretary shrugged and permitted a close-lipped smile to cross her face. She was getting paranoid and she knew the reason why. Her boss, Tommy Kingsley.

She began making plans to begin job hunting as she waited for one of the attendants to fix her an Italian beef sandwich with sweet peppers. Along with the sandwich she bought a container of lemonade and walked to a table set off in a remote corner. She was unwrapping her sandwich when the woman in the straw hat sat down across from her. This frightened the secretary.

"What do you want?" she said with a noticeable tremble in her voice.

"I didn't mean to startle you," Kate Ford replied, "but I thought it was about time we had a face-to-face meeting after all the interesting talks we've had on the phone."

Mary Keenan, the personal secretary of the director of public safety became very still. She recognized Kate Ford. Now she wished that she'd never made that first call.

56

July 10, 1999
12:02 p.m.

Cole entered the Field Museum of Natural History and went to the information booth. He asked to see Dr. Silvernail Smith and the uniformed female attendant directed him to the curator's office on the second floor. En route Cole noticed the vast difference between this museum and the National Science and Space Museum, which had played such a major part in his life. He was still experiencing a lingering sense of shock over the revelations made to him yesterday by Reggie Stanton. Cole pushed them from his mind as he stopped to look at a tomb, which had been carted from Egypt and reassembled in the museum brick by brick.

Cole paused to read the paper mounted under glass on a pedestal in front of the exhibit. The structure, which resembled a two-story building and stretched from the first floor of the museum into the basement, had been the tomb of an Egyptian nobleman. The nobleman had been buried at the base of one of the great pyramids, which was a practice in the ancient culture. Cole briefly considered taking a tour of the tomb before remembering that he had a job to do. Tearing himself away from the exhibit he started once more for the curator's office.

After leaving the site of the snake-infested, destroyed building in Chinatown, Cole had gone home, shaved, and changed into a lightweight tan suit, yellow shirt, and dark brown tie. He'd broken down, cleaned, and oiled his Beretta. After reloading it and placing a fresh bullet clip in the leather ammo pouch on his belt, he was ready to face the bad guys once more.

He reached the door marked OFFICE OF THE CURATOR and entered to find a middle-aged female receptionist seated at a desk. Cole showed her his ID and badge, which caused her eyes to widen slightly in shock.

"I'd like to see Dr. Silvernail Smith," he repeated.

"Is there some problem?" the receptionist said with alarm.

"No. None at all," Cole said with a smile. "I'd just like to ask him some questions related to a case that I'm working on."

"Just a minute," the receptionist said, rising and dashing through a wooden door bearing the word PRIVATE.

A moment later she returned with a young black woman dressed in a gray business suit. She stepped forward, extended her hand to the policeman, and said, "I'm Dr. Nora Livingston, the museum curator."

"Hello, Doctor," Cole said taking her hand and requesting to see Dr. Silvernail Smith for the third time since he'd entered the museum.

The curator's brow knitted in concern. "I hope Silvernail's not in any trouble."

"He's not in trouble. I understand that he's an expert on the occult and I'd like to ask him some questions in connection with a case I'm working on."

He could see that Dr. Livingston wanted to question him further, but something stopped her. She turned to the receptionist and said, "I'll escort Officer . . . uh . . ." She turned to look questioningly at him.

"Cole," he said. "Larry Cole."

Turning back to the receptionist, she concluded, "I'll escort Officer Cole to Silvernail's office."

Cole followed her out into the corridor.

"Are you a detective?" the curator asked, as they descended a staircase leading back to the main floor.

"I'm actually the chief of detectives," he responded.

"I'm sorry, but I don't know much about police ranks."

Cole smiled. "You could call me the curator of the Chicago Police detective force."

"Sounds impressive," she said. They were walking past the stuffed carcass of the giant gorilla Bushman. "Does your detecting often lead you into the realm of the occult?"

"As a rule, no. But we do whatever is necessary to get the answers in complicated cases. And you could say that I am working on a very complicated case."

During their stroll through the museum so far they had passed a number of spectators. As it was summer and the history museum was located so close to the downtown area of the city, it drew thousands of spectators a day. Then Cole and Dr. Livingston descended another staircase leading down to the basement. The number of people they passed began gradually decreasing the farther they went into the bowels of the old structure.

"Well, if you're really that interested in the supernatural," the curator said, "then you've come to the right place. Dr. Silvernail is an expert on the subject."

"Dr. Silvernail?" Cole questioned.

"That's what he prefers to be called. He says that calling him Dr. Smith makes him sound like the comedic villain from an old television series called *Lost in Space*."

"Oh," was Cole's only comment.

They passed the lower level of the Egyptian tomb. Now Cole noticed that this area of the museum was completely deserted.

"Like most museums," Nora Livingston said, "this one is

rumored to be haunted. A number of people, who've gone through this exhibit," she pointed at the exit to the tomb, "claim they've heard strange noises inside the exhibit."

"How old is that tomb anyway?"

"Although the pyramid it was constructed beneath is much older, we've estimated that this structure was built approximately thirty-five hundred years ago."

They reached a door situated between two exhibit cases. It was so out of the way that most visitors to the museum never even noticed it. The curator opened the door and led Cole inside.

Cole had expected to find something dark, dank, and sinister, but instead they were in a well-lighted, air-conditioned office. An office that was currently empty.

"I guess Silvernail is out," the curator said. "He can't have gone far. Would you like to wait?"

"Sure," Cole said, shrugging.

"I'll have him paged, so you won't have to wait long. It was nice meeting you." Then she left.

The office was fairly modern with a PC, fax machine, and new Sony combination TV-VCR. There was also an antique, handcarved desk and a matching desk chair on rollers. Both the desk and the chair looked expensive. Then there were framed photographs, paintings, drawings, diplomas, and citations lining nearly every available inch of wall space.

Cole started with the ones by the door. By the time he'd worked his way halfway down one wall he'd discovered that this Dr. Silvernail Smith was an M.D., who was board certified as an orthopedic surgeon, and had Ph.D. degrees in anthropology, history, and chemistry. There was a shelf filled with textbooks the doctor had authored and a number of photos that revealed a handsome, thin-faced man sporting a mustache and goatee.

Cole began examining the photographs. There were a number of them showing Dr. Silvernail wearing commencement robes and beaming into the camera, while posing with celebrities and every United States president dating back to Jimmy Carter. Then Cole noticed the photos of Silvernail with John F. Kennedy and Richard Nixon.

The policeman paused to do some arithmetic in his head. Kennedy had been dead for thirty-six years. So this photo could not have been taken after November 22, 1963. Then Cole noticed something else. The man in each of the pictures had graying hair, which also dotted his mustache and goatee. Cole checked the later photos. The reproductions were excellent and in each one, from the one with Kennedy to a recent full-color photo of Silvernail with Bill and Hillary Clinton, the doctor looked exactly the same.

There were a few subtle differences. In a couple of the circa early-sixties pictures Silvernail only sported a mustache; however, in all the others he had the goatee and his hair was worn long and pulled back into a ponytail. There was also the stamp of the Native American on his features.

On a hunch Cole glanced over at the opposite wall. The pictures there were noticeably older. He studied them.

They were also of Dr. Silvernail. There was one of him with a group of khaki-clad men and women with the great Pyramid at Giza visible in the background. An inked legend in the lower right-hand corner read: FIELD MUSEUM EXPEDITION—1 SEPTEMBER 1958. That was forty-one years ago. Cole moved to the next set of pictures. In these Dr. Silvernail was shown shaking hands with Presidents Eisenhower and Truman. Cole's mind spat out the numbers. These pictures would had to have been taken a half century ago. Yet Silvernail had not visibly changed.

Cole went to the next group of pictures, which were interspersed with pencil sketches and watercolors. There was a lifelike sketch of Franklin D. Roosevelt, which bore the signature and date in the lower right-hand corner: SILVERNAIL—HYDE PARK, NEW YORK—JULY 13, 1941."

Cole again calculated the years. Fifty-eight. He looked at the last photo of Dr. Silvernail. Cole estimated his age from his appearance in the pictures to be from the mid to late fifties, but Silvernail had looked the same in 1960 as he had in 1998.

Undoubtedly, Cole decided, what he was viewing was elaborate trick photography and the date on the Roosevelt sketch was obviously either an error or an outright falsification. A couple of rows from the Roosevelt sketch Cole found one of Abraham Lincoln. In the corner of this drawing was again Silvernail's signature and another date: WASHINGTON, D.C.—APRIL 1, 1865. Cole smiled. This confirmed his theory about the dates on the sketches being false.

The policeman moved on to the next set of photos.

They looked like old daguerreotypes. In his mind Cole emphasized the "looked like," because they appeared to have been taken during the Civil War. However, again Dr. Silvernail was in each of them. There were three separate photos of Union officers. No dates were visible on any of the pictures, but their grainy quality, the manner in which they were posed, and the uniforms spoke for themselves.

Cole halted his perusal and stepped back. There was something wrong here. Why would anyone go to all this trouble to make up these fakes and then hide them down here in the basement of the museum? It didn't make any sense unless this Dr. Silvernail Smith was on a huge ego trip. And a fantasy ego trip at that. There was another alternative, but Cole refused to give it more than a passing thought, because that would truly be beyond belief.

The rest of the frames on the wall contained sketches. Now Cole felt his skin start to tingle. The drawings were all of snakes. He was about to give each of them a careful examination when a voice from behind him said, "Good afternoon, Chief Cole."

57

July 10, 1999
12:25 P.M.

Dr. Silvernail Smith was dressed in a collarless, blue, long-sleeved shirt, blue jeans, and white jogging shoes with no socks. He came forward with his hand extended. Cole received the strongest handshake he'd ever encountered and the chief of detectives was not a weak man.

"Won't you have a seat?" Silvernail said, indicating the lone couch in the office.

The doctor took a seat across from Cole in the swivel chair behind the desk and spun it around to face the cop.

"Now that we've been introduced, Chief, what can I do for you?"

Cole felt very relaxed with this man, however, he still hadn't gotten over the photographs or the drawings on the walls. But then, first things first.

"Madam Sandra Devereaux sent me to see you. I, that is myself and the department, have been encountering some rather unique problems lately and she said that you might be able to help me."

Silvernail got quickly to his feet. "Where are my manners? Can I offer you something? A cup of tea or perhaps a glass of water?"

"Water will be fine," Cole said.

The historian left the office and returned a few minutes later, carrying a glass of ice water and a steaming cup of tea. Handing the water to Cole, he returned to his seat.

When they were again settled, Silvernail asked, "Did Madam Devereaux send you to see me because the problems you're experiencing have something to do with magic?"

Cole took a sip of the water and said, "Yes and no. We had a discussion last night about energy in the physical world as opposed to energy in the spiritual world." The cop hesitated a moment and made a decision. He decided to trust Silvernail. "Let me tell you what's been going on and let you be the judge."

He began with Christian Dodd attempting to kill Kate Ford with snakes, Cole killing the snakes, and Christian attempting to electrocute Cole. He went on to relate the hunt for Christian in the tunnels beneath the Conrail tracks and the strange storm that had done so much damage to the search party being led by Superintendent Govich. Then, as Cole began to relate what had happened to the gang members on Federal Street, he noticed something change in the historian's face.

Larry Cole had been a cop for a long time and had learned to read people. Now what he was picking up from Dr. Silvernail Smith was a mixture of apprehension bordering on fear and something else. It took Cole a moment to assess what this additional emotional element was, then it came to him. The historian was exhibiting deep sorrow. Filing this away for future reference, Cole continued by relating what had occurred at Sandy's jazz club the previous night, to include the appearance of the strange red vehicle and the incineration of Detective Lula Love. After hesitating a moment, Cole added, "Detective Love was miles away from her assigned area of responsibility and I have a strong suspicion, which I have been unable to confirm, that she was following me."

"Why?" Silvernail asked pointedly.

Cole returned the historian's gaze. "I've made enemies during my career, Doctor. A great many enemies."

The policeman concluded, "We've had some suspicious deaths of career criminals lately and there's a government organization called the National Security Agency, Scientific Research Division, looking for a scientist here in Chicago who could be responsible for what's been happening. Then there's Sandra Devereaux."

Silvernail stood up and walked over to a pastel sketch that Cole hadn't gotten the opportunity to view before the historian came into the office. He said to Cole, "Take a look at this, Larry."

As Cole got up and walked over to join him, Silvernail asked, "You don't mind if I call you by your first name, do you?"

"Not as long as I can return the favor."

"Of course," Silvernail said, continuing to stare at the drawing.

Cole looked at the sketch, which was in the form of a hieroglyph with symbols representing the figures as opposed to a representation of real people. The historian pointed at a red figure, which was the largest one in the sketch. "That is The Man Who Walks in Blood. He is part magician and part warrior. There is an Indian name for him, but for the purposes of our discussion you don't need to know it."

Cole looked more closely at the figure and noticed it wore a headdress that looked like a helmet adorned with feathers and horns. He carried a knife in one hand and a hatchet in the other.

Silvernail continued, "Ancient Native American legend has it that this magical warrior comes forward to combat the powers of darkness and has been at war since the dawn of time. He does not belong to one tribe, nor is he the property of any one nation or race and he must combat evil wherever he encounters it." He turned to look at the policeman. "Do you believe in such legends, Larry?"

Cole managed a smile. "I've found that there is a bit of truth in every legend or fable."

Silvernail graced him with a mirthless smile. "A very politically correct answer, but that really doesn't matter. You'll be forced to believe the legend soon enough."

Before Cole could respond, he pointed at another figure in the sketch. This one was smaller, drawn completely in black and surrounded by squiggly lines that Cole suspected were meant to depict lightning bolts. At the feet of the dark figure were the unmistakable images of writhing snakes. "That is Red Sky. But perhaps you know him by another name."

Cole looked from the pastel sketch to the historian and said, "What other name would that be, Silvernail?"

The historian returned to his seat and said over his shoulder, "The man you are looking for is named Jonathan Gault, Larry, and he is a genius. A dangerous, twisted genius. He is also my brother."

58

July 10, 1999
12:45 P.M.

Jonathan Gault's black Mercedes pulled into the parking lot of the Field Museum of Natural History. He had left Christian in the motor home parked near the private garage where he kept the luxury car on West Eighteenth Street two miles from Chinatown. Since Gault had entered into the deadly security business with Tommy Kingsley, the scientist had been able to afford a number of things. A luxury car, a new motor home, the rental of the Chinatown warehouse, and his hideout in the basement of the Kow Loon Restaurant. Equipment for his experiments had all come within his means due to the director of public safety. And Gault didn't have to report to any bureaucratic dunderheads like the dead Colonel Robert Lee Watkins at Astrolab. But his arrangement here in Chicago also came with its share of problems. Among them was the cop Larry Cole.

After destroying the Chinatown warehouse to test his sound-resonance device, the scientist had returned to Chinatown to see the official reaction. He watched with interest as the snakes he had left behind, slithered from the rubble. He was enjoying the spectacle when Cole showed up.

Once more in his disguise, Gault had watched Cole. When the cop left the scene, the scientist had followed him which, with a little luck and heavy midday traffic, he had accomplished without detection. Now he sat in the parking lot of the Field Museum waiting for the cop to return. However, he was not planning to kill Cole, at least not immediately. Instead he wanted to know what the cop had on his mind. This was because the chief of detectives was obviously tracking him and Christian.

Three times in the past few days, Cole had become involved in their operations. The first time was when Cole killed the snakes Christian had planted in Kate Ford's apartment. The second time was last night in Sandy's jazz club. Then there was earlier today in Chinatown, when Gault had watched the cop prowling around the scene.

Jonathan Gault approached science as a calling that required rigid discipline and strict logic in order to achieve desired results. He also realized that police work was also a science. And from what Gault had been able to find out from Tommy Kingsley, Cole was an accomplished criminal investigator. So, the scientist decided, it would be best to find out what Cole was up to before he was disposed of.

However, now Gault was puzzled. What had brought Cole to the Field Museum? Finding a parking place for the black car,

Gault got out and walked toward the museum entrance. He was becoming more and more intrigued by the manipulations of this policeman. He also found that he respected Cole's courage and intellect. Nevertheless, when the time came, Gault would not hesitate to kill him.

59

July 10, 1999
12:55 P.M.

Our father was the shaman of the Navajo tribe on a reservation in New Mexico," Silvernail was saying after he and Cole had once again taken seats in the historian's office. "My brother rejected the Native American's magic in favor of the white man's technology and he excelled at it. Red Sky, or Jonathan Gault as he called himself, took the European scientist Nikola Tesla as his idol and he was able to do some truly amazing things with science and particularly through various applications of electricity or, more appropriately, the channeling of energy."

"Madam Devereaux mentioned energy channeling in both the physical and the spiritual world," Cole said.

"The ability to channel energy spiritually has been around since mankind first walked upright on this planet," Silvernail said, rubbing his palms together making a rasping sound. "It is the stuff that miracles are made of. Then humanity discovered technology and a way to utilize energy through machines, wires, and computer chips. They have TVs, microwave ovens, and computers to worship now."

Cole could feel his host's sadness as if it was a physical entity inside the office. "Were you and your brother very close?"

Something in Silvernail changed. If Cole wasn't mistaken the historian had become more guarded. "We never knew each other until we reached adulthood and we only had brief contact then. I was always . . ." his eyes shifted to the hieroglyph of The Man Who Walked in Blood ". . . traveling. I spent my early years in the military."

"Just like the magician-warrior you told me about earlier," Cole said quietly. From the slight narrowing of the historian's eyes, Cole could tell that he had hit a nerve. The cop decided to exploit this advantage. "I couldn't help but notice the photographs and drawings on your walls, Silvernail. They are very interesting."

Silvernail never took his eyes off Cole. "Yes, they are, Larry."

"But they strain credulity and you don't strike me as the type who would falsify such things as portraits and photographs of Presidents of the United States."

For just a brief moment Cole thought that he had gone too far. Something dangerous began developing in the office, as if one of the deadly reptiles the cop had been encountering lately had somehow gotten into this place. Then as quickly as it appeared, it was gone and Silvernail Smith laughed.

"You are a very good policeman, Larry. Of course if you weren't you wouldn't be the chief of detectives." He swung his hand up to take in the framed photos and sketches. "Believe it or not each of them is indeed authentic. And the figure of Silvernail in each photo, as well as the signatures on the sketches, are also real."

"Would that be a manifestation of the spiritual energy you and Madam Devereaux mentioned?"

The historian's laugh was forced. "Not at all. The men you

see in some of the earlier photos dating back to the Civil War are ancestors of mine. In each generation someone in the family seems to come out looking amazingly similar to our forebears. I must say that it is a mark of our vanity that we have a tendency to cultivate the resemblance, but merely as a conversation piece."

"And the name 'Silvernail'?"

He shrugged. "With the resemblance comes the label." The historian got to his feet. "Why don't you let me walk you out? I'm sure someone with your responsibilities has a great many more important things to do than hang around old museums."

Aware that he was being sent a message, which was perhaps for his own good, Cole also stood up. "Whatever you say, Doctor."

Jonathan Gault's scientific curiosity was piqued by some of the museum's exhibits. He found the skeleton of the Tyrannosaurus rex in the main rotunda of particular interest. A hundred years ago Nikola Tesla had taken a palm-sized device and placed it against the metal skeleton of a New York skyscraper under construction and vibrated the entire structure from base to apex. Gault knew how to construct such a device, but he wasn't interested in vibrating skyscrapers. Instead he had a more creative use for such an instrument. Beneath his image his mismatched eyes glistened, as he stared up at the gigantic skeleton. The possibilities were mind-boggling.

Gault tore himself away from the dinosaur exhibit. He was searching the museum for Cole when he spied the carcass of the gorilla Bushman. He was about to go over to the glass case it was displayed inside when two men ascended the steps from the lower level of the museum. When Gault recognized them he froze.

* * *

Silvernail had been walking beside Cole idly discussing the museum in which he had worked for the past ten years when he suddenly stopped.

"Is there something wrong?" Cole asked.

The historian was staring off across the museum rotunda. Cole attempted to pick up what the historian was looking at, but didn't notice anything with the exception that the place contained a great many visitors.

Silvernail snapped out of his semitrance and said, "Please excuse me, Larry, but there is something that I have to do immediately. Here's my card. If you need any more help, give me a call."

Cole looked down at the business card, as Silvernail turned and dashed back down the steps. Shrugging, the policeman pocketed the card and started across the rotunda toward the museum exit.

60

July 10, 1999
1:00 P.M.

Cole was about to exit the museum when he heard his name called. "Chief Cole."

He turned around to find Nora Livingston walking toward him. "I'm sorry you had to wait so long, but I couldn't find Dr. Silvernail anywhere."

"I just left him."

"Oh." She seemed surprised. "He must have gotten back to his office without me seeing him."

"Maybe he was outside and came straight back to the office."

She stiffened and seemed momentarily uncomfortable. "Uh, Dr. Silvernail never . . . I mean he seldom leaves the museum."

Cole studied the curator for a moment before something occurred to him. "If you didn't talk to Silvernail about me, how did he know my name?"

She shrugged. "That's something you'll have to take up with him. Have a nice day and come back to the museum soon."

As she turned to walk away he called after her, "I'll probably be back sooner than you think."

She smiled at him over her shoulder and he found that he was smiling back. He continued toward the front doors of the museum just as his beeper went off. It was Kate Ford.

Jonathan Gault was standing behind one of the pillars in front of the museum when Cole came out. He followed the cop down the steps.

Twenty-six years as a cop makes a person develop certain traits. Among these is the ability to sense something different about the landscape through which he is traveling. To be able to detect the detail or the person out of place. The veteran cop also learns that the improbable and the potentially dangerous are not always right in front of him—that peril can be to the right or the left or even behind him.

At the bottom of the stone stairs in front of the Field Museum of Natural History, Larry Cole stopped and turned around. He didn't notice anything threatening. At least not at first. It was summer and there were lots of children, most of them from day camps, tramping up and down the stairs. There were a smattering of young couples and a few senior citizens in evidence. And there was a tall, broad-shouldered man in a tailored black suit. He was the person out of place.

The man had black, shoulder-length hair and wore mirrored sunglasses. He was coming down the stairs maybe ten or fifteen steps behind Cole. Yet the policeman didn't recall seeing him inside the museum. Could Cole have simply missed him? Yes. However, during his exchange with Nora Livingston he had turned around and, as he'd done when he exited the museum, scrutinized his surroundings for possible danger. So the possibility existed that the man had not been inside the museum at all. If he wasn't, then he was waiting outside. And Cole couldn't deny the possibility that he was who the black-clad man was waiting for.

But the man in black reached the bottom of the stairs and walked past Cole without even glancing in his direction. Cole remained standing in front of the museum and watched the man walk off across the parking lot. For a moment the chief of detectives felt very foolish. Was he getting jumpy in his old age?

Cole walked to his car parked in front of the museum. He'd called Kate Ford from a phone booth inside the museum. She had given him the number of her cellular phone. She was in the lobby of the State of Illinois Building. He called her back.

"Larry?" she answered after only one ring.

"What is it, Kate?"

"I need to see you right away." There was urgency in her tone.

"Where are you?"

She told him and added. "There's someone with me that you need to talk to as soon as you can."

"I'm on the way."

Now, as he walked to his car, the man in the black suit was forgotten.

As Cole's car pulled onto Lake Shore Drive and sped north toward the Loop, Gault's black Mercedes followed.

61

July 10, 1999
1:20 P.M.

Larry Cole felt a cold fury building inside of him as he listened to the words of Mary Keenan, the executive secretary to Tommy Kingsley. Once more the evil political machine in Chicago was rearing its Medusan head to interfere with the police department. The fact that he was the target of the current attack did not bother Cole so much as Kingsley making this move while Govich was in the hospital and Cole was immersed in a very complicated investigation.

Cole, Kate Ford, and Mary Keenan were seated in the chief of detective's unmarked police car on LaSalle Street a block north of the Chicago River. At this time of the day the shadows cast by the towers of Marina City were beginning to slide slowly across the street. The terrified secretary sat in the backseat alone.

Mary Keenan had told Kate Ford, and later Cole himself, that Kingsley, using his political crony Alderman Sherman Ellison Edwards as a front, planned to call an emergency City Council hearing the following morning. Although the council had no subpoena power, it could issue strong written summonses that few city employees could ignore. Mary Keenan informed them that the summonses were being prepared for Cole and First Deputy Superintendent Ray Bishop that very afternoon. She had also told them that the objective of the entire proceeding, billed as an accountability session on the workings of the CPD, was to demand the demotion of Larry Cole from his position as chief of detectives.

"But why would Kingsley want to do such a thing?" Kate asked the secretary.

"He hates Chief Cole," she responded with the tight-lipped way she had of talking.

"Why?" Cole and the reporter asked together.

"I think it has something to do with the director's ex-wife."

"What does Anna have to do with this?" Cole said with a frown.

Both women gave him surprised looks. The secretary said, "You knew the director's wife?"

"She worked on the building engineer's staff at Fifty-first and Wentworth when I was the detective commander there. I helped her mother out of a tight spot some years ago. I even helped Anna get her job at City Hall. That's where she met Kingsley."

"You need to tell him the rest of the story," Kate said.

Mary Keenan looked down at the floor and remained silent for a long time. When she finally did speak her voice was so low they could barely hear her. But they did pick up that the city of Chicago's director of public safety had conspired with Jonathan Gault to kill Anna Kingsley and Kevin Quinn.

They sat in silence for a time before Kate asked Cole, "What are you going to do?"

He had been staring out through the windshield at the Municipal Administration Building across the river. A number of thoughts raced through his mind. Among them was going over there right now and confronting Tommy Kingsley. However, Cole realized that this would not be wise. In fact, he needed to take a nice long run at this City Council hearing tomorrow. A hearing that Kingsley wasn't aware Cole, or anyone else at the CPD, knew anything about.

Cole had never been called before the Chicago City Council before, but he was aware of a number of their past hearings that were usually well covered by the media. Some of them were fairly serious affairs aimed at probing issues of importance to the citizens of Chicago. A number were no more than political debates with various factions confronting each other and using verbal one-upsmanship to make themselves appear smarter or better informed than their opponents. A few of them, like the one Kingsley and Alderman Edwards were cooking up for tomorrow morning, had a hidden agenda.

"I've got to get back to work," Mary Keenan said softly.

Kate turned to look at her. "Are you sure it's wise going back there?"

She nodded her head. "I know how to keep my mouth shut and I won't have much contact with Mr. Kingsley for the rest of the day."

"I'm going to want a statement from you later about this Jonathan Gault and his connection to Kingsley," Cole said.

The secretary became visibly tense. "Do I really have to get involved in this?"

"Do you want to see Kingsley and Gault brought to justice for murder?" Cole said with a hard edge in his voice.

She didn't answer him right away. Finally, she nodded her head once more. "I'll do whatever you ask, but you've got to protect me."

"I can provide twenty-four-hour protection for you starting right now."

"No," Mary Keenan said decisively. "I've got to go back to the office. Give me a number where I can reach you and I'll call later after I get off."

Cole gave her one of his business cards. "Where do you want me to drop you off?"

"On the corner of Lake and LaSalle."

"Isn't that too close to the building?" Kate said, referring to the Municipal Administration Building at 180 North LaSalle Street.

"If we're careful, no one will notice me getting out of this car." She paused a moment before adding with a touch of bitterness. "Anybody watching would have paid more attention to who I ate lunch with."

Kate Ford colored slightly, but made no comment.

A few minutes later Cole was cruising south on LaSalle Street. He crossed the Wacker Drive intersection and the traffic backed up bringing the police car to a complete halt in mid-block.

"I'll get out here," Mary Keenan said, opening the back door.

She was already striding off down the block before either Cole or Kate Ford could protest.

The traffic began moving slowly. They were able to maintain visual contact with her until she reached the intersection of Lake and LaSalle. Then she crossed the street and disappeared inside the Municipal Administration Building.

Cole was about to drive across the intersection when he saw a tall man step out of the city parking lot on the northwest corner of LaSalle and Lake. He was also headed for the Municipal Administration Building. Cole froze. It was the same man in black who he thought was following him outside the history museum.

Cole maneuvered the police car to a red zone on the west side of LaSalle. Bounding out he yelled to Kate, "Stay here. I'm going to check something out."

The bewildered reporter watched him trot across Lake Street against traffic and enter the Municipal Administration Building.

62

JULY 10, 1999
1:25 P.M.

The National Security Agency's surveillance satellite was in orbit above the earth. It had been launched after money was obtained from Congress for the NSA to construct it and then carry it into the heavens aboard a space shuttle. The satellite was supposed to be dedicated to keeping tabs on enemies of the United States with particular attention to Middle Eastern dictators and international terrorists. The NSA satellite was a very sophisticated piece of hardware. From distances miles above the earth, the computer-enhanced camera on board the craft could identify an individual on the earth by ultraviolet body signature. Of course to make the identification complete it was necessary to know what the subject under surveillance ultraviolet light pattern was. Such patterns were reputedly as unique as fingerprints.

To this end, prior to the satellite being launched into orbit in 1997, NSA operatives around the world were given the task of obtaining the ultraviolet light signatures of terrorists, violent criminals, and international undesirables. The actual job of collecting the data was fairly simple. All that was needed was a camera equipped with a special lens and light-sensitive, specially treated film. Before long, thousands of ultraviolet signatures began pouring into the NSA's UV signature database. However, the directors of the organization realized that there was room for hundreds of thousands or possibly even millions more.

In January 1998, a secret meeting was held at NSA headquarters near Fort Meade, Maryland. This meeting was attended by the directors of the NSA, CIA, and FBI. There a daring and illegal plan was conceived. They decided to place as many people, both in and outside of the United States, in the system. The heads of the intelligence agencies involved understood the risks they were taking. If it was discovered they would not only be publicly disgraced, but could end up in jail. But the satellite would remain aloft for decades and, if they handled the security right, no one other than those in on the project would ever find out.

Collecting the data proved to be a bit more complicated than anticipated, but with the help of a scientist named Jonathan Gault at Astrolab, the NSA did very well. Special cameras were secreted in numerous locations around the world. When innocent photos for passports, driver's licenses, and official identification cards were taken, an ultraviolet body signature image was also made. Whenever any official pictures were taken anywhere in the world, a signature image went into the NSA data base. By July 1999 the NSA files contained the ultraviolet signatures of Larry Cole and Kate Ford. Jonathan Gault had possessed the foresight of having his signature image erased from the database before he destroyed Astrolab.

Now the NSA satellite passed over California and sped through space in the direction of the central United States. As it approached the Midwest, a computerized transmission was received in the satellite's compact control center and it began to reduce speed. In the area above the Great Lakes in North America, it took up station. A compartment opened in the metal housing and a camera lens protruded to point down at the earth. The powerful instrument began to narrow its focus to cover thousands of miles. Then the focus narrowed to take in hundreds of miles, then tens of miles, down to single miles, and then square blocks. The spy satellite's camera was aimed at Chicago and zoomed in to take in the downtown Loop area. The focus intensified until the area viewed was narrowed to North LaSalle Street between Randolph and Lake Streets.

In the basement of the brownstone in the 4500 block of South Martin Luther King Jr. Drive, the computer screen provided a grainy view of the street below replete with the tiny, indistinct figures of people going about their daily business in the heart of one of the largest cities in the United States. Although the camera was focused on the street, the spy satellite could peer into buildings and even below the ground. However, now only the street was being scanned.

The spy satellite broadcast the ultraviolet signatures as bright circles of light. Over half the figures under surveillance from the sky had been identified and were in the NSA's database. Now Reggie Stanton and Ernest Steiger watched as the figure identified as "L. Cole—CPD #2797339" moved south on LaSalle.

"What's he doing?" Ernest said.

"He's moving pretty fast, so he could be chasing someone." Stanton paused. "It could be our missing scientist."

Ernest frowned. "From what you've been telling me, Cole is an aggressive cop. He could be chasing anyone down there."

Stanton stood up and began putting on his suit jacket. "Let's go check it out, Ernest, and this time you can drive fast."

Clasping his hands to his chest Steiger said a dramatic, "Thank you, big brother."

63

July 10, 1999
1:32 p.m.

Tommy Kingsley was elated. In twenty-four hours he expected to be gloating over his victory. On his desk blotter was a printout of the information that Herb Donaldson had assembled for him concerning Cole's career. He was not interested in anything that had occurred prior to Cole becoming a command officer in 1988. For the average cop, Cole's exploits would have been the raw material from which bona fide legends are made. However, in the hands of Kingsley's political crony Alderman Sherman Ellison Edwards and a few other members of the city council loyal to Kingsley, the stuff from which heroes are made would be turned into the explosive that would blow Cole's career to bits.

It was as Donaldson had told Kingsley earlier, Cole spent too much time playing supercop to be an effective personnel manager. This conclusion was more the result of innuendo than anything that could be proven by demonstrated negligence. But they wouldn't need hard evidence, as the Chicago City Council was not a court of law. What Kingsley was aiming to do was first discredit the chief of detectives, along with using the media to sway public opinion against him. Then the director of public safety would make a closed-door suggestion to the mayor. In the light of the City Council hearings and Superintendent Govich being hospitalized, it would perhaps be prudent to remove Larry Cole from his current position. Kingsley would make sure to drop the word *temporarily* a few times. He would even suggest that Cole be assigned to a less high-profile assignment. Something out of the way and out of the detective division. Perhaps to a district in the patrol division on the midnight watch.

A broad smile split Tommy Kingsley's ebony-hued features. He would make certain to pay the famous, but demoted, *Captain* Larry Cole a visit, while he toiled away in some high-crime rate, ghetto slime pit. There would be no more front-page headline cases for Cole. No more charging around the city like some twenty-first century version of the black knight.

But first things first. He needed to get these documents and the City Council summonses he'd prepared over to Alderman Edwards. Then Kingsley and his political pals would rehearse tomorrow's performance in the council chambers via conference call.

He pressed the intercom. "Mary, would you come in here please?"

There was no answer.

"Mary?"

Still no response.

He got up, crossed the office, and opened the door. His secretary was just coming in from the outer corridor. Kingsley frowned.

"You're just getting back from lunch?" he said angrily.

She lowered her eyes and tucked her chin into her chest. The "I'm sorry, sir," she uttered was barely audible.

"I've got some documents I want you to make copies of," he snapped. "Then I want a messenger to hand-carry them in sealed envelopes over to City Hall."

"Yes, sir," she said, going behind her desk and placing her purse in one of the drawers.

Kingsley started back for his own office, stopped and turned around. "Mary, we're going to have to talk about the length of your lunch periods."

"Yes, sir."

To emphasize his displeasure, as well as ensure he'd made the right impression on his secretary, he slammed the door behind him. Another smile crossed his face as he sat down behind his desk. The image of Mr. Theophilus Weaver, the plantation boss who had called him a "lazy, shiftless nigra" all those years ago, flashed through his mind. He wondered what that old cracker would think if he saw Tommy now?

He'd just finished checking the documents once more when his secretary buzzed him. Keeping the irritated tone in his voice, he answered, "What is it?"

"There's a gentleman here to see you."

"Does he have an appointment?"

"No, but he says that you were expecting him."

"Mary, what in the hell are you talking about?!"

In the background Kingsley heard a deep male voice, but he couldn't make out what was said. Then Mary was back on the line. Her voice trembled as she said, "He says his name is Jonathan Gault."

When the tall, broad-shouldered man in black walked into the office, Tommy Kingsley said, "You're not Jonathan Gault. What is the meaning of this intrusion?!"

The man closed the door behind him and the director of public safety felt a surge of alarm course through him. He was reaching for the telephone to call 911, when Gault spoke. "It is me, Tommy. There are some government agents looking for me so I adopted this disguise."

Kingsley dropped the phone, which bounced off the desktop and dangled to the floor by its cord. "Jonathan, how did you . . . ?" he managed to say before he stumbled backward and actually fell into his desk chair.

"That is not of primary concern right now," Gault said, walking around the desk and hanging up Kingsley's phone.

"What should be of concern to you is that there is an informant in your camp. I've also come up with the perfect method to get rid of this informant and Chief of Detectives Larry Cole, who, if I'm not mistaken, will be here shortly."

Cole entered the lobby of the Municipal Administration Building just as the man in black boarded a crowded elevator and the door closed. There was no way Cole could tell what floor the man would get off on, but then he might not have to, as the cop suspected that he had been following Mary Keenan.

Cole took the next available elevator. The car rose slowly and stopped at just about every floor on the way up to the twentieth. He stepped off into a deserted corridor. He walked to the entrance to the director of public safety's suite and looked through the glass door into the outer office. It was empty and the door to the director's private office was closed. Cole briefly considered entering the office, but quickly reconsidered this. His presence there could unnecessarily endanger Mary Keenan.

Cole was just turning to go back to the elevator when he heard a scream coming from the intersecting corridor. Pulling his gun he ran toward the source of the scream.

Rounding the corner, he saw that the fire-escape door was open. Reaching it he looked down through the bars of the iron structure that ran from the roof to the ground. He saw the man in black scurrying down the steps some four floors below. Then the cop saw the body lying in the alley. Cole put it together quickly enough. The man in black had followed Mary Keenan into the building, forced her from the office, and hurled her off the fire escape. Cole didn't have the time to consider a motive, but was certain what had just happened was linked directly to Tommy Kingsley.

Cole started down the stairs after the man in black.

* * *

Jonathan Gault had reached the tenth floor when he heard the footsteps of his pursuer coming down the fire escape. He looked up and saw Cole. The cop was still eight floors above him, but closing the distance fast. A smile split the scientist's face. Now Mr. Cole was exactly where Gault wanted him.

After hurling Kingsley's spying secretary off the twentieth-floor fire escape, he had started down. As he descended he placed glass tubes containing exactly one ounce of the powerful liquid explosive he had used to destroy Astrolab on the metal housing of the fire escape. He was spacing these vials at eighty-foot intervals near the juncture where metal met the brick wall of the building. On the top of each vial was a cork stopper from which a thin glass filament protruded. The filament extended down into the explosive substance inside the vial. Gault would only need four of these miniature bombs to accomplish the desired result. After all, he didn't want to destroy the entire building and kill Kingsley, although the thought had crossed his mind.

So far Gault had managed to place explosives on the twentieth and the twelfth floors. He planned to place the third on the fourth floor and the final vial in the alley directly beneath the fire escape. Then he would activate a remote-control device, which would cause them to detonate sequentially. When the last one went off, the explosive force above would join with the one coming up from below to completely obliterate the metal latticework along with anything or anyone on it.

Gault was moving quickly and, as he reached the fifth floor with the cop in pursuit, he removed the third vial from his pocket in preparation for placing it on the next landing down. However, running across the metal fire escape was difficult and he lost control of the vial and dropped it. The glass bomb bounced on the metal before rolling off and falling fifty feet to the alley. On contact, it smashed, spilling the contents. Although the loss of one of his weapons alarmed the scientist, he was not concerned for his own safety. The explosive chemical was completely harmless until the proper catalyst was applied. The catalyst to arm the explosive was electrical and he had a transmitter set to the proper frequency in his pocket to accomplish the desired result. First he would have to reach the ground, where the body of Mary Keenan was sprawled in death.

Cole would have tried a shot at the man he was pursuing, but he didn't have a clear line of fire, nor could he be certain that the man in black was responsible for the death of Mary Keenan. So the only course of action left was to catch him.

The policeman narrowed the flights between them from five to four, but realized that the man would reach the ground before he could be grabbed. Cole bounded from the tenth floor to the ninth. He spun on the landing to head for the eighth floor when he stumbled on a bent metal slat and nearly fell. It was all he could do to keep himself upright and hold on to his gun. He'd lost precious seconds. By the time he got to the seventh floor, the man in black was leaping from the second-floor landing to the alley below.

Cole was starting for the steps leading down to six when he noticed the man standing beneath the fire escape. Then the cop watched as he reached into the pocket of his Giorgio Armani suit jacket.

Cole couldn't chance a shot at him, because the fire-escape housing was in the way. The cop could see that the suspect was not holding a gun, but instead what looked from this distance like a portable radio or some type of remote-control device.

Then the figure in black pointed the object at Cole.

Cole started down the steps again. The first explosive went off on the twentieth floor and the housing of the fire escape jerked violently beneath him. He fell heavily and the gun slipped from his grasp.

He managed to retrieve the gun, just as the second explosion rocked the building. The entire iron structure was being wrenched from the side of the building with Cole on it.

The policeman felt as if he was walking across the wings of a plane in flight, as he stumbled to the next flight of steps. He was forced to hold on to the railings to keep from falling. Then pieces of the railings and stairs from above began raining down on him.

Cole realized that he would never reach the ground before the metal collapsed crushing him beneath it. The only alternative open to him was to get back inside the building.

The third-floor exit door was only a few feet from Cole, but the way the metal beneath him was shaking it could have been miles. He managed to take a step forward before the fire escape lurched backward nearly snatching him off his feet. He managed to remain upright and jump forward again. He reached the door, grasped the handle and turned. The door was locked.

The upper floors had been destroyed and Cole's survival time could now be measured in seconds. He couldn't take accurate aim at the lock, but merely pointed and fired. Out of five shots, the fourth and fifth hit the mark. The door flew open. Without hesitating Cole leaped for the opening. His move came at the exact instant the third explosive on the floor of the alley detonated completely destroying the fire escape, which came down in a blaze of flaming metal.

64

July 10, 1999
1:40 P.M.

The black Porsche driven by Ernest Steiger raced into the radar-patrolled area of Lake Shore Drive. He was driving at over a hundred miles an hour and zipped by the traffic cop so fast he barely had time to make visual contact before the car was out of sight.

"Son of a bitch!" the cop said, as he noted the excessive speed. "This guy must be crazy." He pulled the cruiser off the shoulder of the road and was about to hit the emergency lights and siren when his call number came over the radio.

He was accelerating after the Porsche when the dispatcher instructed, "Be advised that a black Porsche convertible bearing Illinois license AB-4076 is a vehicle being operated by government special agents on a priority mission. This vehicle should be entering your patrol area in the next few minutes. You are not, repeat, you are not to attempt to stop them or take any enforcement action per orders of Raymond Bishop, First Deputy Superintendent—Bureau of Operational Services."

The traffic cop decelerated the cruiser and pulled back onto the shoulder of Lake Shore Drive, slammed the gear-shift lever into park, and said, "Special agents, but for what frigging government?"

In the passenger seat of the speeding sports car, Reggie Stanton was securely buckled in and had a portable computer terminal on his lap, which was connected to the NSA satellite. The screen displayed an aerial view of the Municipal Administration Building. The glowing figure, displaying Cole's ultraviolet signature code, was visible racing down the fire escape.

For a long minute the pursuit continued and then the computer screen developed static.

"Something's wrong," Stanton said.

"What did you say?" Steiger shouted to be heard over the howl of the powerful engine's roar.

"There's something wrong," Stanton repeated with a shout.

Steiger executed a hard left turn off Lake Shore Drive to enter Grant Park. They were less than two minutes from 180 North LaSalle Street.

Suddenly, Stanton's computer screen went blank.

65

July 10, 1999
1:42 P.M.

Jonathan Gault had been forced to flee the alley before he could see what had happened to Cole. But he didn't doubt the cop's fate. The last time he'd seen Cole he was on the vibrating fire escape seconds before the metal structure collapsed.

The disguised scientist walked rapidly north on LaSalle Street. The roar of the structure smashing to the ground behind him possessed the sound and fury of a two-ton TNT charge going off. The noise was amplified through the canyons of the Loop bringing all traffic, both foot and vehicular, to a halt. Gault had taken care of two of Tommy Kingsley's problems, the spying secretary and Cole. Now the director of public safety owed the scientist. Kingsley owed him a great deal. With the wail of sirens surrounding him, as emergency vehicles sped to the scene of the disaster, Gault entered the parking lot where he had left the Mercedes. After paying the attendant, he went to get Christian.

66

July 10, 1999
1:43 P.M.

Still seated in Cole's car, Kate Ford heard the horrendous noise made by the collapsing fire escape. Her immediate concern was for Cole. She got out of the car, feeling the same sense of unreality experienced by disaster survivors. The faces of those around her mirrored the stunned shock that she felt. However, her concern for the policeman forced her to move.

The traffic on both Lake and LaSalle Streets had ground to a complete halt. Uniformed police officers were running up LaSalle Street from City Hall toward the Municipal Administration Building. There was an acrid smell of burning metal and smoke was rising into the air, causing the bright summer day to develop an overcast.

Running through the gathering crowd, Kate reached the front of 180 North LaSalle Street just as a bruised, soot-stained Larry Cole staggered out of the revolving front doors.

"Larry," she called to him.

He turned to look at her with a vacant, emotionless expression. She rushed over to him.

"Larry, what happened?"

He looked at her as if he'd never seen her before. He started to walk away. She grabbed his arm.

"What's wrong with you?" she cried.

Cole looked back at the building. "Gault killed Mary Keenan and then destroyed the fire escape."

"Mary's dead?"

Cole turned to look at her. A hint of recognition shown on his face. "Yes," he responded. "He killed her and tried to kill me. I've got to go . . . after . . . him."

"No, Larry. You've got to come with me." She maintained a firm grasp on his arm.

"Where are we going?" he asked in a voice barely above a whisper.

"Away from here."

Kate Ford led Larry Cole back to the police car.

67

JULY 10, 1999
1:47 P.M.

Dr. Silvernail Smith entered the Native American of Yesteryear exhibit, which he had personally assembled artifact by artifact. There were not as many museum visitors in this gallery as there were viewing other, more popular exhibits and after he'd only been there a few moments he found himself alone. A large wigwam, standing fifteen feet tall, was at the center of one of the exhibit chambers. It was surrounded by a wooden railing bearing the admonition, UNAUTHORIZED PERSONNEL NOT PERMITTED. Dr. Silvernail Smith was an authorized person.

The wigwam was an artifact from the Navajo Nation of the nineteenth century. Silvernail pulled the canvas flap at the entrance and lowered his head as he stepped inside. The interior was pitch-black, but the historian did not need lights to find his way around. He had assembled this exhibit and knew every square foot inside the canvas structure, which contained a drum, a spear, an ornamental Navajo chief's headdress, and a prayer rug. This area was never meant for public viewing, so it did not contain much. However, to the man called Silvernail this place was very important. In fact, it was sacred.

He sat down on the coarse rug and folded his legs in front of him. He raised his hands palms up to shoulder level and closed his eyes. He was immersed in darkness and total silence, which was what he needed. Then his spirit reached out.

From the gallery in the Field Museum of Natural History Silvernail Smith was able to touch the past, the present and, to some extent, the future. Now he had come to this place to touch the past.

As the pictures and sketches that adorned the walls of his office testified, the man known as Silvernail had experienced a great deal over a long period of time. To some extent what he had told Larry Cole about the name Silvernail and the resemblance of the men, who bore the name from generation to generation, was true. And to a degree, it was not. The fact that he was The Man Who Walked in Blood was totally accurate.

Now he went back to a time in the New Mexico desert when he and Night Walker, the Navajo tribal shaman, had attempted to demonstrate the superiority of the Native American's magic over the Anglos' technology. To accomplish this Silvernail and

Night Walker had placed a spell on Red Sky. When Red Sky awoke he was high in the mountains above the reservation. There Silvernail and Night Walker demonstrated their magic to him.

In the wigwam in the Field Museum of Natural History in 1999, Silvernail moaned. At the time they had felt that what they were doing to the man who wanted to be known as Jonathan Gault was right. Red Sky had the potential to be a very powerful shaman. Perhaps the most powerful in history. Once he learned the secrets of Indian magic, he would see how superior it was to the pitiful technology Red Sky had learned in the white man's schools. But before he could learn it, he would first have to fear it.

The world of silent darkness in which Silvernail meditated upon the past became filled with sound, light, and fury. By using spiritual energy Silvernail and Night Walker manipulated the forces of magic. They caused violent storms, split the face of rocks, and made the creatures who walked and crawled the earth do their bidding. And indeed Red Sky was terrified. Terrified to the point that he went mad.

The silence of the Native American exhibit imposed itself once more. Silvernail opened his eyes and looked into the dark. Had there been anyone present to witness it, they would have seen tears in the ageless man's eyes.

Although he had gone insane, Red Sky had learned the methods of channeling spiritual energy to accomplish magic. He had applied those same methods to enhance the technology he studied. And with such power at his command Red Sky had become an instrument of evil and destruction.

The historian returned to his meditative trance and focused on what was to come. He knew that Gault hated him and had sworn to some day destroy Silvernail for what had occurred on that mountain. And The Man Who Walked in Blood knew that

Red Sky was close. Very close. Soon he would be here and when he came Silvernail would have to face him. The historian was able to take little comfort from the realization that he would not have to do so alone.

68

July 10, 1999
7:15 P.M.

The blue unmarked police car skidded to a stop in front of Larry Cole's apartment building just north of Grant Park. Manny Sherlock, who was driving, tossed a laminated card on the dashboard which read, CHICAGO POLICE DEPARTMENT—OFFICIAL BUSINESS. Then the four occupants of the car got out and headed for the entrance.

The security guard in the lobby recognized three of the four instantly and buzzed them through the security door without comment. A few moments later they were in an elevator rising to the twenty-second floor. Manny was accompanied by Blackie Silvestri, Blackie's wife, Maria, and Judy Daniels.

Blackie knocked at the door to Cole's apartment. Kate Ford opened it with the chain on and peered out at them. Then she opened the door. They entered.

Cole was asleep in the darkened bedroom. His slumber was troubled. He was dreaming that he was running through a maze of red-hot iron and could not find his way out. Outside the maze, he could see the man in the black suit pointing a metal object at him. In the dream Cole's gun was in his hand, but when he aimed it at the man in black and attempted to fire nothing happened. Suddenly, the metal latticework was no longer beneath him and he fell into a dark void.

From somewhere far off in the distance, he heard his name called. He jerked himself awake.

"Larry," Blackie said.

Cole sat up in the bed. He was drenched with sweat and breathing hard. He was clad only in his shorts and for a moment he couldn't remember anything since he'd leaped off the collapsing fire escape.

"Larry, are you okay?"

Cole saw the lieutenant standing at the bedroom door. "Blackie?"

The heavyset man stepped inside and closed the door behind him. "Kate Ford called and told us what happened to you downtown. We got here as fast as we could."

Cole sat on the edge of the bed and turned on the night-table lamp. "Who's 'we'?"

The lieutenant told him.

"You didn't have to rush over here for this. I'm fine."

Blackie walked over and took a seat in the recliner next to the bed. He pulled a cigar from his inside pocket and placed it in the corner of his mouth. The lines of his face deepened into a scowl.

"Boss, according to Kate Ford you were on that fire escape when it came down. It's all over the news and on the way over here we drove down LaSalle Street and took a look ourselves. Me and Manny flashed our badges at a couple of First District cops who were guarding the scene. They let us go into the alley, where a cleanup crew is trying to clear the debris. What we saw was scary to say the least. Now ever since you started investigating this thing with the snakes, everything has been going haywire. Today marks the second time in less than a week that you came close to getting yourself iced. So, you could say that we had to come over here to see how you were doing. I even brought Maria."

Cole couldn't argue with his logic. The memory of the fire escape collapsing around him was still too recent to ignore.

"Well," Cole said with a forced lightheartedness, "if I've got company I need to make myself presentable."

With that he headed for the shower.

Clad in jeans and a short-sleeved sport shirt, he entered the living room a short time later to find a group of very concerned people assembled. Kate Ford, who'd driven him home and put him to bed, had made coffee, which everyone, except Blackie, was drinking. Instead the lieutenant had raided the refrigerator for a beer.

Cole went to the bar and poured cognac into a brandy snifter. After the day he'd had, he needed something stronger than coffee or beer.

"How do you feel, Larry?" The question came from Maria Silvestri, who was a handsome, gray-haired woman with the soulful eyes of a weeping Madonna.

He took a sip of his drink, feeling the liquid warm him and at the same time provide the reminder that he hadn't eaten since breakfast. He then replied, "I had a bit of a rough time earlier, Maria, but I'm recovering rapidly."

Judy Daniels sat in the easy chair beside the couch on which Maria was seated. She wore her glamour-girl look, as Manny had dubbed it. This consisted of a shoulder-length black wig, exotic makeup, a skintight white dress, and white heels. With the string of cultured pearls around her neck, she looked as if she'd just stepped off the pages of *Vogue* magazine. Now, she placed her coffee cup down on the glass cocktail table and addressed Cole.

"What happened downtown today, boss?"

For a moment Cole lost focus, as he was forced to relive

what had occurred earlier. Setting his brandy glass on the bar, he faced his guests. He paused a moment to look at each of them. Blackie was in the matching easy chair on the opposite end of the sofa. Manny stood behind Blackie. Kate Ford was standing at the entrance to the kitchen. Each of them was waiting for him to tell them about the events that had occurred earlier in the day. And he would tell them; however, he couldn't explain *how* it had happened.

At that moment the telephone rang. There was an extension on the bar within Cole's reach. "Excuse me," he said to his guests. He picked up the receiver. "Hello."

"Chief Cole, this is Dr. Silvernail Smith."

Reggie Stanton and Ernest Steiger had returned to the brownstone on King Drive. They were once more in the basement seated side by side at the computer console. The NSA satellite was again transmitting ultraviolet body signatures with crystal clarity.

Despite Ernest Steiger's kamikaze driving, by the time the NSA agents had reached the Loop, traffic had ground to a complete halt. Leaving his brother with the car, Stanton had proceeded on foot to the alley behind the Municipal Administration Building.

The Chicago Police Department was cordoning off the area, but Stanton flashed his ID and made it to the mouth of the alley. He was stunned when he saw the pile of smoldering metal left in the wake of the explosion. Turning away from the disaster scene, Stanton was certain that Larry Cole, who had been on that fire escape when it blew up, was dead.

Now the UV satellite transmitted to them that Cole had indeed survived the attack by Jonathan Gault.

"Your friend is a very fortunate man," Steiger said, staring at Cole's UV signal on the computer screen.

"He's always been lucky," Stanton said.

"Well, he's going to need luck if Gault goes after him again."

Stanton turned to look at his brother. "I'm counting on our crazy scientist doing just that, Ernest."

69

JULY 11, 1999
7:08 A.M.

Bill "Soupy" McGuire always arrived at the Cook County Morgue early. He had a large cup of coffee with extra sugar and cream in the cup holder of his Ford station wagon. As he pulled into his private parking place, he was feeling pretty good despite it being an overcast, humid summer morning with a definite hint of rain in the air. His high spirits were due to a combination of reasons, foremost of which was that he hadn't been forced to falsify any autopsy reports in the last few days.

Soupy remained in the car with the air conditioner blowing against the heat and humidity. He sipped his coffee and sat in silent contemplation. He hadn't spoken to Tommy Kingsley in three days. Soupy had read in the newspaper about the snake-infested building that had collapsed in Chinatown. Last night he'd watched the coverage on TV of the destruction of the fire escape behind the Municipal Administration Building, where Tommy Kingsley's offices were located. A minicam at the scene got a close-up of one of the twisted pieces of iron from the destroyed structure. A news commentator said that the fire escape had literally been blown off the building, but, no damage had been done to the actual building itself.

Carrying his coffee, the M.E. got out of the station wagon and started for the rear entrance to the morgue.

"Soupy," he heard his name called from across the parking lot. Glancing around he spied the caller and his mouth went dry.

Blackie Silvestri and Manny Sherlock got out of an unmarked police car and began walking toward him.

The M.E. felt his knees go weak.

70

July 11, 1999
10:12 A.M.

The Chicago City Council is composed of fifty aldermen, who represent each of the fifty wards in the city. Each ward has a population of approximately seventy thousand citizens and aldermen are elected for four-year terms. As a legislative body the City Council has not been known to have a great deal of power in modern times. Since 1956, with rare exceptions, the dominant elected official in the Windy City has been the mayor. It was a fact of political life that without the mayor's backing, few aldermen were ever elected and none were ever reelected.

The City Council chambers were located on the second floor of City Hall at 121 North LaSalle Street. The chamber itself was large enough to accommodate the desks of the aldermen. Each desk was equipped with a microphone and the controls for the mikes were located on the raised dais in the front of the room. The chairman of the City Council's seat was at the center of this dais. Other than the microphone controls, which had been utilized to silence obstreperous and out-of-order aldermen in midsentence, the only other items on the chairman's desk were a water pitcher with a single glass and a gavel. By municipal ordinance, the chairman of the City Council was the mayor of Chicago or his designee. On this July morning the mayor was attending a meeting of the American Conference of Mayors in Atlanta. His honor's appointed replacement was Alderman Sherman Ellison Edwards.

Edwards was serving his fifth term as the representative of a South Side ward, which was predominantly African American. The median income of his constituents hovered just below the poverty level and a large number of the residents were either senior citizens or recipients of public aid. Twice Edwards had defeated strong challenges from independent candidates. Both of his challengers had run on platforms stressing the demand for more and better city services for the ward along with hiring more residents to work in highly coveted city jobs. One of the candidates, a self-made millionaire, had obtained a promise from a soft-drink company to build a bottling plant in the ward. The plant would bring a thousand new jobs to the impoverished area. However, Sherman Edwards political influence, know-how, and under-the-table manipulations enabled him to defeat both candidates. No additional city jobs were forthcoming and the incumbent alderman also managed to sabotage the soft-drink deal, forcing the plant into the south suburbs.

Edwards was fifty-seven years old, overweight, and long-winded. He dressed in out-of-date suits and postured in such a way as to appear almost a caricature of a ward-heeling politician. However, beneath that superficial, ludicrous exterior was a man with a sharp intellect, the morals of a five-dollar hooker, and the predatory instincts of a shark. He was a devoted disciple of the old school of politics, Chicago style.

Although he was an elected official, Edwards did not consider himself a public servant. The first priority in any endeavor he became involved in was, "What's in it for me?" Twice he'd been the target of federal investigations into official corruption in Chicago and in 1986, during his second term, he'd been indicted on a bribery charge. A trial had resulted in his acquittal. The Better Government Association (BGA), as well as all the city's daily newspapers, always endorsed his opponents over him and in editorials he was invariably used as an example of everything that was wrong with politics in Chicago. Yet he kept getting elected.

Now Edwards stood at the chairman's lectern and surveyed his temporary domain. The mayor didn't know what Edwards and Kingsley were cooking up for the CPD. When His Honor returned from Atlanta and heard about it, he'd be furious, but by then it would be too late. The police department was one of the sacred cows of the city. It would be up to the director of public safety to provide the explanation for the public bloodletting that was about to occur. However, Edwards had no doubt that Kingsley would acquit himself admirably in this regard.

The alderman had to admit to himself that he was not in Kingsley's league when it came to deviousness. This was indeed high praise from Edwards.

Edwards watched the members of the city council drift in and take their seats. Most of them didn't know about Kingsley's plans to pillory Chief of Detectives Larry Cole. The only ones who were in the know were strictly loyal to Edwards and Kingsley. By the time council members from the opposition block caught on, the damage would be done. Then bye-bye, Mr. Cole.

Edwards glanced at the clock mounted on the wall behind

the dais. It was almost ten-thirty. The two-storied, glass-enclosed visitors' gallery was also beginning to fill up. He recognized a number of the spectators this morning because they were loyal constituents from his ward. The door from the antechamber to his left opened and an usher escorted First Deputy Superintendent Ray Bishop and Chief Larry Cole into the VIP section. To Edwards the area in which the two cops were taking their seats would be more accurately referred to as a prisoners' dock.

The alderman smiled and nodded to the cops. Bishop returned the nod with a solemn face. To Edwards's surprise, Cole smiled broadly and even saluted. *So,* Edwards thought, *the condemned man goes cheerfully to the gallows.*

The chairman of the Chicago City Council Police and Fire Committee picked up his gavel. Before calling the meeting to order he looked out over the assemblage. The stage was set, the hall rented, and the audience waiting in blissful anticipation for the show to begin.

Cole rode with Bishop from police headquarters to City Hall. The first deputy was not only dismayed by the sudden summons for them to appear before a special session of the city council, but also by Cole's cool, unconcerned manner. Bishop had been around long enough to know that Alderman Sherman Ellison Edwards had something up his sleeve. Bishop also knew that Edwards was a close political ally of Tommy Kingsley, whose animosity toward the Jack Govich–run CPD was no secret. And the fact that the chief of detectives had been summoned specifically, indicated that he was the primary target of the witch-hunt, yet Cole seemed totally indifferent.

The first deputy started to question Cole about his nonchalant attitude, but decided against this. The chief of detectives had a reputation for easily overcoming adversity. However, in a way Edwards's tactics would pose a different type of challenge from those Cole was used to, like armed maniacs, insane murderers, and serial killers.

They were dropped off at the LaSalle Street entrance to the hall and were met by a uniformed police officer, who was assigned to the city hall security detail.

The officer, who had thick white hair and sported hash marks on the left sleeve of his uniform blouse denoting thirty years of service, saluted the two high-ranking cops and said, "Director Kingsley assigned me to escort you gentlemen to the council chamber."

"The VIP treatment," Cole quipped. "I would expect nothing else from our esteemed director."

Bishop had had enough. "Do you think you could work up a modicum of concern over this thing, Larry? I mean we haven't been invited over here because Edwards and Kingsley want to congratulate us on what a great job the department's been doing."

"Don't worry, Ray," Cole said confidently, "I've got everything under control."

Bishop rolled his eyes.

They followed their escort to the second floor of City Hall.

"We're all interested in public safety," Alderman Edwards began, deepening his Alabama drawl to a ridiculous level. He adopted the Foghorn Leghorn accent to make his opponents think of him as a dumb sharecropper. Generally, this caused them to underestimate him, which was a fatal mistake. "This mornin' we wanna look at one of the most critical areas of our public safety. That is the Chicago Po-lice Detective Division." Edwards paused and turned to motion with his right hand to the two cops. "To this end we've invited two of Chicago's Finest, First Deputy Superintendent Raymond Bishop and Chief Larry Cole."

Edwards was about to go back to his prelude to the inquisition when he noticed a stir in the ranks of his fellow aldermen. Momentarily he was confused. Then he noticed all eyes turn to the entrance to the VIP section where Bishop and Cole were sitting. Turning, he saw Jack Govich, his legs encased in ankle-to-knee casts, struggle on crutches into the city council chamber. Bishop and Cole leaped to assist him. Bishop took the crutches, while Cole helped the superintendent to a seat. Although flushed and in pain, Govich smiled at Edwards, who appeared stunned speechless by this development.

Alderman Jeffrey O'Hara, an ex-cop who was sympathetic to the CPD, spoke into his microphone. "I would like to congratulate our esteemed acting chairman for having the foresight to invite the renowned superintendent of police here this morning. I would also like to commend you, Superintendent Govich, for leaving your hospital bed, after you suffered such serious injuries in the line of duty, to be with us today."

Govich managed a smile, which brought a resounding round of applause from the assembled council. For once in his long, loud, meaningless career, Alderman Sherman Ellison Edwards was at a loss for words.

"You knew about this all the time," Bishop said with mock anger as he, Govich, and Cole rode back to police headquarters. Govich had been delivered to City Hall in a fire ambulance courtesy of the Chicago Fire Department Commissioner. After his arrival Edwards had mumbled something about the necessity for a postponement and abruptly adjourned the meeting. Now Govich was on his way back to the hospital.

Cole responded to Bishop's comment. "Actually I didn't know that the superintendent was coming, but I did have a surprise or two for Edwards and his buddy Kingsley."

Bishop frowned. "But Kingsley wasn't there."

"He was there, Ray," Govich said. "He just kept out of sight. Now you're free to go after him, Larry."

"Go after him for what?" Bishop questioned.

Cole's face became set in hard lines. "For murder, Ray, and more than one."

71

July 11, 1999
12:20 P.M.

Tommy Kingsley was in a panic. He was in his office with the door locked. He had also shut off the phones, except a secured private line, for which only a select few possessed the number. He was waiting for a call from Sherman Edwards. It had been two hours since the alderman had abruptly ended the City Council hearing and Kingsley wanted an explanation from his political crony as to why he hadn't followed instructions.

On cue, the telephone rang. Before it could do so twice, he snatched up the receiver. It was Edwards.

"What in the hell happened?!" Kingsley exploded.

"Well, Tommy boy, that pal of yours Jack Govich showed up."

"Save the down-home bullshit for someone who might swallow it, Edwards. Now I laid it out for you on a silver platter. All you had to do was follow the scenario and Cole would have been dead and buried."

There was a change in Edwards's voice. The Alabama cornpone drawl vanished to be replaced by a voice that was infinitely more cultured and as hard as granite. "You know you did a good job of ousting your predecessor, Kingsley. In a lot of ways E. G. Luckett and you are very much alike. Both of you came up from nothing and both know how to get what they want by playing the political game the only way it can be played, without rules."

"I don't need a lecture on political science from you, Edwards."

"Yeah, well you're going to get one, because what I'm about to tell you might save your worthless ass."

Kingsley was frozen rigid with outrage, but he was too fascinated by the alderman's gall to hang up.

"The downfall of E. G. Luckett was that he went after Larry Cole and failed. Now it looks like you've made the same mistake."

"I didn't make the mistake, you did."

"*Au contraire,* my dear director. I didn't do anything. It's obvious Cole and Govich found out about the party you planned this morning and they countered it nicely. Seeing the superintendent limp in wearing those casts nearly made my heart skip a beat. That is if I had a heart."

"Govich had nothing to do with it. All you had to do was go after Cole like I told you," Kingsley argued.

"You still don't get it. Cole's a fucking hero, Tommy. Govich has two broken legs he got protecting the citizens of this great city. To challenge them separately is dangerous enough; to take them on together is tantamount to committing the same political suicide that Luckett did."

Kingsley felt a chill go down his spine. "What are you talking about?"

"My sources at police headquarters tell me that Blackie Silvestri, who is Cole's right-hand man, brought in the Cook County Medical Examiner for questioning earlier today. They've had him behind closed doors all morning, but word is that your name came up once or twice in connection with some thieves or some such that got suddenly dead. In my book that spells trouble for you."

Without saying another word, Tommy Kingsley hung up the phone. Quickly he got up and went to the door. Unlocking it and opening it a crack, he peered across his secretary's office. He could see through the glass door into the empty corridor beyond. He crossed the outer office and checked outside. No one was there.

He slipped out and started for the elevators but stopped. Retracing his steps he went to the stairs and started down. He encountered no one during the descent. On the ground floor he found the alley exit blocked due to repair work proceeding on the collapsed fire escape. This forced him to leave by the front door on LaSalle Street.

Exiting the building he found the area literally crawling with uniformed cops; however, all of them were busy handling the vehicular and pedestrian traffic around yesterday's disaster scene.

Kingsley walked rapidly north on LaSalle Street keeping his head down in the hopes that no one would recognize him. He made it to the municipal parking lot on Lake Street where he kept his car. He fumbled with his keys dropping them on the floor before he was able to retrieve them and start the engine. He was breathing heavily and sweating profusely as he put the car in gear and pulled from the lot.

He glanced frequently in the rearview mirror as he sped south. However, he failed to notice the fifteen-year-old burgundy Ford traveling a block behind him. The driver of this car was a nerdy-looking man with thick glasses and slicked-back hair and the passenger was a silver-haired grandmother, who wore a strawhat decorated with artificial flowers. If Kingsley did catch sight of them he would never recognize this innocuous couple as Sergeant Manfred Wolfgang Sherlock and Detective Judy Daniels, the infamous Mistress of Disguise/High Priestess of Mayhem, who were following the director of public safety.

It took Tommy Kingsley nearly an hour to get to his Southwest Side home. When he drove into his driveway he failed to notice the old Ford park a half block away. In a self-absorbed panic, he rushed into the house.

He went directly to his den to grab the two thousand dollars in cash he had stashed in a safety deposit box along with his passport and a bankbook containing a quarter of a million dollars on deposit in Weaver, Alabama. This would be enough walking-around money until he could figure a way out of this situation with Cole. He was counting the cash as he started for the stairs to go to his bedroom and pack when he noticed movement coming from inside his living room. Kingsley froze.

Christian Dodd, whom Kingsley had only seen once before, crawled across the living room entrance and stared at him.

"What are you doing in here?" Kingsley said in a voice so choked with fear his words were barely audible.

The young double amputee smiled, which gave his features an angelic glow, although it was that of a dark angel. "Dr. Gault sent me to give you something, Mr. Kingsley."

"What?"

"This," Christian said, removing a tube-shaped device from his belt, which resembled a miniature nightstick. He pointed it at Kingsley.

72

July 11, 1999
3:13 p.m.

Cole and Blackie were about to leave headquarters to serve search and arrest warrants on Tommy Kingsley. Judy and Manny had tailed the director of public safety home and were now sitting outside his house. Cole saw this as a stroke of divine providence, as he had not wanted to seize Kingsley at his downtown office. There would be enough publicity connected with this thing as it was without turning the arrest into a downtown political and media circus.

The interrogation of Soupy McGuire had revealed a series of events so bizarre as to seem initially unimaginable. In collusion with Tommy Kingsley, whom Soupy claimed had intimidated him into cooperating, they had covered up the murders of at least eight people. Things didn't look too good for the medical examiner, but Cole and Blackie promised to do everything they could for him.

Then First Deputy Superintendent Bishop called.

"I know you're on your way out to pick up Kingsley," Bishop said, "but could you drop by my office before you go?"

"Sure thing," Cole said. "Wait for me in the car, Blackie. This should only take a minute."

When Cole walked into the first deputy's office and saw Reggie Stanton and Ernest Steiger waiting for him, the chief of detectives made no attempt to hide his displeasure.

Seeing his colleague's reaction, Bishop said a contrite, "It comes right from Washington, Larry. We are to cooperate with the NSA in the person of these two gentlemen in connection with the investigation we are currently conducting involving the director of public safety and Jonathan Gault."

Cole looked about to protest, thought better of it and said, "Okay, guys, come along, but please keep out of the way. We're doing real police work here."

The two agents glared at the policeman as he turned and walked out the door.

A short time later they pulled up in front of Tommy Kingsley's Southwest Side home. Ernest Steiger was driving the Porsche and Blackie was behind the wheel of Cole's police car. The battered burgundy Ford Judy and Manny had tailed Kingsley in was parked across the street. Now the disguised cops met the chief and his entourage in front of the director of public safety's residence.

"Okay, Stanton and Steiger, make yourselves useful and cover the back," Cole ordered. "Blackie, give them a radio." He turned to the nerdy-looking Manny and the grandmotherly disguised Judy Daniels. "You two cover the front."

The NSA agents didn't appear too enthused about being given orders, but grudgingly they complied.

Cole and Blackie gave the NSA agents a moment to get in place. When Blackie figured they had reached their destination he keyed his mike and said, "We're going in the front."

Stanton's voice came over the radio. "For your information, there was a black Mercedes in the alley when we came around back. It just took off like a bat out of hell."

Blackie looked at Cole.

"Do you think he had a getaway car waiting?" the lieutenant asked.

Cole looked at Kingsley's official sedan parked in the driveway. "There's only one way to find out."

The two cops flanked the door. Cole rapped heavily on it three times. They waited fifteen seconds for a response and when none came Cole repeated the manuever. They waited a brief period before exchanging nods. Then Blackie stepped in front of the door and aimed a kick at the lock. The door flew open.

With guns drawn, they entered.

"Police!" Cole shouted.

Blackie was on the walkie-talkie. "We're inside."

The house was silent. Cole and Blackie began moving forward, keeping an eye out for danger. They didn't really expect resistance from Kingsley, but many officers had been put in their graves after underestimating suspects.

Cole was about to call Stanton and Steiger, along with Judy and Manny, into the house to assist them in a room-by-room search when he glanced into the living room. There he saw Tommy Kingsley, or rather what was left of him.

Blackie was unaware of anything amiss until Cole audibly exhaled. Following his boss's eyes, Blackie also saw what was in the living room. They continued to maintain their vigilance with guns raised, as they moved to the living room entrance. There they stopped. This was the scene of a violent death, but it was also now a crime scene. Cole and Blackie were not about to tramp across it and spoil any evidence.

The body lying a few feet away was not easily identifiable as that of Tommy Kingsley. It had been burned to a crisp. However, there were no signs of fire damage to any other part of the house. The smell of burned flesh was strong. Cole and Blackie exchanged looks. Jonathan Gault had struck again.

The crime lab technicians finished processing the scene. One of Soupy McGuire's people, a young pathologist named Dr. Darlene Johnson, finished examining the body prior to it being removed to the morgue. Cole, Blackie, Manny, Judy, and the

NSA agents were waiting for her in Kingsley's study. Cole had it dusted for prints before they went inside. Now, the chief of detectives sat behind Kingsley's desk staring at a photograph of the former director of public safety and his deceased wife, Anna.

Dr. Johnson, who was in her midtwenties, wore horn-rimmed glasses but adopted a cheerful, lighthearted manner, knocked on the door frame before entering. Cole motioned her inside.

She consulted a notebook, smiled, and said, "The deceased was electrocuted by an application of high voltage until he was literally incinerated. I couldn't find anything in this house capable of expending that amount of energy."

After the medical examiner left, Cole turned to Stanton and Steiger. "Do you two have anything to add to all this?"

"It's obvious that what happened to your murder victim was the result of a falling out among thieves," Stanton said.

"Gault was obviously in business with your esteemed director," Steiger said, sarcastically. "So it's obvious that Chicago still ain't ready for reform."

"Look who's calling the kettle black," Blackie shot back.

Before an argument could erupt, Cole held up his hand, "We haven't got time for this. That scientist is dangerous and we need to work together to get him off the streets before someone else is killed."

"We've got a plan to nab Gault, Larry," Stanton said. "You keep walking around and he'll come to you. Then we'll nail him."

"So you guys are using Chief Cole as bait?" Blackie asked.

"It's in the interests of national security, Silvestri," Steiger said.

"Don't you people ever get tired of hiding behind that bullshit?"

The telephone on the late director of public safety's desk rang.

They all looked at Cole. He let it ring twice more before picking up the receiver. He held it to his ear without speaking.

"Larry?" Kate Ford's strained voice came over the line.

Surprised, he said, "Kate? How did you know I was here?"

It took her a moment to respond, "Jonathan Gault told me."

Cole sat on the edge of his chair and tightened his grip on the phone. "Where are you?"

She started to answer, but was cut off. When she spoke again, she was close to tears. "He said to tell you that he'll be waiting for you."

Cole fought to control his anger. "Why doesn't he tell me himself, Kate?"

There was another pause from her end. Then, "He says he doesn't want to, but that you'll figure it out."

The eyes of the other cops in the room were on Cole, but no one moved or spoke.

"Has he hurt you?" Cole asked.

"No," she said in a more controlled voice.

"Where does he want to meet me?"

Again, she paused before answering, "He says you'll know."

Then the connection was broken.

Slowly, Cole hung up the phone.

"What's wrong, boss?" Blackie asked.

Cole's jaw muscles rippled as he responded, "Gault has kidnapped Kate Ford."

73

July 11, 1999
4:17 p.m.

It was the lull between the lunch crowd and dinner show at Sandy's. From four until six no food was available from the kitchen, but the bar remained open. There was a smattering of patrons and Benny Little was the lone bartender on duty when the man wearing the expensive black suit and mirrored sunglasses walked in.

Benny walked down the bar to wait on him.

Sandra Devereaux was in her office when she experienced an odd chill. Getting up from behind her desk she walked over and checked the thermostat. The temperature registered seventy-two degrees, but the chill she felt remained.

Leaving the office, she walked onto the balcony overlooking the club. The place was empty.

"Benny?" she called.

There was no answer.

Madam Devereaux realized that this was the slow time of the day, but she'd never seen the place completely deserted.

"Benny?!" There was an edge in her voice, which she recognized was due more to panic than anger.

Except for Ray Charles crooning a ballad over the speakers, Sandy's was as quiet as a tomb.

She turned to descend the stairs when she saw the man in black standing at the far end of the bar. The sight of him froze her in place. Sandra Devereaux had never set eyes on him before, but she knew who, or rather what, he was. She was sensitive enough and sufficiently schooled in the black arts to feel the power emanating from him. Without a second's longer hesitation, she ran back to her office.

With a sinking despair, she realized that she had no magic to use against the evil entity that had invaded her club. But she did have a gun. She snatched open the bottom drawer of her desk and removed a stainless steel snub-nosed Smith and Wesson revolver.

Sandy decided not to wait for him to come up after her. The office possessed the confines of a very effective trap. Instead she would go down and face him in the club. In that way, if she got the chance, she could make a run for it.

She went back out on the balcony and peered down into the club below. The man in black was nowhere in sight. Steeling herself she started for the stairs. She reached the main floor and there was still no sign of him. Now, her jazz club seemed like an alien place. Besides there being no bartenders and patrons, even the music had stopped.

She advanced slowly past the stage and the dance floor. She kept the gun raised and she was prepared to open fire at *anything* that moved. Her heart was pounding so furiously the sound was like a kettledrum beating in her head. She reached the halfway point of the bar without encountering anyone. The front door leading onto Fifty-third Street seemed at once enticingly close and at the same time miles away. But she realized that if she was going to escape, now would be the time to do so.

Summoning her resolve and holding tightly to her revolver, she broke for the door. She had taken a couple of steps when the first explosion rocked the building. The entire structure was being shaken from the foundation to the roof.

The air was suddenly filled with dust and the mirror behind the bar, along with all the bottles and glasses, shattered. The floor beneath her buckled and she tripped and fell, screaming when a sharp pain lanced up her right leg. She attempted to get to her feet when a huge chunk of the ceiling fell pinning her beneath it. Then the whole building imploded.

74

July 11, 1999
5:17 P.M.

The Field Museum of Natural History closed at 6:00 P.M. on weekdays. Now, with less than forty-five minutes to go before this time, there were only a handful of visitors remaining inside the immense structure.

Curator Nora Livingston was in her upper-level office and Dr. Silvernail Smith was working inside the Egyptian tomb when all the electrical power to the building was cut off. This plunged most of the museum into pitch blackness, as the few windows inside the place were of frosted glass and set high in the walls above the main gallery.

In the dark Nora was able to find a flashlight inside her desk, which she used to illuminate her office. She picked up the telephone and dialed the single-digit number for maintenance. But when she placed the receiver to her ear the line was dead. She pushed buttons for the outside lines and found that they were also not functioning. Apparently everything was off including the air-conditioning unit, as it was not emitting its characteristic hum and the office was becoming stuffy. Then she smelled the smoke.

Shining her flashlight beam around the office she picked up

the haze, which was thickening rapidly. Fighting panic, she got up from her desk and crossed to the outer office door. Her secretary had gone home at five, so the office was vacant. The smoke here was thick and she began coughing as she made her way to the exit. Out on the second-level balcony the air was fresher, but the smoky haze still hung in the air. She was en route to the staircase when she heard a bloodcurdling scream coming from somewhere below.

The only illumination in the bowels of the Egyptian tomb, where Silvernail was working, came from dim exhibit lights. The semi-darkness was for effect, as it gave the ancient edifice a sinister atmosphere that added mystery. But it was never intended to be totally dark, which Dr. Silvernail Smith discovered quite evidently when the museum's power was cut.

The historian realized that this was no ordinary power failure, but instead sabotage. Had the power supplied by Commonwealth Edison been interrupted accidentally, the museum's backup generator would have kicked on immediately. When this did not occur, after the lights had been off for over a minute, Silvernail accurately surmised the reason. He also ventured an accurate guess as to who had caused the power failure.

Then he smelled the acrid smoke.

The historian knew the tomb well enough to find his way along inside of it even if the interior was pitch black. The passages were narrow and crisscrossed each other with the intricacy of a maze. In the dark, going was slow and the closeness of the walls nearly claustrophobic, but he managed to climb back to the upper level. He was about to step out of the tomb when he heard a scream, which originated close by.

He was about to dash outside when an eerie feeling gripped him. He hadn't felt this way in a very long time. He realized instantly that he was in grave danger.

The historian melted back into the shadows of the ancient

Egyptian tomb. As silently as he could he climbed to the roof of the tomb, which provided a view of the museum's main rotunda. Crawling to the roof's edge, he peered over the side. What he saw below made him emit an involuntary gasp.

There was an odd-looking red vehicle down on the floor of the rotunda. Silvernail had never seen anything like it before, but its unique sophistication instantly transmitted to him that the confrontation he had foreseen in the Native American exhibit the day before was imminent.

The origin of the scream he had heard was a male museum visitor wearing a loud blue and yellow Hawaiian sports shirt and shorts. The man was lying on the floor in front of the red vehicle. Silvernail could see the curly brown hair of the driver and his face. He couldn't have been much older than twenty, but the stamp of cruelty on his features made him appear years older. And he was torturing the museum visitor utilizing a combination of fire and electricity.

The victim of the attack was trapped against the wall of the Egyptian tomb. The operator of the vehicle was deriving great enjoyment from shocking the visitor with a metal rod protruding from the front of the red housing and when he attempted to escape the trap, a jet of red flame licked out and blocked him.

Watching the sadistic demonstration sickened the historian, as he realized who had taught the young man such cruel games. Then the spider grew tired of the fly.

Suddenly the jet of flame intensified to envelop the tourist. The man emitted a final scream, as he was incinerated. Insane laughter echoed through the dark rotunda and then the murderer became aware of Silvernail's presence.

Spinning around, he spied the historian on the roof of the tomb. Then a voice Silvernail had not heard in many years came over the museum public-address system.

"Silvernail, my brother," Jonathan Gault said, "I know

you're here. It has been such a long time, but I really can't stop to chat. I have a great deal to do before the guest of honor arrives at the little party I'm throwing here in your museum. But I will make sure that you won't be bored. I've brought my friend Christian along to entertain you. That interesting vehicle Christian is operating is called 'Red Lightning.' He named it himself, but its unique significance fired my wicked imagination. I am to introduce something of a red lightning effect into your museum this afternoon. I think you'll find it interesting, but hardly enjoyable." Then the PA system became silent.

Silvernail started for the stairwell leading back into the tomb when he heard a strange buzzing noise coming from the rotunda below. Turning he looked back over the edge and what he saw froze the blood in his veins.

On the red vehicle, between the area where the electric rod and the flame emitting nozzle were located, the beam of a powerful laser shone. The crazed young killer was using this laser to slice into the foundation of the ancient structure. Silvernail could already feel the floor beneath his feet starting to vibrate as the tomb was destroyed.

75

July 11, 1999
5:20 P.M.

Fifty-third Street, in front of what used to be Sandy's jazz club, was clogged with fire trucks, rescue vehicles, and police cars when Cole and Blackie arrived. The chief of detectives and the lieutenant flashed their badges at the officers manning the street barricades and were directed to the female lieutenant in charge of the scene.

She recognized Cole and gave him a sharp salute. "Another strange explosion, boss," she said. "With what happened down at the Municipal Administration Building yesterday, it looks like the Windy City's falling apart."

She had expected this comment to draw a smile from Cole. When it didn't she became all business.

"Were there any survivors?" Cole asked.

"Just one. The owner, Sandra Devereaux. She's pretty banged up, but she's alive. They're stabilizing her in that ambulance over there before—"

But Cole was already running toward the ambulance. Blackie followed.

Sandra Devereaux was weak, but conscious. She had sustained a broken arm, a broken leg, four cracked ribs, and numerous cuts and bruises. But she was, as the lieutenant in charge at the scene had said, still alive. The paramedic, who was attending her, cautioned the chief of detectives that she needed to be on her way to University Hospital. Cole agreed and kept his questions brief and to the point. When he stepped out of the backdoor of the ambulance, Blackie was waiting.

"So what do you think, boss?"

Cole looked at what had once been the building that had housed Sandy's. It had been destroyed with the same exotic efficiency as the Chinatown warehouse and the Municipal Administration Building's fire escape. Then there was the death of Tommy Kingsley. Cole turned to Blackie.

"Stanton and Steiger are again working their side of the street, but I don't think they're any closer to finding our mad scientist than they were when this thing started."

"If you ask me, those two couldn't find their behinds with both hands," Blackie said. Then he noticed the frown on his old friend's face. "But I think you've come up with something from the look of that crease in your forehead."

Cole stared at the remains of the jazz club for a long time. "Gault's wrapping things up in Chicago, Blackie. Tying up loose ends, so to speak."

"But what does he want with Kate Ford?"

"She's the first one who spoiled his plans when she uncovered the booby-trap murders of the career criminals. When he tried to kill her I intervened and Christian tried to kill me. From that point it all comes back to this. Now he's expecting me to follow him to the next step and that's why he kidnapped Kate."

"And that next step is?" Now it was Blackie's turn to frown.

"I'll fill you in later. Now I want you to go back to headquarters and see if you can keep our NSA agents occupied. I'll call you later."

"Where are you going?"

"To see Dr. Silvernail Smith at the Field Museum of Natural History."

76

JULY 11, 1999
5:30 P.M.

Nora Livingston was attempting to organize what visitors she could find into a group so she could lead them out of the museum. There had been no more screams, but she was forced to fight a rising panic as she made her way through the dark, smoke-filled rotunda.

She had managed to corral five people for the evacuation: a

young woman with two preschool children and a couple clad in traditional East Indian attire. The children were crying and the East Indians couldn't speak English very well, but the curator was doing a good job of ushering them along toward the front door. She kept an eye out for any more visitors she could add to her little band, but there was no one in sight. She assumed that everyone else had gotten out.

They made their way around the dinosaur skeleton and were closing in on the desired objective when they encountered a woman tied to a straight-back chair. She was gagged.

Leaving her group, Nora rushed over to help her. The curator had never seen fear like she saw in the eyes of this woman. She went to work on the ropes binding the captive, but found them tied with a knot she found impossible to undo. She turned to ask for help from her group. They were gone, but the rotunda was not empty. A man in a black suit stood a few feet away staring at her. What she saw in his eyes terrified her.

77

July 11, 1999
5:35 P.M.

When Larry Cole pulled up in front of the Field Museum of Natural History he realized that something was very wrong. There were a number of people in front of the museum. In and of itself this was not unusual, as it was summer and the museum was in Grant Park in the downtown area. However, a number of people were standing around looking at the front of the museum.

Getting out of his car, Cole went over to a uniformed security guard, who was standing at the bottom of the steps leading up to the main entrance. "Is there something wrong?" the cop asked.

"The power failed inside and there was smoke in the main rotunda," the guard said. "We tried to evacuate everybody as quickly as possible, but I think there're still some people inside."

"Did you call the fire department?"

The guard nodded. "They should be on the way."

"I'm a cop," Cole said, flashing his badge. "I'm going to take a look inside."

The guard shrugged. "Suit yourself."

When Cole entered the museum a fire alarm echoed through the building. Then, as he advanced past the reception desk, the alarm suddenly ceased at the same time that the iron doors at the entrance slammed shut. How this had occurred was a mystery. Then a voice came over the loudspeaker.

"Good evening, Mr. Cole. I see that you got my message."

Cole stopped, but remained silent.

"I am Dr. Jonathan Gault. This is the perfect place for us to finally meet, although I don't think you're going to enjoy the occasion."

Cole pulled his gun. "If you're so eager to meet me, show yourself."

"That gun really won't do you much good," Gault said calmly.

"Don't bet on it," Cole said, hefting the automatic and advancing into the shadows of the rotunda. He had to locate the room in this building where the public-address announcements originated. He proceeded cautiously into the dark museum.

Cole's gun was equipped with night sights, which gleamed with green fluorescence in the dark. There was still no indication of anything moving out there. Then he heard the sound of glass breaking. Cole moved in that direction.

The second-floor gallery overshadowed the display cases along the west wall of the rotunda. However, even in the dark he was able to tell that one of them was broken. Carefully, he examined it.

The plate-glass pane in the front of the case had been shattered. Inside there was a stone pedestal surrounded by small artificial trees arranged to resemble a jungle. There was nothing else there, which forced Cole to surmise that the exhibit had been removed. He read the card mounted at the base of the pedestal. BUSHMAN: THE LARGEST AFRICAN GORILLA EVER . . .

Cole heard a noise behind him. He turned and what he saw made his blood run cold. The gorilla Bushman had died in captivity and then been stuffed to become an exhibit in the Field Museum. As far back as Cole could remember the animal's carcass had been on display here. Now, the gorilla, which had grown to full size before its death, stood on all fours a few feet away. And it was alive.

"What do you think of my little mechanical toy?" Gault crowed from the shadows. "Want to see it in action?"

The animal bared its teeth and stood up to begin hammering its chest; however, it made no sound.

"I think he's mad at you, Cole. Very mad at you."

Then the giant gorilla charged Cole. The cop managed to get off three shots before it knocked him to the floor.

78

JULY 11, 1999
5:37 P.M.

Silvernail Smith was trapped on the roof of the Egyptian tomb, as the laser cut through the walls. He was feverishly attempting to come up with a way to counteract the maniacal operator of the red vehicle when Gault's voice again echoed through the rotunda. "Christian, leave Silvernail alone and take your position. He won't be going anywhere for a while."

The laser beam stopped and the vibration caused by the tomb being destroyed ceased. Silvernail moved cautiously to the roof's edge and looked down at the rotunda twenty-five feet below. The red vehicle vanished into the shadows. Quickly, the historian dashed to the exit leading down into the tomb. Instantly, he realized what Gault had meant when he said that he wasn't going anywhere. The passageway leading down was completely blocked and there was no way he could climb down the outer walls.

He returned to the edge of the roof. The only way to reach the main floor was to jump. He realized that he could break a leg or, worse, his neck, but he had to chance it. Silvernail took a deep breath and leaped out into space.

It took Cole some time to come to the realization that terror had erased his ability to think rationally and that he was not being attacked by a giant gorilla, but nothing more than a large mechanical toy. One of the bullets he'd fired before Bushman jumped him, had ripped a hole in the physical shell and some of its stuffing was coming out. The gorilla carcass was big and moving independently by way of a mechanism Gault had placed inside of it. However, the carcass didn't possess the enormous strength such a beast would have possessed in life. With little effort, Cole managed to throw it off. It landed on the floor and in an instant became the same lifeless creature it had been for over thirty years.

"That wasn't much of a challenge, was it, Cole?" Gault's voice purred over the speaker.

Wherever the crazy scientist was broadcasting from was obviously equipped with closed-circuit video cameras. Cole peered into the shadows of the huge rotunda, but couldn't locate any cameras. But he knew they were there.

"You'll have to do better than that," Cole said defiantly.

"Oh, I shall. Actually, that was just a warm-up for things to come. Now it's time to up the stakes a bit."

A woman's scream echoed through the museum. It came from the east wing adjacent to the Tyrannosaurus rex skeleton exhibit.

Cole ran across the rotunda into the wide corridor from which the scream had originated. He was only vaguely aware that he had entered "The Hall of Reptiles." Halfway down this exhibit area he saw the source of the scream.

Kate Ford and Nora Livingston were tied to chairs at the center of the corridor. The glass cases surrounding them were filled with stuffed snakes, snake skeletons, snakeskins, photographs, and drawings of snakes. And the reason why one of the women had screamed was a snake; however, unlike the contents of the exhibit cases, the one coiling less than a foot away from her was very much alive.

Gun raised, Cole skidded to a stop ten feet away from them. Gault's voice was heard once more. "Allow me to introduce my sole surviving pet. This is Satan and he is a cobra from Sri

Lanka, where their species is considered to be not only sacred, but extremely deadly to humans."

The serpent extended its cowl and hissed. It was between Cole and the women, so he couldn't chance a shot. Cole began circling to the left.

"A single bite from Satan can inject two ounces of a particularly potent venom into the body," Gault said with a noticeably growing excitement in his voice. "The nervous system is attacked and the limbs begin to spasm making it impossible for the victim to move. But the most agonizing aftereffect of the bite is that the respiratory system is paralyzed and the victim slowly suffocates."

Cole was now in position to attempt a shot. He lined up his sights and was applying pressure to the trigger when Gault said, "It's too late."

The cobra struck so fast there was no time for the cop to react. Kate, who had maintained a terrified silence and seemed hypnotized under the serpent's unblinking gaze, screamed as the fangs punctured her exposed right calf muscle. Before it could turn on the curator, Cole shot the snake five times, hitting it every time and severing its head before it could bite her again. Bloody pieces of Satan were smeared across the gallery floor. Cole rushed over to Kate Ford.

She was already bathed in perspiration and her breathing seemed labored. Twin trickles of blood oozed from the marks left on her leg by the snake's fangs. Quickly, he cut the ropes using his pocketknife, then picked up Kate. He was about to carry her out of the museum in his arms when Nora Livingston said, "The man who did this said that the doors are sealed. The interior is electrified and the outside is booby-trapped with high explosives set to go off if anyone attempts to force their way in."

"She's right, Cole," Gault said over the speaker. "You can't leave and if you try to get out you'll receive a shock a great deal more potent than the one Christian gave you a few days ago."

Cole realized with a sinking heart that he had been set up. He looked into the snakebite victim's face. She was obviously terrified, but also displayed signs of the onset of the fatal sickness resulting from the snakebite. Carefully, he placed her down on the floor.

"Now I understand that the primary mission of the Chicago Police Department is to protect life. In order for you to save Ms. Ford's life you'll have to get help for her here inside the museum."

Slowly, Cole looked around the gallery until he spied the television camera mounted high up on the north wall. "And where is that help?" Cole asked quietly.

"There is a metal case containing a sterilized syringe with the exact amount of antivenom needed to save her on the staircase leading to the second floor at the south end of the rotunda. All you have to do is go and get it, return and give the injection to Ms. Ford. However, I suggest that you hurry. Satan's bite will prove fatal in less than an hour."

Cole turned to the curator. "Stay here with her. I'll be back as soon as I can."

"I'll do everything I can for her, but please hurry."

Then, with no other options open to him, Cole ran from "The Hall of Reptiles."

He rushed into the main rotunda just as a loud screeching noise was heard. Cole turned and at first thought his eyes were playing tricks on him. Then the movement became more pronounced and was accompanied by the nerve-shattering sound of metal grating on metal. The skeleton of the Tyrannosaurus rex, which stood twenty feet tall and had been on display at the center of the central hall of the museum, began moving toward him. The skeleton's jaws, lined with rows of dagger-sized teeth, snapped shut with a threatening click. The monster was heading straight for the cop.

79

July 11, 1999
5:40 p.m.

Jonathan Gault was enjoying himself immensely. He had what he needed right at at his fingertips. He could see and hear everything that was going on inside and in the immediate vicinity of the exterior of the museum. He had devices controlling his animated "toys," as he had designated them.

It had been a simple matter to abduct the meddling journalist from her town house. He had tied her up, gagged her, and locked her in the trunk of his car. He'd untied her long enough to make the call to Cole at Tommy Kingsley's house from a public telephone on Lake Shore Drive. He put her back her in the Mercedes while he blew up Sandy's jazz club. Then they had gone to the museum. He had begun planning what was taking place in the main rotunda since the moment he saw Cole with Silvernail. Now he would deal with both the cop and his old nemesis from the New Mexico desert.

Gault watched the monitor depicting the north end of the main rotunda, where Cole was battling the skeleton of the Tyrannosaurus rex. The cop was doing pretty well, but would never survive the encounter. The monster was being animated by devices the size of a package of cigarettes, which contained enough electrical relays and memory chips to make what had once been no more than a dust-collecting exhibit, a true challenge for the gun-wielding cop. And even if Cole did come through the attack by the skeleton, there was always Christian.

To some extent, although he was criminally insane, Gault possessed a sense of warped honor, so there was indeed a vial of antivenom waiting for Cole on the staircase at the south end of the rotunda. But he didn't expect the cop to ever reach it. In fact, he planned to do everything that he could to prevent Cole from achieving the designated objective.

Gault spent a moment or two more watching the conflict between man and machine going on in the north rotunda. Then he checked briefly on the monitor covering Christian's position at the center of the museum. Finally, he switched to the camera trained on the Egyptian tomb. He expected to see Silvernail still standing on the roof of the ancient exhibit. Then what he did see made even the calculating, diabolical Jonathan Gault gasp with shock.

Silvernail leaped from the roof of the tomb to the rotunda floor. Gault watched the maneuver experiencing a depth of emotional concern he didn't believe possible. The historian landed on the balls of his feet with his knees bent and then went into a roll to dissipate the shock of the impact. He remained motionless on the floor for nearly a full minute before he slowly got to his feet and began limping away. Gault started to send Christian after him, but decided against this. Cole was more important right now and Silvernail wasn't going far.

Turning back to the monitor covering the north rotunda, Gault's eyes momentarily lost focus and he recalled the concern he had felt for Silvernail's welfare. Then his features hardened once more and he went back to his devices of destruction.

The historian had severely sprained his left ankle and bruised his right shoulder when he struck the floor. Ignoring the pain he struggled to his feet and limped off across the rotunda. He only hoped that the young maniac in the red vehicle didn't show up, because if he did the historian was defenseless. However, if he made it to "The Native American of Yesteryear" exhibit on the second floor he would see how much the man, he had once known as Red Sky, had learned about the transmission of energy.

Unlike the encounter with the animated gorilla, Cole found the moving dinosaur skeleton a great deal more dangerous. He took aim and fired at the skeletal head. The bullet ricocheted off the surface of the skull and smashed into the ceiling below the second-level gallery. The bullet didn't appear to do any damage or even slow the creature down. He looked for an alternative weapon.

He spied a display case on the east side of the rotunda depicting a full-size display of Native Americans of the early North American plains. There was a male, a female, a child, and a dog depicted in the display. The man was carrying a spear.

Cole ran to the case and fired three shots to shatter the glass. Holstering his weapon, he leaped inside and snatched the spear from the mannequin's hand. The entire arm came off and fell to the floor of the display. As he ran back to confront the moving dinosaur skeleton, Cole was comforted by the fact that the spear was made of wrought iron.

He jabbed the spear at the monster's leg and made contact. It didn't affect the beast at all. The skeletal head came down and its jaws opened. It snapped shut within inches of Cole's arm.

He thrust the spear upward and the jaws opened again, grasped the tip of the spear and ripped it from Cole's hands. Then, as the cop watched, the mechanical beast snapped the iron in two as easily as if it had been made of balsa wood. One of the legs came off the floor and swung at Cole. He dodged out of the way, but was still struck a glancing blow that knocked him twenty feet across the marble floor. He skidded until he rammed into a marble pillar and was knocked momentarily unconscious. He shook his head, forced himself to his feet, and leaned against the pillar. The dinosaur skeleton was now standing directly over him. There was no escape.

Silvernail made it inside the wigwam on the second floor. He barely managed to keep from crying out because of the agony caused by his injured ankle and shoulder. Forcing the pain from his mind, he squatted on the prayer rug and crossed his legs. Shutting his eyes he concentrated with every fiber of his being to become one with this place.

He began with the canvas structure he was in and moved out through the gallery and the rotunda to encompass the entire museum. Slowly, he became one with it, feeling it as more than just a structure of concrete and steel. He felt it as a living entity with a past and present, although he did not attempt to delve into its future. If he failed there would be no future.

He began feeling its energy rhythms in the physical as well as the spiritual universe and he even became aware of the many ghosts that haunted this place from the past going all the way back to the dawn of humanity. But his concern for the living was greater than for the dead.

He first became aware of the two women in "The Hall of Reptiles" exhibit. One of them was seriously ill. Then he found Cole and discovered that the policeman was only seconds away from death.

Silvernail Smith used every ounce of magic he possessed to help Larry Cole.

80

July 11, 1999
5:45 p.m.

Jonathan Gault was manipulating the remotes that controlled the thousand-pound Tyrannosaurus rex skeleton as it menaced the cop. Now the scientist decided to terminate the contest. He had expected Cole to pose a greater challenge; however, the cop had been up against truly formidable opposition. Now it was time to end it. And he expected it to be messy. Very messy. Gault could only characterize what he was going to do to Cole as similar to a bug being smashed against the windshield of a speeding car.

He manipulated the remote that controlled the dinosaur's head. The jaws opened and the head descended toward the trapped policeman. In a second it would all be over. Suddenly, the remote stopped working.

Cole watched the jaws of the huge skeleton open to envelop and then rip him to pieces. Finally, he had met a deadly challenge he could not overcome. There was no way that he could combat this threat, which meant that not only would he die, but Kate Ford would succumb to the snakebite. The chief of detectives steeled himself and prepared to join his father permanently in the hereafter when the deadly double row of dagger-sized teeth stopped within inches of Cole's chest.

The seconds ticked by rapidly and neither predator nor prey moved. Then, recognizing the opportunity to survive, Cole began inching his way from beneath the giant skeleton. He made it six feet when a voice whispered through his mind, "Disable it, Larry."

He was certain that the voice had been that of Silvernail Smith, but the historian was nowhere in sight. Cole looked back at the motionless monster.

"Disable it, Larry," the voice came again.

"How?" Cole said into the emptiness of the shadowy museum.

His eyes frantically swept the skeleton without seeing anything that he could use to stop this thing.

"Hurry! You don't have much time left!"

Cole felt a frustration building inside of him and he drew his gun as a purely defensive gesture. Then he saw it, or at least he saw the first one. The device was square-shaped and of such a shade as to blend in with the dark coloring of the skeleton. Cole scanned the rest of the skeletal structure. There were three such devices arranged at the juncture of neck and head and at the top of each leg.

"Disable it now!"

Cole took aim at the device closest to the head, lined up the fluorescent sights and pulled the trigger just as the dinosaur began moving again. Sparks flew as the cop's bullet hit the mark. The jaws shut and the head went motionless, but the rest of the body continued moving. The cop ran toward the south end of the rotunda. He could feel the monster getting closer as the marble floor vibrated beneath his feet. He looked back over his shoulder and saw it gaining on him.

"Go around the fountain, Larry. Use the fountain."

There was an ornate water fountain in the center of the central rotunda. The power cut had stopped the flow of water and its spotlights were out. Now, with the skeleton less than six feet behind him, Cole veered to the left and skirted the edge of the fountain. His feet slipped on the marble surface and he barely maintained his balance. Then he heard the scraping noise as the mechanical predator attempted to duplicate the manuever. The skeleton never made it.

Cole turned to watch as the dinosaur lost its footing and crashed to the floor of the rotunda. It shattered on impact and lay motionless at the cop's feet.

Breathing heavily from a combination of fear and exertion, Cole stood over the jumble of bones and smashed remote-control pieces spread out over the floor in front of him. Then he remembered Kate Ford and rushed toward the south end of the rotunda.

He skirted the debris and was sprinting as fast as he could when Christian drove from the shadows in the Red Lightning vehicle and intercepted him. The cop froze when he saw the glare of sadistic cruelty on the young man's face.

"You survived the first time we met, Larry. You won't be so lucky now," Christian said.

81

July 11, 1999
5:47 P.M.

Silvernail was in agony, but he continued to concentrate on his movement through the spiritual universe, which had enabled him to stop Jonathan Gault from killing Cole with the dinosaur. Now he could sense the policeman confronting a new, infinitely more dangerous nemesis. The historian, who had once been known as The Man Who Walked in Blood, only hoped that he possessed enough remaining strength to help Cole.

82

JULY 11, 1999
5:48 P.M.

Manny Sherlock was sitting in Detective Division Headquarters across the office bay from NSA agents Reggie Stanton and Ernest Steiger, who were hunched over a portable computer. Sherlock also had a computer in front of him with which he was attempting to tap into the NSA unit. But at the exact instant he made the interface he would have to distract them or they would know what he was doing. A keystroke away from accomplishing his mission, he looked around for a diversion. He saw Judy coming out of Blackie's office.

Checking to make sure that the NSA agents were still occupied, Manny motioned for her to come over to his desk.

"What's up?" she said, perching on the desk's edge. She was wearing a baggy pink-flowered dress called a muumuu and her hair was piled on top her head. She had on a pair of open-heeled sandals that made flapping noises when she walked. Manny would have preferred her to have adopted the glamour girl look of yesterday as opposed to today's hausfrau.

He checked first to make sure Stanton and Steiger were still occupied before he lowered his voice and said, "I need you to go over there and get them to look away from that computer screen for a few seconds."

"You're kidding?"

At that moment Steiger stretched and turned his head to glance in their direction. The cops froze in wide-eyed shock, but the blond agent's eyes swept over them and he returned to looking at the computer screen.

"C'mon, Judy," Manny urged. "If anybody can do it, you can."

"Let me tell you something, Sergeant Manfred Wolfgang Sherlock," she hissed through clenched teeth, "those two men are certifiable homicidal maniacs. They're dangerous simply to be around, much less talk to."

Manny shrugged and looked back at his computer screen. "Well, if you can't do it I understand, but I never thought a simple job like this would be too much for the Mistress of Disguise/High Priestess of Mayhem."

This got to her. She bit her bottom lip as she slid off the desk, smoothed the folds of her dress in front of her, and said, "Well, you don't have to get nasty."

Then she walked across the room toward the NSA agents.

"Hi," Judy said, standing over them. "Remember me?"

The two pairs of menacing gray-blue eyes came up to glare at her. She felt a momentary panic, but then recalled what Manny had said. She was the Mistress of Disguise/High Priestess of Mayhem.

"I was the undercover officer inside Antonio DeLisa's house the night you two were shot."

Now Stanton's eyes narrowed a bit. Steiger continued the same hostile stare, because on the night she was talking about he had sustained three .45 caliber gunshot wounds, which he barely survived. Stanton had carried Steiger's unconscious body into the DeLisa mansion, which had been damaged by a round fired from an antitank weapon. Judy was being held hostage by the Mafia-connected DeLisa at the time. Larry Cole had rescued her, but was forced to shoot Reggie Stanton in the process.

Despite Stanton's and Steiger's unflinching glares, they still hadn't spoken. Judy wondered how much time Manny needed.

"You know," she said awkwardly, "the way you guys looked

that night I didn't think either of you was going to make it."

Finally, Stanton managed what could have passed for a smile and said, "So, how have you been, Officer Daniels? Still putting on your disguises?"

She hoped Manny had what he needed, because she wasn't about to stand here and withstand the stares from these two escapees from *The Village of the Damned* a second longer.

"It's *Sergeant* Daniels now and you two have a nice day." With that she walked back to Manny's desk.

"You owe me, Manny," she whispered, angrily. "I'd rather go back undercover with the Mafia than talk to those two again."

But Manny wasn't listening. Instead he was staring at his computer screen, which he had managed to surreptiously interface with the NSA computer. "They're tracking the chief, Judy. He's over at the Field Museum, and from the looks of this he's in trouble."

At that instant Stanton and Steiger closed up their portable unit and headed for the door. Judy and Manny had a pretty good idea where they were going.

83

July 11, 1999
5:50 P.M.

Christian pushed a button on the Red Lightning vehicle's control panel and the laser licked out and, with deadly accuracy, knocked the Beretta from Cole's hands. Now the policeman was totally at his mercy. Christian was overcome by a blood lust. He had never experienced such a sense of unbridled power in his life. He could maim, burn, or destroy anything he desired. Nothing could escape him, which was evidenced by the museum visitor he had first tortured and then incinerated. Now he wanted to kill again and then again. And at this moment he had the object of one of his murderous fantasies standing defenselessly in front of him.

Christian had attempted to kill Larry Cole once before and failed. This time he planned to succeed, but first he would have a little fun with the flamethrower and possibly even the laser. Despite Christian being somewhat intelligent, his education had gone no farther than the fifth grade. This left him mentally unprepared for what happened to him now in the south rotunda of the museum.

He was reaching for the button to activate the flamethrower when Cole changed right before his eyes. Christian gasped in shock and horror when the man that he planned to slowly torture to death became Jonathan Gault.

"Doctor," Christian said, "why did you . . . ?" But he was unable to complete the question raging in his mind.

However, Christian's horror was just beginning. Suddenly, there was a great deal of movement at the south end of the museum rotunda. Figures began moving back and forth in an eerie tableau, because none of them seemed to be coming from or going anywhere. Then the terrified murderer understood why.

What Christian Dodd was viewing, courtesy of his mind being manipulated in the spiritual universe by Dr. Silvernail Smith, were the numerous restless souls from the next world, who had made the museum their home. There were men, women, children, and even animals populating the army of ghosts parading through the rotunda. And they appeared in the spirit world in much the same manner as they had in the world of the living at the instant of their deaths. So Christian was seeing the beheaded, the maimed, and the horribly burned passing within inches of the Red Lightning vehicle. Then when the spirit of a young woman, who had been split in two from head to crotch with a band saw, walked right through him, Christian screamed.

He took the Red Lightning device into a wild turn and raced off across the marble floor. He was too busy watching the ghoulish souls to pay attention to where he was going and rammed headfirst into what was left of the lower level of the Egyptian tomb. On impact he was knocked unconscious and a large gash split his forehead. The Red Lightning vehicle's front end was destroyed and a trickle of the combustible chemical from the flamethrower began leaking onto the floor.

Jonathan Gault screamed in frustration after watching what had just occurred in the rotunda. Instead of killing Cole, Christian had gone into a panic. Now, with the destruction of the dinosaur skeleton and what had happened to Christian, the scientist began searching for Silvernail. And Gault vowed that the historian had interfered with him for the last time.

Nora Livingston was kneeling on the floor beside the unconscious Kate Ford. She had removed her suit jacket and covered the snakebite victim with it as best she could. Kate was shivering violently, but was bathed in sweat. She was also breathing heavily and making a harsh rasping noise at the end of each exhalation. Nora realized that if Cole didn't return with the antidote soon, this woman was doomed.

Then Larry Cole returned.

After his strange encounter with Christian Dodd, Cole retrieved his gun and went in search of the vial of antivenom Gault had said would be on the south steps. He found the metal case and started back for "The Hall of Reptiles."

The cop didn't know what had kept Christian from killing him, but along with the stark fear he had witnessed on Christian's face, Cole had experienced an odd feeling himself. It was as if he was in a graveyard at midnight. But his concern for Kate overrode his anxiety.

Now he injected the antivenom into her arm and prayed that Gault had prepared the correct dosage. He didn't know how long it would take for the injection to have any effect. He needed to get her medical attention as soon as possible, but first things first.

"I'll be back, Nora," Cole said. "I'm going to get Silvernail."

84

July 11, 1999
5:52 P.M.

Silvernail's work in the spiritual world and his injuries in the physical one had succeeded in completely exhausting him. He didn't think he possessed the energy to crawl out of the wigwam and make his way to safety. A smile creased the grimace that had set his face into a mask of pain. The reason for his mirth in the midst of such dire circumstances was that he didn't know if any such place of safety existed as long as his brother was alive.

Finally, he struggled to his feet and using the ceremonial spear for support, made his way out into the Native American exhibit and began moving as quickly as he could toward the rotunda. Although imminent disaster had been averted, Silvernail realized that the danger for him and his friends on the main floor of the museum was far from over.

The historian reached the balcony, which ran completely around the upper level of the rotunda. As fast as he could, he made his way toward the staircase leading down to the main floor.

Jonathan Gault was not physically in the museum as he manipulated the devices of destruction he had created and used to monitor those trapped inside. Instead he had tapped into the closed-circuit TV and public-address systems from his van, which was parked in the east parking lot of the Soldier Field football stadium. Now that Cole, assisted by Silvernail, had managed to survive, the scientist decided that a more direct, hands-on approach to the problem was required.

After he watched Christian ram the Red Lightning vehicle into the wall of the Egyptian tomb, Gault drove the motor home from the parking lot onto McFetridge Drive at the south end of the museum. Parking his van in a tow-away zone, Gault got out and headed for the rear entrance. He had wired all of the entrances to the museum with explosives, which could only be deactivated in one of two ways; by an extremely capable bomb technician or by detonation. The latter method would destroy a substantial part of the Field Museum of Natural History.

Deactivating the booby trap connected to the exterior rear door and turning off the electrical field inside, the renegade scientist was about to enter the building when he heard the sound of approaching sirens. He smiled. "You're probably on your way here to rescue, Mr. Cole," he said out loud. "However, I guarantee you, it won't be easy." Laughing, he entered the museum and reset the booby traps.

"That guy must be out of his mind," Blackie said, as they followed the Porsche Ernest Steiger drove from police headquarters to the Field Museum. Without the use of emergency equipment and displaying a total disregard for the traffic laws,

Steiger managed to proceed at breakneck pace, barely managing to avoid horrendous collisions at every intersection. The trailing police car, with Manny driving, Blackie in the front passenger seat and Judy in the backseat, was barely able to keep up with the NSA agents despite their flashing headlights and siren being activated.

"When this is over," Judy said, "we need to cite this guy for each and every violation he's committing."

Keeping his eyes on the road and the black sports car he was following, Manny said, "That won't do any good, Judy. We'll never be able to make any traffic charges stick."

"Why not?"

Blackie, who was securely buckled in and braced against the dashboard, responded with a sneer, "National security."

The Porsche skidded to a stop in front of the museum and the cops pulled in right behind them. There was a group of people standing at the top of the staircase outside the main entrance to the museum. The NSA agents, followed by the cops, ran up the steps.

The small crowd surrounded what was left of a man in a security guard uniform.

"What happened here?" Stanton demanded with authority.

"I think that's fairly obvious," Blackie said. "This guy looks like he stepped on a land mine, but used his face instead of his feet."

A teenage girl wearing a baggy sweatshirt and cutoff jeans said, "The lights went off inside the museum and we smelled something burning. Everyone came out here and this policeman showed up and talked to the guard." She motioned to what was left of the man lying a few feet away. "Then the policeman went inside and a few minutes later the guard tried to follow him. There was an explosion and . . ." She looked down at the dead guard and fell silent.

"Blackie," Manny called from one of the entrance doors. "Take a look at this."

The scoring on the metal door, where the explosion that had killed the guard had originated, was evident. The other explosives were also visible.

"This whole thing is wired to blow," Blackie said, examining the metal surface. "One of them can go off alone, explode in sequence or all blow at the same time."

"Well, we've got to get inside this place," Judy said. "Chief Cole is in there."

Ernest Steiger had been studying the doors. Now he said, "I can defuse this, but it's going to take time."

Reggie Stanton, Blackie, Judy, and Manny stared at the blond agent.

With a weak smile, he added, "I suggest that you evacuate this area in case something goes wrong."

85

July 11, 1999
5:55 P.M.

Cole retraced his route from the north to the south end of the rotunda. He skirted the lifeless, stuffed carcass of Bushman and the remains of the dinosaur skeleton. He was about to check on Christian when he saw Silvernail Smith struggling down the staircase. Cole rushed to help him.

"Are you hurt?" Cole asked the historian.

Silvernail placed his arm around Cole's shoulder, managed a smile, and said weakly, "I've been better, but I'll live."

They began moving slowly across the rotunda.

"Gault managed somehow to seal the doors after I came in. I don't know if we can get out," Cole said.

"We'll find a way to break out, Larry."

"But we've got to do it soon. Kate Ford was bitten by a cobra."

When Silvernail stiffened in alarm, Cole explained, "Gault provided an antidote, which I managed to give her after you helped me."

"Yes," was Silvernail's only comment. "But we must hurry."

"There's no need to rush, gentlemen," Jonathan Gault said from the shadows. "You see there's really nowhere to go. So why don't we visit for a while?"

Cole reached for his gun.

"Don't do that, Cole!" Gault shouted. "You've caused me enough problems with your primitive firearm. Now I want you and Silvernail to go over to the fountain."

The area he indicated was only a few feet from where the cop and the historian stood. They slowly made there way over to it being forced to step around the remains of the smashed dinosaur skeleton.

"Toss the gun into the fountain," Gault ordered.

"And if I don't?" Cole said.

An electrical charge crackled from the darkness and enveloped them. Silvernail and Cole were frozen rigid for ten seconds. When the charge stopped, Gault purred, "I could expose the two of you for a longer period of time, but that wouldn't be healthy. In fact, a full minute could prove fatal. Now throw the gun into the fountain."

Grudgingly, Cole complied.

"Now sit down on the edge of the fountain, gentlemen."

They sat.

86

JULY 11, 1999
6:00 P.M.

Outside the museum, Blackie, Manny, and Judy, with the help of responding police units, had evacuated the front of the museum. The spectators had been forced back to the edge of the museum parking lot two hundred yards from the location at the top of the staircase where Ernest Steiger labored to diffuse Gault's explosives. Reggie Stanton stood a short distance away and watched his brother work. The black man exuded a pronounced tension. Ernest was relaxed to the point of being almost casual. And he talked incessantly.

"After I completed my studies at the Sorbonne, Daddy arranged for me to attend the British commando demolitions school," Ernest was saying, as he used the tips of his fingers to trace the edges of one of the explosive mechanisms. "How he did that was beyond me, but you could say one thing for old Karl, he did have his contacts. Got it!"

Stanton flinched as Steiger pulled the device away from the door.

"Now this is a nasty piece of ordnance, Reggie. I don't know how powerful the explosive is, but if I don't miss my guess, it is deadly to anyone within fifteen meters."

Placing the device on the ground, Steiger returned to his work. "So I learned how to make bombs, diffuse bombs and—"

"Ernest," Stanton said, quietly.

"Yeah, Reg."

"Don't you think you should concentrate on what you're doing?"

He had just pulled another explosive from the doors. Looking at his brother, he said with a grin, "I am concentrating, Reg." He turned back to his work. "There are three more of these left and then we should be able to get in."

87

July 11, 1999
6:02 P.M.

Jonathan Gault stepped from the darkness into a dim cone of light near the fountain where Cole and Silvernail were trapped. When the historian saw his brother and the way he was dressed, he gasped. Cole was also surprised, even though until this moment he had never gotten a good look at Gault.

The man with the odd eyes was wearing a ceremonial headdress made from the head of a buffalo replete with horns. There were ceremonial beads hanging from it and the scientist had painted his cheeks and forehead red and white. A smile split the killer's face. "Does this remind you of anything, Silvernail?"

In a grim, quiet voice, which rose barely above a whisper, the historian replied, "It was our father's. I thought it perished on his funeral pyre."

"I wouldn't let it!" Gault screamed, his voice booming through the huge, empty rotunda. Then as quickly as his anger flared, it vanished. "The shaman's headdress, along with you, was all that I had left of the old ways."

"Did you miss me?" Silvernail said with a bitterness that matched his brother's.

Gault's eyes flared and he answered, "How can I miss what has only caused grief in my life?"

"I tried to help you."

"You," Gault said, pointing an accusing finger, "and my father tried to force me into your world of primitive magic. Now I have returned to show you and the world that what I am capable of is far superior to the magic of your world, Silvernail, or the technology of yours, Cole."

Since Gault had addressed him, Cole responded, "Is that what this was all about, Gault? Proving to your big brother that you made good?"

The scientist smiled in humorless amusement. "I was very impressed with the way you handled yourself earlier, Cole. By rights you shouldn't be alive. I plan to rectify that condition for you before I leave, but then first things first." Turning back to Silvernail, Gault asked, "How did you rescue Cole from Christian? Mind control?"

"I played on some of the young man's deep-seated fears," Silvernail began. "As I recall, years ago you had many such fears of your own."

Cole heard something moving out there in the darkness of the rotunda behind Gault. Attempting to conceal his scrutiny, the cop looked past the scientist off into the shadows, but it was too dark to see anything. It was evident that whatever was out there was coming closer.

"And what about your fears, Silvernail?!" Gault demanded. "Or does The Man Who Walked in Blood no longer succumb to the weaknesses of us poor, weak mortals?"

As if the words Gault had spoken were physical blows, the historian lowered his head. Cole turned to look at him and was unable to mistake the emotion he generated. That emotion was shame.

Gault's voice now held a tone of triumph. "Tell me, Mr. Chicago Police Department Chief of Detectives, did the man who now calls himself Dr. Silvernail Smith tell you who or actually *what* he is?"

Cole continued to stare at Silvernail, who remained sitting on the ledge of the fountain with his head down. The cop was trying with all his might to get his attention, but Gault's words had dropped the historian into a deep depression. In fact, Cole didn't know what he was going to do once he did get Silvernail to look at him. Whatever was out there in the rotunda was getting closer and one thing was certain, it was not going to be good news for Jonathan Gault's captives.

"You didn't tell him your secrets, Silvernail?" Gault crowed. "No? So I guess it's up to me."

At that instant Christian Dodd, bleeding badly, but still astride the Red Lightning vehicle, rolled into view.

Gault was not aware that his diabolical assistant was behind him.

Silvernail's head came up and he saw Christian. He looked back at his brother and then whispered urgently to Cole, "Fall backward into the fountain, Larry!"

"What?!"

"Do it now!"

Together the two men leaned back until they toppled into the waters of the fountain, which was five feet deep.

Gault raised the electronic weapon just as he became aware of movement behind him. Spinning around he was initially relieved to see that Christian was alive. Then he realized that something was very, very wrong with his young friend.

The ghosts Christian Dodd had encountered in this place were still with him. Now what he saw in front of him was another apparition from hell that was half man-half beast with horns protruding from its head. Dazed and in pain, Christian's fear jolted him into action and he pushed the button to activate the flamethrower. A burst of fire erupted from the front of the Red Lightning vehicle and enveloped the man-beast just as Gault shouted, "Christian, don't!"

However, Christian had no time to dwell on the fact that he had just incinerated his friend, as the leaking fuel ignited beneath the vehicle and exploded with a force that hurled pieces of it and the maniacal young killer all over the museum.

Cole and Silvernail stayed beneath the waters of the fountain until their lungs screamed for air. When their heads finally broke the surface, it was all over.

EPILOGUE

August 4, 1999
1:40 p.m.

The luncheon, hosted by the Field Museum of Natural History Curator Nora Livingston, was concluding in the museum's executive dining room. Present were the museum historian Dr. Silvernail Smith, Kate Ford, who had recovered completely from the snakebite, Chief of Detectives Larry Cole, Lieutenant Blackie Silvestri, Sergeant Manny Sherlock, Detective Judy Daniels, National Security Agency Deputy Director Donald Hildebrand, and NSA Special Agents Reggie Stanton and Ernest Steiger.

The catered menu consisted of tossed salad, broiled white fish, new potatoes, boiled carrots, and coffee, tea, or lemonade. Dessert was strawberry yogurt. Everyone seemed satisfied with the meal with the exception of Blackie Silvestri, who planned to order a cheeseburger when he got back to police headquarters.

Judy, who was dressed in a conservative blue business suit, wore horn-rimmed glasses with plain lenses and her hair tied back in a spinterish bun, was attempting to come up with a plan to deal with Ernest Steiger's advances. She didn't know how she had done it, but somehow her spinsterish appearance had turned the blond agent on. Since she'd walked in the door, Steiger had been following her around like a lovesick puppy. The situation was amusing to Cole, Blackie, and Manny, but Judy didn't think she was going to let this budding romance go too far. She was very much aware of what Steiger and his broad-shouldered brother were capable.

However, for the most part, the lunch had been a cordial, pleasant affair. Cole and Stanton had even reminisced briefly about the case Cole had been working on when he first met the NSA agent. At the time Stanton was a Chicago police officer.

"So Larry takes me out to the parking lot where this hooker and a dope dealer were murdered by a vigilante. He estimated the distance that the killer was standing from his victims, but he can't figure out what happened. You see, the perp used a throwing knife and the dope dealer had an automatic pistol. Larry asked me what I thought."

Kate Ford was listening to Stanton's tale with open interest. "What did you think?"

"Why don't you tell her, Larry?" Stanton said.

Cole managed a smile and said, "He told me that a weapon was only as good as the person using it. Initially, I thought it was something that he'd picked up from the police academy. That's when he told me that his uncle said it."

Deputy Director Hildebrand looked warily from Cole to his special agent. However, Kate didn't understand the significance of Cole's revelation. "Did you ever catch the killer, Larry?"

Cole looked at Stanton. "He never went to jail, but we had a pretty good idea who was responsible. Didn't we, Reggie?"

Stanton's gaze rested on Cole for a moment. "If you say so, Chief."

But the affair concluded amicably and just about everyone got what they wanted. The NSA had uncovered a treasure trove of scientific data from Jonathan Gault's motor home, which they found on McFetridge Drive behind the museum.

The CPD had solved the series of murders that had begun with the deaths of the career criminals and in the process had uncovered and defeated another evil plot by a few nefarious politicians to take control of the department. Soupy McGuire was indicted for criminal conspiracy and was scheduled for trial in mid-September. But Blackie had talked with the state's attorney assigned to prosecute the case and, in exchange for a plea of guilty, Soupy would receive a suspended sentence. His days as a pathologist were over, but even Soupy had to admit that he had been lucky. It could have been a great deal worse. And Kate Ford had one helluva story.

Everything was neatly wrapped up. For everyone that is except Larry Cole.

After lunch Cole accompanied Dr. Silvernail into the main rotunda where the Tyrannosaurus rex skeleton had been reassembled and was back on display.

"We managed to conceal the mark your bullet made on its skull," Silvernail said. "No one will ever be able to detect it."

Cole looked up at the massive skeleton and felt a chill go through him when it appeared to move. He forced himself to look away.

The rotunda had been almost completely restored to the state that it had been in prior to the invasion of Jonathan Gault and Christian Dodd. But Cole still had a few questions for the historian.

They began walking slowly across the rotunda in silence. They were passing the water fountain, which was again lighted and spewing jets of water at the rotunda ceiling, when Silvernail said, "I assume there are some unanswered question you have, Larry."

"Why would you say that, Silvernail?"

"Historians are detectives of a sort. We also have a tendency to notice things in much the same manner that police officers do."

They stopped at the restored Bushman display. Cole stared

in at the gorilla carcass with less than fond memories. "Right before he died, Gault wanted to tell me something about, and I quote, 'who' or 'what' you are."

Silvernail stared at the display. For a long time they stood that way in silence. Finally Silvernail said, " 'Who' or 'what' I am, other than an historian at this museum, ceased to exist for me and my late brother so long ago that it no longer matters to me or should it to anyone else."

He started to walk away. Cole reached out and gently grasped his arm. Silvernail turned to look at the cop.

"Since we're friends now and have been through so much, maybe someday you'll share the long forgotten 'who' and 'what' with me. Of course it will remain confidential."

Silvernail smiled. "Of course."

Reggie Stanton was waiting for Cole in front of the museum. The black Porsche was parked at the curb.

The NSA agent said. "Ernest loaned it to me for the afternoon. Why don't we take it for a little spin?"

"I don't think so," Cole said, starting to walk away.

"It won't take long, Larry," Stanton said to his back. "Just call it my way of repaying you for all we've been through over the years."

"Repaying me?" Cole said with a frown.

"Yeah," Stanton repeated. "Repaying you. I'll even let you drive."

Edna and Josie Gray, aka Eurydice Vaughn, were jogging on the five-hundred-acre wooded reserve situated on a private lake near Michigan City, Indiana. The property was surrounded by a six-foot wooden fence, which was liberally posted with the admonition PRIVATE PROPERTY—KEEP OUT.

Armed guards, wearing black jumpsuits and leading trained attack dogs, patrolled the perimeter. To date no one had attempted to trespass on the land and if anyone ever did, it was unlikely they would survive the encounter.

There were two structures surrounding the small lake. One resembled a country club building, which this land had been slated for before the NSA took over. The other building, on the opposite side of the man-made lake, was a twelve-room mansion. The security contingent occupied the country club; Edna and Josie Gray lived in the mansion.

Everyday the two sisters went for a five-mile run around the sixteen-hundred-yard gravel running track encircling the property. They were monitored every step of the way by the guards. The security personnel didn't know why these women were there and the only visitor they'd had was a doctor named Vargas from Chicago. How long they would be there, the guards didn't know, nor did they care. It was simply none of their business.

For the most part, Edna and Josie, who was sometimes referred to as Eurydice, kept to themselves. The guards knew their names, but nothing else about them. Again, this was by design.

Now the women jogged past the country club building and started another circuit around the lake. Once they had gone a few hundred feet, a sliding door in the lakeside wall of the country club opened and two men stepped out. They watched the sisters receding into the distance.

"You could stop in over at the mansion and say hello when they finish their run," Stanton said. "I know you'll be discreet and keep this place secret."

Cole watched Edna and Eurydice a moment longer. "I think they're doing pretty good without me, Reggie. And I think that I'll be just fine without them." Turning to the NSA agent he concluded, "We've just got enough time to get back to the city before rush hour."